Shooting Angels

Nicolas Sansone

ISBN 13: 978-09840984-8-4

Library of Congress Control Number: 2009909817

Cover design by All Things That Matter Press
Cover Art By Eric Portis
Published in 2009 by All Things That Matter Press

*This book is dedicated,
with great love and appreciation,
to my family.*

Acknowledgments

I would like to thank Chris Bachelder, Melvin Bukiet, Rosemary Laughlin, Elizabeth Majerus, Brian Morton, and Sabina Murray, not only for teaching me about writing, but also for providing so much support and encouragement over the years. It's thanks to their mentorship that I am able to trust my own imagination to guide me.

I am indebted to the editors at All Things that Matter Press for their professional support, and to Lily Barback, Lucy Barnes, Durga Chew-Bose, Laura Clark, Adam Cogbill, Paul Costello, Erin Coughlin, Alex Fox, Eric Glover, Akiva Gottlieb, Mike Harang, Sarah Hassan, Amy Laburda, Nehemiah Luckett, India Morgan, Brian Morton, Eric Portis, David Sansone, Eric Sansone, Lauren Schott, Aiyanna Sezak-Blatt, Allison Speicher, Beth Slattery, Melinda Taub, Emily Tuttle, Michelle Vider, and anybody else who looked at early drafts of this work. The feedback of these readers proved invaluable, and their willingness to spend their time and mental energy on this story is deeply felt.

Special appreciation goes out to Eric Buchakjian, Sean Coyne, Georgeann Koch, Jean Orr, Kara Shemeth, and Jon Wolfe for enduring twenty-five days of hell with me on the Space Shuttle Columbia search mission.

I am extremely grateful to Eric Portis for his offer to do the cover art for *Shooting Angels* and no less for his unflagging artistic and personal support.

Additional thanks to all of my beloved friends and family—and also to God or Whatever It Is for allowing me so many liberties with His/Her/Its representation.

The Landing

Arlo Saunders set out to survey his land, beginning from the western edge of his property just behind his one-story ranch house, and walking due east through the bristly grasses of east Texas pastureland. His cattle grazed mildly somewhere beyond the brook, Amanda's morning biscuits cooled in his stomach, and the chill, boggy air of February pressed like a cold compress on his arthritic joints. He'd been calling himself "king of the ranch" for forty years and now, as creaking old age settled in upon him like autumn hoarfrost, every pang and complaint of his body portended a shift in climate. Today, however, not a single ache plagued him and, though his morning strolls took longer now than they had four decades ago, a glimmering sunbeam of youth radiated somewhere within him.

The smell of sulphur bubbling up from the swamps on the margins of his land hung heavily in the clammy morning air. Arlo didn't mind the stench; these days, he'd lived with "the stink of earth's indigestion," as he said, for so long that he almost enjoyed the sulfurous vapors. As he sucked in the malodorous air today, however, he noticed an unexpected scent. Arlo knew his land so well that he could immediately notice any foreign aroma, however subtle. Arlo couldn't identify this new odor as the musty cardboard smell of an imminent rainstorm, nor the acrid blastings of a discharged skunk, nor the pungent reeking of a new stand of noxious weeds. Arlo had never encountered this smell before — a smell like diesel mixed with scorched chicken. The smell of something awful about to happen.

***

Back at the house, Arlo's wife, Amanda, turned on the television to watch the commodities reports. Suddenly, a well-dressed government official broke into the program. Amanda's television screen filled with an image that, at that selfsame moment, her husband was watching over the western horizon. A white arc streaked across the pale blue sky, as though a rock wrapped in a cloud were plummeting to earth. Amanda, gone pale, clicked off the television and went out to the porch to watch.

***

Chris Lester sat alone on the roof of his fire crew's bunkhouse, scratching his pencil over the stark white surface of his sketchbook, and quickly filling his paper with gray lines, whorls, planes, and points that, when all taken together, more or less resembled the New Mexico sunrise in front of him. Chris's imagination, however, had prompted him to include a moldy mass grave, wherein severed limbs, bloodied torsos, and screaming, half-rotted faces clambered over one another in torturous agony. In all other respects, Chris's sketch quite replicated reality.

Chris considered where to position the wrecked airplane he meant to draw, when a sudden female voice startled him. "Chris, you'd better come back downstairs."

Chris turned around to see Juliet Davies, a lithe redhead and the rear flapper on his squad. Their crew boss, Ana, had given Juliet the most degrading possible position for a returning hire in an effort to make her resign. However, Juliet had taken the insult in stride, proudly declaring to the crew after every fire, "If it weren't for the rear flapper, all your sorry asses would be roasted." Juliet's self-assurance – utterly unorthodox in the world of wildland firefighting, where the prevailing culture encouraged women to defer to the superior intellect and godlike brawn of their male counterparts or, better yet, attempt to become men themselves – inspired Ana to want her off the crew. Ana feared that, if she showed weakness in dealing with her fellow females, she might herself be accused of possessing feminine instincts.

"I'm drawing now," Chris said. Juliet watched for a moment in concern. Chris's eyes locked onto his sketchpad and his pencil raced almost frantically over the page. Chris had always been Juliet's best friend on the crew; she felt that he evinced a sensitivity absent in some of her more macho colleagues. However, he had recently grown more aloof – almost distracted – and this change had been concurrent with his growing dependence on his sketchbook. Though Chris had possessed a creative mind as long as Juliet had known him, he recently clung more and more to his drawings. He sketched with a compulsiveness that alarmed Juliet.

"That's messed up shit," Juliet said softly, gazing over Chris's shoulder at the images of perdition. "Why are you always drawing that morbid stuff? Just draw a regular fucking sunrise for once."

Chris didn't immediately reply. He wished that Juliet would leave him in peace, yet regretted that wish. Juliet, after all, had gone out of her way to befriend him. Nonetheless, these days she always looked at him with a sympathetic concern that irritated him. Ever since Vince Markham had joined the squad, Chris found himself less patient in the presence his crewmates.

"Catastrophe is beautiful," Chris finally said. He paused for a moment in his sketch, visualizing the cracked airplane fuselage that he would next pencil in.

However, Juliet preempted him. "I'd stifle that sentiment, buddy, and get your brooding ass downstairs. We're watching the news."

Chris's pulse quickened. The Las Cruces crew never wasted time watching the news. Something big must have happened – a natural disaster or a terrorist attack. A part of himself that he couldn't silence felt excited by the prospect.

"Something wrong?" he asked, hoping that his voice didn't betray his eagerness.

"The Daedalus Space Shuttle has just come down. It broke up on re-entry."

At the mention of the space shuttle, Chris dropped his pencil, his incomplete sketch already forgotten. True, the actual physical fallout of the accident would be far from catastrophic and the death count wouldn't exceed seven, but something about the idea of humankind's ballsiest technological marvel being swatted back to the imperfect world from which it came appeared significant and almost apocalyptic to Chris. He couldn't exactly say why, but he felt that, in some way, the news of the space shuttle drew him.

"Chris, come back to Earth," Juliet said, troubled by the faraway look in her friend's eyes. "You'd better get downstairs pronto. Ana's already on the phone with NASA. We might be on search and rescue."

Juliet took a moment to ensure that her instructions had registered before bounding back downstairs. Chris closed his sketchbook, leaving his fictional plane crash unrendered. His ears buzzed. The monumental glory of a disaster, in his eyes, increased in magnitude relative to his proximity to it. Only a second-year firefighter, Chris hadn't yet done a search and rescue mission — and he burned to experience pulse-stopping catastrophe firsthand. He stood up quickly and followed Juliet downstairs.

***

God eased Himself onto the davenport in His living room, looking down at His rum and Coke. A little fruit fly glutted itself on the sugary drink. God picked it out and took a long, satisfying slurp. The sounds of mortals puttering around on earth far below Him blended into a

3

cacophony not unlike radio static. The omnipresent noise, formless and almost comforting, never bothered Him. He kicked off His shoes and reclined on the davenport, the muddying bliss of the rum lightening His concern for mankind.

Mrs. God, a curvaceous blonde in a skimpy red dress, entered the room, carrying a newly mended fedora. "Oh, God. Thou consistently surpasseth all understanding, but this surpasseth most of Thine usual shit."

"I beg Your pardon?" God asked coolly. He loved to hear His wife challenge Him on policy issues.

"Why kill those kids on the space shuttle? Thou beith retired, for goodness's sake," Mrs. God said, moving God's feet off the couch and sitting down beside Him. She placed the fedora on His head, adjusted it so that the brim covered one of His all-seeing eyes, and nodded with satisfaction.

"My dear," God replied, taking one of Her hands in His and pressing His tender lips against Her skin. He looked into Her eyes, smiling slightly. "Sometimes bad things have to happen."

The Ground Rules

That morning, Ana Jenkins, the crew boss of the Las Cruces Ranger District, received the following fax from NASA:

"15 February 2008– Space Shuttle Daedalus down. Area of debris est. spread 50,000 sq. miles. Sensitive information. Urgency of materials recovery: highest. Requesting: USFS, National Guard manpower, 3,000 strong, to undertake S&R mission. Objective: scan projected area of debris dispersal via wildland gridding techniques. Goal: recover no less than 85% of ship; recover human remains as possible.

Due to scale and secrecy of deployment, extra measures necessary. Please note the following:

1) Individual squads to be conducted to search quadrants by NASA liaison. All rigs to be surrendered to NASA liaison until completion of assignment. GPS data to be unavailable. Location highly classified.

2) Length of deployment to be contingent on success of mission. Initial contract to be twenty-one days, extended as necessary to facilitate goal accomplishment.

3) Once admitted to search quadrant, no possibility of demobilization without proper clearance. EMT on call for emergency medical aid. All other necessities provided.

4) Daily duty to begin at 0500 hours. Coverage of 1.5 sq. mi. per diem. Expected per diem timeframe: 15-16 hours. Crew to report back nightly at precisely 2100 hours.

5) Each crew member permitted: backpack (1), change of underwear (1), change of socks (1 pr.), toothbrush (1), toothpaste (3 oz.), contact lens solution as needed (not to exceed 8 fl. oz.), water bottles (6 qt.), fusees (4), headlamp (1), batteries (8), rain poncho (1), Nomex (1 shirt, 1 pr. pants), boots (1 pr.), Kevlar chaps (1 pr.), helmet (1), safety goggles (1 pr.), work gloves (1 pr.), tampons (4, women only), first aid kit (1), prescription medicine (to be cleared with physician before deployment to search quadrant), sleeping bag (1), tent (1 per 2).

Any personal item in excess of the above to be confiscated.

Expressly forbidden: cellular telephones and/or other communication devices, cameras, audio/video recorders, and/or other recording devices, GPS devices, compasses, paper and pencil – anything not listed above.

To facilitate check-in procedures, please bring nothing but the above-listed permitted items."

Next, Ana read a fax specifically written for the Las Cruces Ranger District:

"15 February 2008– Your squad has been assigned to the East Texas Search Zone, Quadrants A74-A93BB. This falls in the domain of the East Texas Deployment Zone located in Longview, TX. Please tie in with NASA liaison Ross Tucker at the Longview Armory by 2000 hours, 17 February. You will receive further instruction at that time."

***

"Four tampons?" Juliet asked. The crew sat together in the common room of the bunkhouse for its assignment briefing. Now in the off-season, the crew fell short of its usual twenty members. Along with Ana, Juliet, Chris, and Vince Markham, three guys from Kansas and a male sawyer from Hawaii made up the roster of the yearlong crewmates. At the moment, Ana stood in front of the crew with a clipboard in her hands, a scowl on her face, and urgency in her voice.

"Four is plenty," Ana snapped. "We'll only be gone three weeks."

"I don't know about you, but I'd rather play it safe than sorry. It's always men that write these fucking lists."

"Anybody with serious questions?" Ana asked.

"Fuck you, Ana! This is a serious question! If I'm going into Texas for God-knows-how-long, I'm not going to let some asshole guy pack for me."

The first time Juliet had told Ana to fuck off last year, the crew had been completely aghast. By now, though, her antagonism failed to astonish anybody. Juliet and Ana had never really gotten along — but, cheeky or not, Juliet was too good a firefighter to be laid off.

"Juliet, your disrespect to me is disrespect to your entire crew and it will absolutely not be tolerated on this deployment," Ana said, before shooting a "What are you going to do?" look at the guys from Kansas. Ana stood nearly seven feet tall, with enormous biceps and a long, equine face. Feeling that she had defended herself as was appropriate, Ana continued in a softer voice, "Anyway, you can have my tampons; let's just move on, please."

Juliet remarked to Chris under her breath that Ana had used so many steroids that she no longer menstruated. Everybody heard her but, for the sake of saving time, Ana made no further reprimand.

"Any further questions?" she asked.

In the ensuing silence, Ana surveyed her crew. Now in her second year as crew boss, she had begun to wear her authority with greater comfort. The secret, she always told herself, lay in showing no weakness. She needed to keep the boys in line. If her crewmates needed compassion, they had one another. However, it fell to her to make sure that everybody in her crew stood tough enough to face a twelve thousand-acre wildfire without shitting himself. Playing *Joy Luck Club* and talking emotions wouldn't cut it.

Ana felt good about this year's crew. The Kansas boys were pretty new–they had come in about a month ago–but they seemed to have their shit together. The guy who seemed to be the leader of the three, Roger Chalmers, could run six miles in under thirty-five minutes, thus making him the fastest person on the crew. He had worked on a wildland crew in Alaska for a year prior to relocating to Las Cruces. He had brought along two of his newbie friends from high school–Scott and Francis–when he joined the crew. Ana couldn't get excited about Roger's friends, but they hadn't yet given her any reason to complain. Polite and athletic, they created no friction in the smooth operation of the squad.

Takeshi, the Hawaiian, also seemed acceptable. He couldn't hike quickly, and he struggled with his English, but the accuracy with which he could fell a tree had simply astounded Ana when she first saw him brandish a chainsaw. He had joined the crew in November and, since then, Ana had been pushing his abilities further and further by asking him to fell the most difficult snags in the entire district. Two weeks ago, he had leveled a cat's-eyed leaner on a 60% grade onto a dime Ana had placed in the space between the trunks of two neighboring trees. No matter how difficult a challenge Ana set for Takeshi, he never failed to meet it. Furthermore, he never talked back.

Ana's star performers, though, were Chris and Vince. Both were machines. Tempered by the relentless fires of the previous season, they could now work for hours without stopping to rehydrate. Though neither had the speed of Roger or the chainsaw skills of Takeshi, neither exhibited the extraneous bullshit that men so often resort to. Free of ego, free of horseplay, free even of the tendency towards casual conversation, the two seemed to be ideal firefighters. They were competing for head pulaski and their performances in Texas would undoubtedly figure into Ana's final ranking decisions.

The only point against Chris in Ana's mind was his remorseless interaction with Juliet. Ana wanted to like Juliet–she honestly did. However, Ana felt that Juliet was hell-bent on receiving special treatment as a woman. Ana had had to fight to be taken seriously in the firefighting community and she had no intention of allowing Juliet an easier ride. Furthermore, Juliet's frank disrespect mortified Ana. After nearly two decades of firefighting, Ana had only gained the necessary respect to be promoted to crew boss within the last two years. Now that she finally had the position she had wanted for the past eighteen years, she had no intention of allowing a spoiled bitch from New Hampshire to yank all authority from her.

Juliet aside, the crew was a good one, and Ana had no doubt, as her eyes wandered over the face of each squad member in the common room that morning, that it would perform well in Texas.

When nobody spoke up with a question, Ana adjourned the meeting. "Pack your bags, make your phone calls, and be in the rigs–ready to go–in an hour."

***

Robin Rodriguez had been on his feet all day by the time he walked up the driveway of the Saunders homestead. When he signed on for his internship at NASA, he had been excited at the prospect of seeing firsthand the quick, resourceful decision-making of the ground crew. He had been drawing rockets on the margins of his class notes since fourth grade social studies. His first day at NASA, he had been so lucky as to meet with Ross Tucker – the brains behind the Daedalus Space Shuttle mission, and quite possibly the most intelligent man Robin had ever come into contact with. That night, exhilarated by the new contact, Robin had already been planning what he would say to Mr. Tucker in order to land a position on his next mission. However, Robin hadn't been in Texas for a month before his easy, charming personality, which had always served him well, proved an unsurpassable obstacle – he was assigned to PR. As the technicians sketched out the latest aerodynamic models, Robin shook hands, smiled, and answered telephone calls.

Today, the scientists were back at HQ, tossing back rounds of coffee, rolling up their shirtsleeves, and pointing angrily at hasty diagrams to hypothesize on "What went wrong?" Robin, in the meantime, had been assigned to go door to door through the East Texas Search Quadrant in order to explain to residents why they were going to be seeing squads of Nomex-clad government agents marching through their ranches in the near future. Robin hated going door-to-door. The majority of East Texas ranchers had moved out to the hinterlands specifically to avoid unexpected guests; most did not have a flattering opinion of the government. At this point, Robin was unsure even of his own opinions. The Daedalus had crashed first thing in the morning and, there he was, ten hours later, already facilitating the search and "rescue" operation. He had never seen such a quick mobilization. NASA had already set up three base camps throughout Texas and squads were expected to begin trickling in the following day. Although it was standard operating procedure to have a firm emergency plan in place, a malicious voice in Robin's head kept muttering, "This disaster was entirely anticipated."

He cringed as he walked up the dirt path to the front door of the Saunders homestead. He had been to at least fifty houses just like it today. It was a dumpy one-story brick house that must have been standing since pioneer times. He could see rotten curtains hanging inside the dusty windows. He wasn't sure if they were yellow fading into green, or green fading into yellow. The grass was the same necrotic color. Meanwhile, the yard was littered with rusted hoes, threadbare tires, and a decimated trampoline whose exposed springs jutted out lethally at all angles. Bracing himself for the odor of mothballs, Robin stepped up to the door and knocked.

After several minutes, he heard shuffling inside the house. The door was opened by a crumpled old woman with stringy white hair falling like sea snakes around her brownish head. Robin could hear that the television was on. The President was saying, "In times of tragedy, the most important thing is to keep our heads." His speech had been playing all day.

"Mrs. Amanda Saunders?" Robin asked, his habitual diplomatic grin spreading like melted butter across his boyish face.

"That's me. Come in, please," she said, shuffling off into the house as though Robin had been an expected guest.

Robin followed Amanda in surprise. Not only was her familiar manner off-putting, but there was something odd about her voice, too. It sounded young. Though she was about four and a half feet tall with cottony cataracts over her eyes, she spoke with the breathy seductiveness of a nubile screen ingénue. She suffered from none of the vocal static that typically accompanies old age.

Amanda shut off her television and had Robin sit at a seemingly hand-hewn wood table in the center of a peeling linoleum kitchen. "Ginger snap?" she asked, holding out a chipped tray of stale biscuits. She spoke as though she were offering a romantic tryst, rather than an old cookie. It took all of Robin's discipline to keep his shudder in check. He retreated further into his smile as he waved away the proffered cookie.

"Ma'am, are you the wife of Mr. Arlo Saunders?"

"I am, indeed," she replied, pouring iced tea into two dirty glasses. "Arlo'd be out in the fields this time of day. Gotta wait until sundown if you're wanting to lay eyes on him."

"That's okay, ma'am. My name is Robin Rodriguez. I work for NASA. I'm going to ask you to pass along some information to your husband, okay?" Amanda did not respond, but instead set a glass of iced tea in front of him. It smelled of rotten eggs. Robin continued, "Today there was an enormous accident. At 0800 hours, the Daedalus Space Shuttle…."

Amanda cut him off, tears bleeding through her cataracts. "I know, dear. I saw it. All those dear kids." She took a swig of iced tea. It left a brown froth on her hairy upper lip.

"Then you certainly understand the necessity of an immediate search and rescue operation." Every time Robin said "rescue," he felt sick. Those astronauts would be lucky if all their digits had landed in the same time zone. "NASA is organizing a nationwide rescue effort, drawing together as many as 3,000 wildland firefighters and National Guardsmen to scour the area of dispersal. In order to facilitate this search, we will be passing through your property. We ask your cooperation in providing no hindrance to our agents as they conduct their search. If you have any fences, we ask that you…." Robin trailed off, seeing that Amanda was absently considering a point above his head. "Ma'am?" he asked, trying to get her attention. "Ma'am," he said, a bit more sharply.

Amanda turned to him guiltily. "I'm sorry," she said. "I'm thinking about those kids."

Robin didn't quite know what to say, so he began his speech again from the beginning. "NASA is organizing a nationwide rescue effort, drawing together as many as…."

"Those poor kids," Amanda interrupted, shaking her feeble head. A mucousy tear dripped on to the table. She continued in her soft, smooth girl's voice, "Arlo and I never did have kids. Just couldn't have 'em. They didn't take to me. Doctors say Amanda's poison." She spoke as if in a trance. "Always wanted a young one, dear. Kept the old trampoline in case a little boy came along. You saw our trampoline?"

Even Robin's diplomatic smile faltered at the pathos of the ancient woman lost in senile candor. He wanted to say something reassuring, but her airy, singsong voice made him so uneasy that he couldn't collect his thoughts. "An old woman shouldn't sound like that," he thought. "It's as though she were possessed by some little elvish girl."

Amanda turned to look at Robin. "And who are you?" she asked, as though seeing him for the first time.

"I'm Robin," he said. Amanda was now peering hard at him. Robin gulped and shifted his weight uneasily.

"Robin," she said, knitting her brow in consternation. Suddenly, her eyes lit up hopefully yet somehow bashfully. "My son, Robin?"

"Um. Yes, Amanda. I'm your son." Robin felt sick to his stomach. He had no idea why he had spoken such a brazen, troubling lie; his NASA training had not prepared him for such an eventuality. All he knew was that he wanted to get out of the house as quickly as possible and to somehow avoid the unseeing gaze that Amanda had turned upon him.

"I'm your son, and I love you very much, but I have to go now."

As Robin stood up, he noticed another quick change in Amanda's features. She seemed abruptly angry. She creased her forehead and puckered her mouth sternly.

"I'm sorry?" Amanda asked, suddenly with ultimate lucidity. "Are you making fun of me?"

"No, ma'am!" Robin could feel the blood running to his cheeks. He smiled, found it insincere; frowned, found it severe; and then allowed his panic to overtake his face.

"I have no children."

"I know that, ma'am."

"Then why'd you be going around here speaking that you're my son? You're playing the fool of me."

"No, ma'am. I just...." Robin realized that there was absolutely nothing for him to say. With a shudder, he wished himself back at headquarters, debating with the scientists over the durability of the space shuttle's heat tile. Robin hated PR.

"I think you'd best see yourself out, young man," Amanda said, picking up Robin's glass of iced tea and emptying it into the sink.

Shakily, Robin spotted the door and started towards it, uncertain whether or not he ought to say "Thank you for your time."

***

Chris stuffed his sketchbook into his backpack and zipped it. Juliet was sitting on his bunk, watching him pack. She had packed within ten minutes of the crew's briefing. Packing to go on dispatch was never difficult – particularly when the government told you exactly what to bring. The rest of the crew was outside, bidding farewell to the sparse New Mexico landscape. East Texas could get particularly gnarly, in terms of terrain, and everybody was going to miss the open expanses and knee-level scrub brush of Las Cruces. Chris had deliberately waited until the crew had gone outside before beginning to get his supplies together. He wanted to take advantage of his last opportunity to be alone before he became wedded to his crew for the foreseeable future. Juliet, unfortunately, proved incapable of reading his psychology and had followed him into the boys' room, gracing him with her opinions on the assignment.

"I don't like it, Chris," she complained, picking at Chris' bedspread. "I've never heard of an assignment put together so quickly. Ana got that fax like an hour after the crash."

Chris shrugged. "It's NASA. They've got emergency plans."

Juliet continued to speak. Her discontentment with the assignment was fairly general and so, as long as she was complaining about something, she wasn't too concerned with what that "something" was. "You know, you can't bring your sketchbook, Chris. They'll confiscate it from you. Fucking government, telling us what we can and can't bring."

"I don't understand why you're so upset, Juliet. They always tell us what we can and can't bring." Chris picked up his colored pencils from his bedside table and decided on the three most indispensable colors – black, gray, and red – before stuffing them into his pocket.

"You can't bring those," Juliet said. "It's bullshit, but you can't."

"I'll take my chances," Chris said.

Juliet stopped talking for a moment, taking a few deep breaths. She tended to get worked up very easily and realized that she needed to be better at keeping her head. "I'm sorry, Chris," she said. "I don't know why I'm being so obnoxious today."

Chris forced a smile. He, too, couldn't shake the feeling that something seemed funny about NASA's orders, but, unlike Juliet, he rarely felt comfortable discussing his convictions.

"I guess I'm just nervous about the assignment," Juliet admitted. "I haven't shared a tent with Ana since we've started fighting. It's going to be so uncomfortable."

Juliet had finally gotten through to Chris. He sat down next to her on his bed and patted her knee. "She's not going to go easy on you."

Juliet exhaled heavily, touched that Chris was being genuine with her. His tender moments had been growing scarcer over the past several months. She could see that something about the assignment was making Chris uncomfortable, so she decided to ease off her own anxieties and lighten the mood.

"Well, at least you'll have an easy go of it. Aren't you sharing with Markham?" she said.

At the mention of Vince Markham's name, however, Chris stiffened. His hands began trembling slightly and his mouth went dry. Juliet was stunned by the change that had come over her friend; she had no idea why it would have been inspired by what she had said. Vince was a gentleman and, though incredibly introspective, was easy to get along with. In Juliet's mind, it was far better for Chris to share a tent with Vince than with any of the three vulgar Kansas boys or with Takeshi, whose constant unearthly silence closed him off entirely to the rest of the crew.

With some effort, Chris turned to Juliet. She could see that his eyes were moist. This alarmed her. Chris had been acting recently as though he were guarding some monumental secret. Whatever it was, Juliet didn't want her friend to suffer alone.

"What's wrong, Chris? Something to do with Markham?" Juliet asked.

Instead of answering directly, Chris hesitantly asked, "Do you find him attractive?"

Though Chris had said nothing outright, Juliet understood immediately. She hoped her astonishment didn't register on her face. Ever since Vince had joined the squad, Chris had become surlier and more reticent. Juliet had unconsciously made the assumption that his behavior stemmed from his competitiveness – Chris and Vince were the two best firefighters on the crew and neither one had yet firmly established himself in top place – but the tenderness in his voice now revealed the secret that Chris himself could not. He loved Vince Markham. Juliet never would have guessed, but, now that the supposition had entered into her head, she was certain of it.

Chris saw the surprised empathy in Juliet's eyes and immediately regretted having said so much. Juliet's compassion only irritated him. He felt embarrassed and longed to be alone.

"Have you told him, Chris?" Juliet asked softly.

"Are you off your nut?" Chris replied, suddenly replacing all of his former vulnerability with antagonism. He glared peevishly at Juliet.

"Chris. Nobody's going to care that you're gay. Not even Vince Markham."

"I didn't say I'm gay," Chris said.

"It's okay, Chris. It's totally normal."

Chris rolled his eyes and stood up. He grabbed his backpack and slung it on. "I don't care if it's 'totally normal,'" he whispered angrily. "I'm not gay, so it doesn't matter. This is one stupid, meaningless attraction, and I shouldn't have told you."

"I'm sorry," Juliet said, standing up and putting a hand on Chris's shoulder. "I know it doesn't mean anything."

"I don't want to talk about it."

Juliet was still searching for something to say when Vince Markham himself walked into the room. Juliet could understand Chris's attraction. Mystery clung to Vince. He rarely spoke, and moved about with his eyes always cast on the ground. Most of the crew members chalked this up to his humility. Vince was self-effacing to an extent that few people can accomplish without devolving into ostentation. He wore only the plainest dark clothes, never looked anybody in the eye, and prayed at regular intervals throughout the day. When he prayed, he remained absolutely motionless, eyes shut, for as long as thirty minutes together. Not even the most sudden noise could draw him out of his prayerful state once he had begun his meditations. The only ornament that Vince allowed himself was a little golden crucifix. He would hold his crucifix when he prayed. Some members of the crew swore that it glowed within his grasp; however, such rumors were entirely apocryphal, as far as Juliet was concerned. She acknowledged that Vince had a strong spiritual presence, but she was loath to think of him as supernatural. He was just a guy, like any other – he simply happened to be a little quieter and more serious than most.

Physically, Vince was a model specimen. His skin was dark brown, like the coating of a well-toasted marshmallow, and he kept his thick black hair cropped close. His body was streamlined for maximum efficiency – graceful and powerful at the same time, his muscles worked with the flexible ease of a cat's. A secret smile never seemed far from his lips. Nobody ever caught him actually smiling, though; he always simply seemed about to smile. Juliet would have been attracted to Vince herself, but his closed personality was a turn-off for her. Nonetheless, she thought that he would be a good match for Chris. The two rarely spoke to one another, but, physically – Chris's pale skin next to Vince's black skin, Chris's short, stocky frame next to Vince's tall, lithe body – they complemented each other perfectly.

Trying to force down the discomfort she felt as a result of her conversation with Chris, Juliet issued a sunny "Hello, Vince!" Ever since Vince had joined the crew last year, Juliet had been devoted to drawing him out of his shell. As usual, however, her attempt met with nothing more than a seemingly self-amused nod.

"I'm heading out to the rigs," Juliet said. "I'll meet you boys in ten minutes."

Vince nodded again.

"Hang on, Juliet," Chris said, still a little pale-faced. "I'm ready to go, too." As Chris followed Juliet out of the boys' shared bedroom, Vince removed the crucifix from around his neck, knelt in the center of the room, and began to pray.

***

God sat on the swing hanging from the oak in His front lawn and puffed on an old cigar. He surveyed the skyline of Heaven through His smoke. God had chosen to move fifteen miles out of the downtown with Mrs. God to a suburb called Greater Heaven because of the quickly skyrocketing crime rate in the city center. As Central Heaven filled with more and more souls, each having suppressed its most brutal urges on Earth, the city gained a rapidly worsening reputation for freewheeling libertinism. Nobody had the threat of eternal damnation to act as a deterrent to his darkest actions. Those with enough political clout to be granted favors had fled from Central Heaven to the multitude of smaller suburbs cropping up in the neighboring countryside.

God sighed and tightened His necktie. Sooner or later, He would have to step in and create another Heaven. Mrs. God was always pushing for the idea of Purgatory. "After people spendeth two centuries suffering, you're going to seeith a certain amount of discouragement in them. People will giveth up trying to get into Heaven and hedge their bets in Hell," She would usually say over dinner. However, God found the idea of Purgatory to be inherently inhumane. No, no. He would just have to start conceiving of New Heaven. It wouldn't take long – seven days at the most – but God found it bothersome all the same. He had thought that, by inventing Deism, He had absolved Himself of the need to take any more responsibilities on His shoulders. He had wanted to enjoy His retirement in peace.

Mrs. God stepped onto the porch. She was rolling a blunt.

"God!" she cried. "Do You haveth any more of that good shit You picked up in Colombia?"

God looked at His wife from beneath the brim of His fedora. He let out a low whistle. She grew more beautiful every time He beheld Her. The couple went together well. Her hair was blonde like the sunshine, Her skin was white like a wisp of cloud, and Her eyes were blue like a clear wintry sky. God was Her complement: His hair was black like moist topsoil, His skin was brown like the trunk of a Mediterranean palm tree, and His eyes were the vibrant green of newly mown grass. Whenever the two made love, luminescent colors vibrated out from the friction of their bodies and filled the firmament. Those observing the phenomenon from the Earth below referred to it as a "sunset."

"You're a right broad, My love," God said around His cigar, a manly sneer overtaking His stubbly face.

Mrs. God smiled flirtatiously. "You didn't answereth Mine question," She said. She put a slender hand on God's shoulder.

"The thing is," God teased, "when a dame around here opens her mouth, all a gent hears is 'Danger.'"

Mrs. God wrapped Her other hand playfully around God's waist. "Then I sayeth to Thee, 'Danger.' And Thou needeth to shaveth, or Thou'll be gettingeth no celestial action." She tightened her grasp on His waist, kissed Him ferociously on His unshaven cheek, and released Him. Neither said anything further. Mrs. God, giving up on the possibility of getting at the Colombia stash, held out Her blunt to God, who lit it with a flourish of His Zippo. Mrs. God took a few puffs, scanning the Central Heaven skyline meditatively. Black smog had long ago enveloped the cityscape, making the individual buildings almost indistinguishable at such a distance.

"What a shithole," She pronounced. "You've got to setteth up a police department and environmental regulations."

God shook His head. "I'm retired, and even a buxom duck like You won't get this old hand back on the saddle."

"Thou art a hypocrite," Mrs. God said, with a ghost of a smile. "Thou haven't doneth a damn thing in six hundred years and then, out of nowhere, Thou smitethed the damn space shuttle that never dideth a damn thing to Thee."

God shrugged and winked at His wife, whose face betrayed its placidity behind its veneer of reefer smoke. "Can't a slick cat prowl on his own, without old Mother Hen pecking at his motives?"

Before Mrs. God could make Her objections to God's sexist vernacular, the clouds beneath Their feet rumbled, split open, and vomited up Vince Markham from the world below. He looked around, nonplussed.

"You guys have moved again."

Mrs. God shrugged before enwrapping Vince in a passionate hug.

"Crime!" God cried, in response to Vince's observation. "Pollution! Prostitution! Central Heaven's mean streets have gone to the rats!"

"God and I have to keep movething. The downtown just keeps gettething worse and worse," Mrs. God said by way of a more coherent explanation, releasing Vince from Her hug and holding him at arm's length. "You've growneth."

"I can't have grown, Mrs. God. I saw you this morning before the space shuttle crashed."

God shook His head and indicated a small white pimple brewing beneath the surface of Vince's dark skin. "This sucker's new. And there's a new hair about to sprout on your left arm. A private dick, such as Myself, is always in the know." God spoke with a great degree of self-satisfaction, but His smirking sense of superiority did not alienate Vince in the slightest. Vince loved God and Mrs. God with all his heart. Though They sometimes behaved in an overly dramatic manner, Their hearts were good, and They had always been there for him. Vince had begun praying when he was eight years old and desperately wanted a bicycle for Christmas. It was then that he had first been transported to Greater Heaven and encountered the Heavenly Couple. God had given Vince a stern lecture on greed and materialism, but, like any loving father, had gotten the bicycle for him anyway. Since then, Vince tried to drop in on his friends five times a day: first thing in the morning, last thing at night, and directly before meals.

"I can't stay long, Guys. My crew is leaving for Texas in ten minutes," Vince said. Mrs. God offered him a puff on Her roach, which he declined. "I'm a little worried. I have a really awful feeling in my stomach about the crash. Something doesn't seem quite right about it."

God nonchalantly scooped up a handful of cloud from the ground and began wadding it into a compact ball. "Why might that be?"

Mrs. God looked angrily at Her husband. "I don't know, God," She said, answering for Vince, "but I thinketh that it beith a good question. Why?"

God simply shrugged and rolled His ball of cloud around in His hands. "Vince, buddy, I'd be a dirty scoundrel if I lied to a cheeky young pipsqueak like yourself. It's My work."

"You've always told me You were retired," Vince said.

"I am," God replied, "but sometimes a man has to step up and fill a need what needs filling, read me?" He hurled the ball of cloud at Vince playfully, and it spattered into an infinity of wispy fragments that slowly floated down to the ground. Vince, smiling benignly, brushed the stray cottony bits of cloud from the front of his black dress shirt. "Just try to enjoy yourself down there," God continued, "and don't give yourself indigestion over the 'why' of it. Leave the indigestion to Me – I've built up a hearty constitution after an eternity of the old ball-and-chain's chicken cacciatore."

"Thou loveth My chicken cacciatore," Mrs. God said, rolling Her eyes.

17

"All I mean to say," God said, stubbing out His cigar on the heel of His wingtip, "is that you can't let yourself get the heebie-jeebies down there. You just stay in touch and, no matter how bad it starts looking for you and your crew, you'll be fine as long as you keep faith in Me."

"In Us," Mrs. God corrected, jabbing God in the ribs. "Thou beith such a chauvinist."

Despite God and Mrs. God's encouraging words, Vince had only heard "no matter how bad it starts looking for you and your crew." The ill feeling he had regarding the whole assignment doubled. He had no specific reason to feel that something terrible was coalescing, but he was scared. He knew that God worked in mysterious ways, but why He had stepped out of retirement to meddle in worldly affairs and why He imagined that things might go badly for the Las Cruces Ranger District were troubling mysteries. Before Vince could open his mouth to question God further, the clouds beneath his feet ripped apart and he found himself suddenly back in New Mexico, kneeling in the center of his vacated bedroom, head bowed, with his crucifix in his hand.

It was time to leave for Texas.

The Find

Two days after the crash, Arlo was out on his daily stroll through his land. He had been finding bits and pieces of shuttle here and there around his property. They were infrequent and typically no larger than his hand. Some were metal – rings, hinges, and screws – and some were charred chunks of frothy foam tile. If he hadn't heard about the heat tile on the news, he would have assumed that the bits of tile he kept finding were nothing more than fragments of an old Styrofoam coffee cup. However, Arlo knew that his land was in the area of highest concentration of debris fallout and so he kept his eyes open for anything unusual.

His property spanned several square miles, so, at his creaky pace, it would take him weeks to get through it all. All the same, he had heard on the news that the government was organizing a search mission and he wanted to cover as much ground as he could before the Feds arrived. He was amassing a little collection of old space shuttle fragments. Though he had no practical use for them, and though he knew that the government probably had more of a right to them than he did, he could not convince himself to overlook the opportunity of owning some historical mementos. No major news had ever happened in his neck of the woods; Arlo felt that his ranch's brief era of national significance merited commemoration.

The other issue on Arlo's mind as he slowly hobbled through his fields, casting his eyes around hungrily in search of extraterrestrial treasure, was Amanda's recent submersion into dementia. When he had returned to the house on the evening of the crash, Amanda had been sitting at the kitchen table, rocking back and forth and muttering, "Robin, Robin – he flew up in the sky, and then came a-crashing down!" Arlo, gravely concerned, had tried to get her to snap out of it, but he couldn't exhort her to leave off chanting or rocking until well after sundown.

Later, after rationality had once again recaptured Amanda's mind, Arlo asked her, "Who's Robin?" She had looked at him as though he were mad and told him that she had never known any such woman.

Amanda, at eighty-six, was three years younger than Arlo, but, nevertheless, had always worn her age less heartily than her husband. Arlo knew that he couldn't expect her to last forever, but the sight of her staring into space and reciting what seemed to be a children's verse had brought him closer to tears than he had ever been in his life. The next day, he had gone out into the fields as always. Hardship or no hardship,

Arlo saw no use in hand wringing, and he welcomed the monotony of his routine in bringing his mind away from his wife. He couldn't cure senility, so he focused on a goal he could accomplish: to collect as much of the space shuttle as he could.

Now, the February sun was burning brightly, undistorted by any sort of cloud cover or humidity. The air was cold enough that Arlo could see his wheezy breath materialize before him as he trudged over the frozen soil. He had only found one small chunk of heat tile that morning and felt that he was bound to make a big discovery soon. After all, he had discovered six pieces on the day of the crash and ten on the following day. He was hoping for something metal, or maybe even plastic, a button or a knob, maybe. If it had writing on it, it would be all the better.

About a quarter of a mile past the creek, a warm glint sparkled on the ground near the edge of the woods. Arlo didn't speed up as he approached. He had been walking more than usual in the past few days, and so his spine was plagued with firebursts of pain. Rushing might overtax his heart, causing him to collapse before he got the chance to see what was causing the light.

It took Arlo fifteen minutes to hobble close enough to make any sense of the object. It was a laminated plastic spheroid object. It was lying against a rock and, amazingly, seemed rather undamaged by its passage through the atmosphere and its impact with the earth. There were a few chips in the plastic, but, largely, the surface was flawlessly smooth. In fact, the object was so intact that it seemed almost to have been gently placed on the ground like a giant Easter egg for Arlo to discover.

Ignoring the riotous protest of his back, Arlo leant down to pick up the sphere. He brought it up to his chest, turning it over as he did. With a sudden scream and a shudder of revulsion, Arlo dropped the object and averted his eyes. His heart thrummed frantically and its pulse echoed throughout his body. He forcefully squinted again and again, in the hope that he could erase the image that the object had forced into his consciousness. However, when, after several minutes, he felt brave enough to look again at what he had dropped, it remained just as ghastly as before.

He had discovered a head, still neatly enclosed in its space helmet.

The head staring at Arlo through the plastic window of the helmet was not an unattractive one. The astronaut had had a sharp, defined jawline and a subtle nose. His lips were open, as though he were preparing to inhale. However, the especially chilling thing about the head was that its eye sockets were empty. Delicate tongues of blood crisscrossed its cheeks. Arlo found himself transfixed, gazing into the black depths of the fallen spaceman's skull. In spite of the head's lack of eyes, Arlo felt that it was watching him. His heart was palpitating rapidly and he took several deep breaths. Even so, when he closed his eyes he could still feel the sightless gaze of the eyeless head scrutinizing him.

Arlo wasn't sure what to do. An astronaut's severed head was lying on his property. He couldn't just pick it up and take it home – he wouldn't want to, anyway. But, on the other hand, he couldn't just leave it there. Sitting at home, caring for Amanda, and lying in his bed at night, Arlo would be constantly plagued by the knowledge that there was a severed head out there at the edge of his woods, waiting for somebody to do something with it. He thought maybe he should call the police and have them come and take care of it. However, he didn't want to let the head out of his sight. It might take him two hours to get back to the house to call the police. What if a coyote got at the head in the meantime? Arlo figured that the best thing was probably to bring the head back to the house with him; the difficulty in that, though, was that he didn't want to touch the thing again.

"Help."

Arlo was startled from his calculations by a low, raspy voice speaking just on the edge of audibility. He looked around for the source, but, of course, the dread conclusion was already immediately obvious – the head was speaking.

"Help me, you shitheaded geriatric."

At Arlo's age, running away was not an option. Instead, he looked down at the head to see that its healthy, boyish lips had twisted into a fiendish grin beneath its cavernous eye sockets. "It's happened," Arlo thought. "I've gone senile." He tried to remember the name of his wife, his parents, and his home state. He could – or, at least, he thought he could. What if he were wrong, though? What if he had, in his dementia, constructed an elaborate fantasy universe, entirely removed from reality? But, then, if that were the case, why should he find it incongruous for a decapitated head to be addressing him as a "shitheaded geriatric?"

"Snap out of it, Oldie Hawn!" the head suddenly yelled. "You're not senile, your wife is. You're going to be just fine, as long as you help me. And I'll throw a little something into the bargain: help me out and I'll see to it that Amanda pulls herself out of this chasm of crazy she's lately fallen into."

Arlo looked around once more, but he only saw the quiet, slowly flowing stream, the dark trees at the edge of the woods, and the immaculate blue February sky. In his youth, he might have spent such a cloudless day playing fetch with his father's dog, Gorgeous; picking out rushes to adorn the bouquet he planned to present to his eighth grade teacher, Miss Forester, with whom he had been hopelessly in love; or working on the raft which he never actually finished building. Now he was eighty-nine, all the best times were behind him, and he was about to enlist himself in the aid of a grotesque, eyeless head.

"What kind'er help d'you mean, sir?" Arlo asked, fighting to keep dizziness from overtaking him.

"Grandpa speaks at last! I thought I'd lost you. We don't have any time to waste, geezer. We've got hell to raise. Pick me up, take me home, and hide me. I'd hide myself, but I seem to be immobile, annoyingly enough. I've got revenge to pay. It's God that blasted me to Earth, and it's God that we're going to throw down with." Arlo made no move. "What are you waiting for, you dander-headed shitrag?"

"I ain't...well, sir, but I mean to say that God...well...." Arlo hesitated. After years of ceaseless operation, the clockwork in Arlo's head was beginning to wear down; the teeth of his gears were worn into impotent nubs, his gaskets were slippery, and his screws were stripped of their tracking. To an ancient mind, operating inefficiently from overuse, no ready answer is available to the demands of an embittered head seeking revenge against the Creator of All.

"Look, leatherbutt," said the head. "The Feds are already swarming all over East Texas like coeds at an orgy. They're looking for me – and when they find me, they're gonna slice up my skull and have my brains for brunch. I'd rather that didn't happen. In short, I'm making you a proposal, you chimp-faced codger. Hide me in your cellar with a bottle of Seagram's and I'll bring the missus back to the age when she could bang like a bunny all night long. Youth, eh? Whattaya say to that?"

Arlo, hopelessly mashing his jaw up and down in an agitated attempt at speech, had nothing coherent to say to that.

Sensing that its case was not being won, the head changed its approach. "If we're playing hardball, we're playing hardball, you wrinkle-brained son of a bitch. I can make your life pretty damn pleasant if you do what I'm asking; conversely, I can make your life pretty damn unpleasant if you don't."

With that, a lightning bolt of electric pain sliced through Arlo's body, leaping from his feet to the top of his bald head. He began shaking – his muscles were spasming uncontrollably, his heart beat with agonizing ferocity, and his jaw was locked. He thought that the head might be laughing, but he couldn't hear very much over the sounds of his own tortured screams. Just when Arlo thought that he would die of the torment, the pain drained from his body and endorphins rushed in to soothingly fill the vacated space. His heartbeat slowed and his breathing returned. He looked at the head in horrified panic.

"Feel that, you salami-titted troglodyte?" The head spoke with cocky assurance, as though visiting such excruciating pain on Arlo had cost it no effort whatsoever. "You've got an eternity of far worse than that to look forward to if you don't pull me out from under the Fed's radar." The head paused. "So, what's it gonna be, you pantywaisted marmoset? Pleasure or pain?"

With a trembling hand, Arlo, still unable to speak, picked up the head and tucked it under his arm like a football.

"You made a good choice, Stonehenge-teeth," the head said as Arlo started with it back to the ranch house, wondering how, exactly, he was going to explain his new acquaintance to Amanda.

The Loss

While Arlo was gaining the friendship of a head, the Las Cruces crew was finally nearing the tie-in point with the NASA liaison, Ross Tucker. Ana was driving the crew's fifteen-passenger van, with Takeshi asleep in shotgun. Chris was sitting in the back, staring out the rear window. He had been sketching a series of gory executions for much of the two-day drive, but, as the van drew closer and closer to Longview, his attention had been arrested by the changing landscape. West Texas had resembled New Mexico in its broad expanses of arid desert, but East Texas was proving to be a gnarled jungle. Chris could see unruly patches of dense forestland sprawling up to the side of the highway. The roads were deserted, the shadowy thickets were backlit by the setting sun, and, as the van passed through eerie fields of illuminated corn set against a darkening purple sky, Chris felt poised on the brink of a nightmare.

Juliet was sitting next to Chris, stacking her six tampons – Ana had given her two – into little fortresses on her knee before knocking them down again. With no pens, no books, and no Discman, Juliet's restless fingers had no other diversion; any attempts she had made at conversation with Chris had met with inattentive grunts. Now, however, as the darkness of night closed around the van, and the steady breathing of her sleeping crewmates made her feel like the last living person, her chill sense of loneliness was motivation enough for her to try talking to Chris again.

"Quite a sunset," she whispered to Chris. For a moment, she imagined that he wouldn't turn away from the window to acknowledge her, but eventually he did.

"I think it's awful."

"Why?" Juliet had the same feeling herself, but she wanted to keep the conversation afloat. At the same time, she was curious – perhaps Chris had a more tangible reason for his feelings of dread than she had for her own.

Chris disappointed her, however, by shaking his head and returning his attention to the passing Texas landscape. With a sigh, Juliet stuffed her tampons back into her pocket and mumbled, "Are we stopping soon? I have to pee." Receiving no answer from Ana, or from anybody else, Juliet shut her eyes and tried to silence herself into sleep.

***

The crew arrived at the armory, as scheduled, at 1900 that night. The armory was a tiny, glum brick building on the outskirts of Longview. A rusty mockup of a tank sat in cobwebbed grandeur in the middle of the empty, unlit parking lot. A pale light shone through the building's front window; otherwise, the crew found itself stepping out of the van into complete darkness.

"Let's hustle, guys," Ana barked, clapping her hands to rouse her half-asleep crew. She had been the first one out of the van and the first one to grab her backpack from the back. She had always held the firm conviction that nobody – particularly men – should ever take longer to do anything than she.

"Are you sure this is the place?" Roger – one of the Kansas boys – asked as he stepped into the blinding darkness of the Texas night. "There's nobody here."

"I'm aware of that," Ana snapped, rolling her eyes, though conscious that nobody could see her do so. "This is where we were instructed to go, and I have not been notified of any change in the operating procedures."

Despite her brusque tone, Ana could not deny that she was nervous. If there had been a mistake and they had ended up in the wrong place, her crew might begin to question her. She couldn't afford any surprises.

Thankfully, as she was meditating on the possibility of having misunderstood NASA's seemingly plain orders, a man in a crisp white shirt came out of the front door of the armory and asked, "Are you the Las Cruces crew?"

"We are," replied Ana. She strode up to the man, grabbed his hand, and pumped it once before letting it fall. "Ana Jenkins, crew leader. We were told to report to Mr. Ross Tucker."

"Ah." The man smiled, the greenish fluorescent light from the armory's interior casting an otherworldly pallor over his youthful face. "Mr. Tucker has been unexpectedly detained elsewhere. I'm filling in for him temporarily. My name is Robin Rodriguez."

***

The "elsewhere" in which Mr. Ross Tucker had unexpectedly been detained was Shultz and Morgan Funeral Parlor. The blood had been gently scrubbed from his wrists, his self-inflicted knife wounds had been neatly sewn up with barely visible thread, and his face had been massaged out of its agonized expression, entrenched by rigor mortis, into one of attractive, calm self-assurance. A dusting of rouge gave a deceptively lifelike quality to his cheeks, his premature wrinkles were glossed over with beige foundation, and his hair had been washed, combed, and pomaded. In short, enclosed in his coffin, clad in his best Sunday suit, Mr. Tucker appeared better put-together than he ever had in life.

Tucker's suicide had followed quickly upon the crash of the Daedalus. Robin had been notified later that same evening. He had just arrived home from the Saunders' ranch when he received the phone call.

"Mr. Rodriguez?"

"Speaking." Robin was still shaken by his manipulation of Amanda and was calmed somewhat by the neutral, businesslike voice on the other end of the phone. The ultimate goal of a PR man is to be able to respond to all anomalous circumstances with no emotional interference; the fact that he had failed in this at the Saunders' was fresh in his mind as he spoke to the anonymous caller.

"I'm calling from HQ with a special mission," said the man on the other end of the phone.

"I'm sorry," Robin said, walking into his dim kitchenette and grabbing an apple, "but I cannot follow orders given anonymously. What's your CID number?"

"Ross Tucker went down with his ship."

Suddenly, Robin felt as though he were in a dream. He looked quizzically at the apple in his hand, as though he had no conception of how he might have come to be holding it. His murky grey kitchen seemed to be swimming in fog. Ross Tucker had been, simply, invincible. Barely five feet, skinny, and constantly looking as though he had just been roused from bed, Ross Tucker possessed NASA's quickest mind. He could multiply a chain of five-digit numbers in his head faster than his colleagues could write down his dictated calculations. He had been central to designing the Daedalus mission, and even the specifics of the search and rescue mission had been drawn largely from his excruciatingly detailed contingency plans. For Robin, to think that such an airtight mind could fall victim to mortal ailments was sacrilege.

"Tucker is dead, in other words," the caller continued. "He was found at his console, bleeding all over the damn equipment. I know you know how much the success of this mission mattered to him. He couldn't live with the consequences."

Robin tried to collect his gauzed-over mind. "I'm sorry," he said, shaking his head. "Couldn't live with what consequences? Who are you? If you don't identify yourself by your CID number immediately, it is my duty to end this conversation."

"Tucker took a gamble and failed. It is important that nobody realize how high the stakes were; therefore, we cannot allow the search and rescue mission to be deterred by his death. Tucker had wanted to meet each crew assigned to the mission. Of course, that is impossible now – it would have been impossible, even had he lived. There are simply going to be too many crews coming in throughout the next several days. In the interest of time, we are splitting up his responsibilities among our entire PR staff. Your assignment is the East Texas Deployment Zone, in and around Longview. You will be briefed tomorrow, and will meet and brief your crew at the Longview Armory at 1900 on the 17th. Please suspend your private party notification assignment – we will notify the remainder of the area ranchers of our presence by phone. Specific instructions will be faxed to you at your office by 0900 tomorrow."

Robin unconsciously began rapping the apple hard against his stainless steel counter. He could process none of what he was hearing, except that Tucker was dead. If that were true, then there was no limit to what surprises the world was capable of presenting. It was as though water had begun flowing upstream, or gravity had suddenly decided to switch directions.

"I'm sorry," Robin said for the third time, falling back on the PR-man tactic of alleviating speechlessness through self-effacement. "I have no qualifications for such an assignment."

"You'll be faxed full instructions tomorrow by 0900. There is no qualification necessary, aside from an ability to follow protocol."

"What's your CID number?"

"Are there any further questions?"

"Why did you say that the stakes were high?"

"Unless there are any further questions, I will wish you goodnight. Thank you for your time."

Robin was about to pose his question again when he realized that the man had hung up, leaving him with a dented apple in his right hand, an impotent telephone in his left, and a thundering headache.

***

The Las Cruces crew had entered the armory and was currently having its bags and vehicle searched by Robin, who, having read through NASA's explicit instructions with the greatest attentiveness twelve times over the last two days, was finding his new responsibilities not only simpler than expected, but even satisfying. The fax had been very detailed as to NASA's precise demands on him. After greeting the crew and searching its belongings, he was to deliver a scripted briefing before ferrying the Las Cruces crew to its preordained search sector. Hairy questions were simple to deal with – they were not, under any circumstances, to be answered.

"Where is everybody?" Juliet asked, as Robin leafed through the contents of her backpack. Ana glared at her as a mother might glare at a precocious child, but said nothing.

"In order to ensure security, we are dealing with each crew individually," Robin replied automatically, not pausing in his search. Juliet's was one of the few questions he could answer with certainty. That response had been spelled out in the faxed instructions with great emphasis.

Robin put Juliet's bag aside and picked up Takeshi's. It checked out, as did Roger's. However, Roger's friends did not fare as well. Robin extracted a pack of cigarettes from Francis's pack and three pornos from Scott's.

"Aw, c'mon, don't be a buzzkill!" Scott said, blushing in spite of himself.

"Yeah," Francis agreed. "Scott only wanted to bring along some pictures of his mom to remember her by!"

Ana maintained a straight face, Juliet rolled her eyes, and Scott slugged Francis forcibly on the shoulder. Robin diplomatically avoided any indication of his personal thoughts on the matter, but simply deposited the magazines, along with Francis's cigarettes, in a bin he had reserved for confiscated items.

Throughout the searches of his crewmates' bags, Chris was conscious of his own trepidation. He had brought his sketchbook out of necessity. It wasn't recreational, like Scott's pornos. As Robin began to leaf through Chris's bag, Chris tried to think of how he could phrase his objection without sounding petulant or, worse, nutty.

Wordlessly, Robin came across the sketchbook and took it into confiscation. Chris felt himself blushing. He felt the eyes of the entire crew on him. Vince was looking at him with unexpected sympathy. Chris wanted, on principle, to reject Vince's compassion, but his gratitude exceeded his pride and he smiled slightly – and, he felt, stupidly. His blush deepened, and he hated himself for it.

"Aside from the book, your backpack meets specifications," Robin said, already moving on to Ana's bag.

"Um, sorry, but…." Chris said, feeling that his voice was weak and even a little feminine. He noticed that Ana was glaring at him with fire in her eyes and that Vince's compassion was quickly hardening into irritation. Even Juliet seemed to be urging him to hold his tongue. Chris gulped and continued, "You can't take that." His fingers began to tingle; he had the sudden annoying impulse to draw, and it was all he could do to keep from rushing to Robin and grabbing his sketchbook back.

Robin was too busy looking through Ana's backpack to notice the grave insecurity in Chris's tone. "Don't worry," he replied, without looking up, "It will be returned to you."

"Chris," Ana snapped, "Shut up."

Chris felt exposed. He had always been intimidated by Roger, Scott, and Francis because of their enormous statures and their collective conviction that his drawing habit was "gayer than a San Francisco prom king." At that moment, they were giving him their most cutting "you've got to be kidding me" looks. Even Takeshi, typically quiet and unobtrusive, seemed impatient. After two days in the van, the entire crew just wanted to set up camp as soon as possible. Chris gulped and continued nevertheless, "Uh, yeah...." He saw a muscle twitch above Ana's right eye. "I mean, sir, that I have to keep that with me at all times." His palms were sweaty and he wished he were dead.

At this point, Robin finally glanced up from his work. He was startled by the anxiety in Chris's eyes. "We will return all your confiscated items to you after the completion of your assignment."

"C'mon, dweeb," Scott said. "I gave up my porn; you can give up your diary."

Chris wanted to say that it wasn't a diary and, moreover, that its confiscation could lead to enormous problems. Before Chris could decide what to say, he dared once more to steal a glance at Vince. The compassion-cum-irritation had transformed once again – Vince was now looking at Chris with pleading eyes. Vince was tired, everybody else was tired, and Chris was being selfish by holding up their in-processing. With downcast eyes, Chris kept silent this time, attempting to quiet the insistent voice in the back of his head that was telling him he was making a huge mistake.

***

Juliet watched Chris's relinquishment of his sketchbook with great concern. She had never seen him quite so vulnerable, and his insecurity seemed quite abrupt. In the days since he had confessed to her his feelings towards Vince, Chris had been snippy and almost showily peevish. This unexpected break in his recent defenses only served to reinforce the suspicion with which Juliet had viewed Chris's sketchbook ever since he had become attached to it a month ago. There was something about the violence with which Chris would blast bloody reds, fiery oranges, and smoky blacks onto the pages that made Juliet think there was something more than a repressed crush kindling in his heart.

"Juliet, I need your help out at the rig," Ana said, snapping Juliet away from her thoughts. Without waiting for Juliet to acknowledge that she had heard, Ana strode out of the armory into the hazy Texas night.

The rest of the crew watched Juliet follow Ana out. Robin was still at work searching bags and didn't notice the interest with which the crew observed Juliet's exit. Under most circumstances, Ana called on male crew members when she needed help, and so everybody on the crew recognized her selection of Juliet as nothing more than an opportunity to get her alone for a conversation. Everybody but Chris, who was still focused on his separation from his sketchbook, wondered what the conversation was to be about.

As Juliet stepped outside, she was hit by the sudden chill of the air. Though she was wearing her Nomex, the insistent February wind snaked through the thick material effortlessly. A heavy fog had rolled in while the crew was inside the armory, causing the little light seeping out of the window to have no effect on visibility. Juliet could feel her small nose growing ice cold. She put her hands under her armpits, hunched her shoulders up to her ears for warmth, and groped towards the van.

If the unexpected coldness of the night had an effect on Ana, she did not betray it. She was standing erect at the van, not allowing herself the slightest shiver. She peered into the gauzy blindness around her until she could make out Juliet's dim figure silhouetted against the gray fog. Once she was confident that Juliet was near, she began speaking without preamble. "I don't like to keep the crew waiting, Juliet, so I won't mince words. You hate me and that's fine, but it's a new season and I won't have you disrespecting me openly. Say what you will behind my back, I need the assurance that my direct orders will be met with respect and obedience. Believe it or not, I have this job because I have fought to deserve it. When I speak to the crew, it is out of eighteen years' experience." Ana tried to see if Juliet was listening, but in the darkness she could barely see her. With a sharp exhalation, Ana continued. "Contradiction of my imperatives is not only disrespectful, but dangerous as well. I know the forests, and I know safety out here. You're still new. Maybe someday you'll prove yourself and then you can fight fire in a bustle and a hoop skirt for all I care, but today you're under my command. I expect this mission to go flawlessly, but I require your grudging cooperation. Are we agreed?"

Juliet was glad that Ana could not see her face throughout this lecture. Angered by her superior's condescending tone, worn out from two days in a cramped van, stung by frozen winds, and troubled by Chris's desperate expression in the armory, even the sheerest exertion of her dignity could not prevent a handful of frustrated tears from escaping her eyes. Juliet felt utterly trapped. Nobody on the crew listened to her. Scott, Roger, and Francis were a pack of howling frat boys who could think no further than the length of their boners. Takeshi was nice enough, but got embarrassed whenever Juliet spoke to him. He rarely opened his mouth – even at mealtimes, he would open his tiny slit of a mouth as narrowly as possible, pop in a morsel of food, and slam his lips shut again before anybody could claim to have caught him with his mouth agape. Vince, while pleasant, was too busy communing with God to take notice of his fellow mortals; Juliet had tried and failed time and again to get him to open up to the crew. Ana, of course, was impossible to speak to without getting berated, and even Chris had recently become testy and full of angst. Chris used to be Juliet's salvation. He would listen to her gripes, speak to her without performing a tired routine of macho posturing, and, more than anything, take her seriously. When Chris had spoken of Vince to her, she had assumed that his candor would bring them even closer together; instead, he seemed to resent Juliet for her knowledge of his weakness and had left her abandoned in a team of people who couldn't understand her.

Now, rubbing her hands together for warmth, flummoxed by the cold and impersonal manner in which Ana – who, as a woman, ought to be her ally, for Chrissake – had just addressed her, Juliet hated her tears. They were weakness. Here, in God-knows-where Texas, forty hours from home, with nobody to talk to, no property save the contents of her backpack, and not even the simple acknowledgment from her boss that her feelings of loneliness were valid, Juliet began to wonder if maybe she was too weak a woman to be a firefighter after all.

"Juliet," Ana said severely. "Please. The crew is inside waiting for us, and we are all very tired. I ask that you either agree to show me more respect or that you explain to me what is unreasonable about my request. In either case, please don't waste any more time."

Juliet nodded before realizing that, in the foggy darkness, it was unlikely that Ana could distinguish her gesture. She steadied her voice and said, as evenly as possible, "You won't have any problems with me."

"Good." Even in the darkness, Juliet could tell that Ana's condescending smile had snaked across her lips. "Thank you, Juliet. I'm glad that we can agree to behave as mature women. Now let's get inside; you sound cold."

Ana moved briskly back into the armory, leaving Juliet to plod slowly behind her. Cold as she was, Juliet needed a moment alone to process what had just occurred. She was furious at Ana, but her mind was primarily occupied with the doubt her conversation had just unearthed. "All along I've been pissed at Ana," Juliet thought, trying in vain to halt a shiver that ripped across her body, "but maybe I'm just jealous of her composure. What if nobody takes me seriously because my attitude is not one to be taken seriously?"

Juliet tried to shake off her self-doubt as nothing more than textbook internalization of her insecurities. She had taken a psychology course in high school and knew that her mind was just seizing her loneliness and frustration and trying somehow to justify them. Nonetheless, it was only with considerable force of will that Juliet was able to step back inside the armory to face the rest of the crew.

***

While Juliet and Ana were outside speaking, another confiscation was occurring inside the armory.

"Why could you possibly need to take it?" Vince asked, his angry blush turning his brown face a purplish bruise color. "It is ungentlemanly, unreasonable, and unchristian."

Robin wiped his sweaty palms against the thighs of his jeans and imagined that he was in a rocket ship, soaring thousands of miles outside the earth's atmosphere. Staring out the triple-paned console window, he could see galactic whorls, bleary gas giants, and jagged chunks of obsidian space ice. This was what he had envisioned when he joined NASA; he had never planned to be sitting in a hollowed-out armory in East Texas with a golden crucifix dangling from his left thumb and a group of fatigued firefighters glaring at him with peevishness.

"I'm sorry," Robin said, an artificially sincere smile unconsciously melting across his face. "Regulations specify that no materials beyond what is accounted for in the Deployment Manual may be brought into the Search Sector."

Vince puffed out an unsteady breath. He was trying very hard to restrain his anger, but he couldn't understand what the goal in taking the crucifix could possibly be. Chris had never seen such a display of feeling in Vince before; the shock of seeing such a mild individual struggle to keep a surge of emotion in check was enough to distract him from his own recent loss.

"Sir, I apologize if this comes across as disrespectful," Vince began, a tremor in his voice betraying the fact that he was not entirely in control of himself, "but I cannot go through with the mission if my crucifix is taken from me."

Every one of Vince's well-formed muscles was flexed, displaying the rounded contours of his powerful body even through his heavy Nomex. Unprecedented animation flickered behind his chocolate brown eyes. Chris felt a surge of passion for Vince; his head was dizzy from the level of electricity in the room – between his love for Vince, his anger about the sketchbook, and Vince's anger about the crucifix, Chris felt as though he were at the center of some cosmic confluence of energy.

"Agreed," Chris interjected, feeling all of the eyes in the room sharply redirected towards him. He astounded himself with his confidence. "I'm not going without my sketchbook."

Chris received a jab in the ribs from Scott, whose thin, angular frame made his elbows lethally bony. "Don't be a doof," Scott growled.

"Yeah," Francis agreed wearily, coming to Chris's other side and readying his fists, in case their destructive power should be called upon.

Robin was taken aback. Refusal to participate was not addressed in the instructions he had received from NASA. He knew only that his responsibility was to get the crew out into the Search Sector and to sidestep uncomfortable questions. However, after a moment's hesitation, Robin instinctively began to do what had qualified him for PR in the first place – he started spinning an elaborate lie with the utmost sincerity.

"I understand your hesitation, fellows. I know there are things I depend on that I wouldn't want to be without for three weeks – religious tokens and whatnot." Robin's smile deepened, exposing his cherubic dimples. He had the crew's attention, but he didn't know for how much longer. He needed to come up with something fast. However, before he had even started to consider what to say, his mouth was speaking with such authority that he didn't dare to stop it.

"Yes, indeed, I understand your hesitation," Robin repeated, "but all of our measures are in place for your own safety. Upon reentry into the atmosphere, a number of the radioactive components on the Daedalus shuttle were exposed to a sudden increase in atmospheric pressure. Certain elements – xenon, for one – can be alloyed with certain others in order to produce what we call supercharged elements. These supercharged elements have greatly increased half-lives and also bear the ability of transforming the simple iterative motion of gamma radiation into a more obliquely directed quarter-adjusted circular path. Under most circumstances, the conduction of these supercharged elements occurs in highly controlled environments…." Robin coughed, at once proud of his creative diversion and yet slightly depressed by the fact that he would never actually understand the atomic processes on which he was currently riffing.

"But my crucifix…," Vince said.

"Is made of gold, or at least of a gold-bearing alloy. I know the odds of a misaligned magnetism are slim – probably one in ten, if it's an alloy – but that's too much of a risk. You could instigate a tonal reattribution in the supercharged elements, creating a radiation overflux."

Robin had graduated in the middle of his class in mechanical engineering at Rice. With a twinge, he realized that if he had spent his time studying for his tests, rather than developing elaborate excuses as to why he had flunked them, he might have been better suited to his dream job as an astronaut. Instead, he was little better than an actor, weaseling his way out of tight situations as a career.

"I'm not even me right now," Robin thought with dissatisfaction. "I'm Ross fucking Tucker, the brilliant scientist who touts more accolades than Robin Rodriguez ever will."

"Hear that?" Roger said, patting Vince on the back. Of the three Kansas boys, Roger was the crudest to his friends, but the most gentlemanly to the other members of the crew. He was Catholic and, though he saw Vince's faith as rather over the top, he respected the ethic behind it. "They've just gotta look out for us, bud. Nobody's trying to disrespect you here."

Francis's comment to Chris was less conciliatory. "Let's just fucking get on with it, you grabass."

Vince was not entirely convinced by Robin's pseudoscience. He couldn't follow Robin's argument, but it seemed to him that he wasn't meant to. He eyed his cross reluctantly. He couldn't doubt that it was an object of incredible potency, but he knew that there was no logical way it could actually create a "radiation overflux" – whatever that might be. There had to be a reason NASA needed to take his cross, just as there had to be a reason they had taken Chris's sketchbook. The entire situation sat uneasily with him. He wished that he had even just ten minutes to break off from the group and consult God.

At that moment, Ana stepped inside, dragging a wisp of frosty air with her. "Let's go," she said and, without bothering to consult the appearance of her crew, began piling backpacks near the door. "We all through here?" she asked Robin.

"Yes, ma'am." Robin dropped Vince's crucifix into the bin with Scott's porn, Francis's cigarettes, and Chris's sketchbook. "Everything checks out. Unless there are any problems among your crew, I can drive you out to the camp site immediately."

The crew looked at Vince. He felt profoundly uncomfortable, but he remembered what God had said before he had left New Mexico: "You just stay in touch and, no matter how bad it starts looking for you and your crew, you'll be fine as long as you keep faith in Me." He felt that he was meant to be with his crew, so, silencing his unease, he picked up his pack and said, "Let's go."

Chris decided almost immediately to relinquish his resistance as well. He felt safe wherever Vince went, and the prospect of Texas without his sketchbook was less frightening than the prospect of New Mexico without Vince. Chris wordlessly picked up his backpack as Francis exhaled, a little disappointed that he would not have an excuse to pummel Chris into obedience.

When Juliet came back into the armory, she was gratified to discover that her crewmates were too busy reviewing the Search Sector Transit Procedure to notice the dejected expression on her face. She slid unnoticed into the room, grabbed her pack, and listened to the tail end of Robin's briefing.

"…at which point I will depart in order to facilitate the in-processing of newly arriving crews. The primary difficulty you will encounter in the woods is communication. For reasons of safety and security, we are not able to equip all of you with radios – only your crew boss will be given a radio for communication with our headquarters. In light of this, it is absolutely crucial that you all stick together out there and that you contact headquarters regularly. At this time of year, most of the wildlife out there is pretty subdued. Your biggest threat is going to be hypothermia. Stay alert to what your body is telling you, remain hydrated, and don't attempt to cover too much ground in one day. Move swiftly but efficiently. Are there any questions?"

"Actually, yes," Vince said. "What, exactly, are we looking for?"

Robin smiled. NASA had given him an answer for this one. "Absolutely anything out of the ordinary."

***

Mrs. God rolled over in Her sleep, Her slender arm instinctually groping the side of the bed where Her husband usually lay. Tonight, however, Mrs. God's slumber was disturbed by the discovery that Her husband was not beside Her. His half of the bed was warm, but empty. Puzzlement worked its way into Mrs. God's dreams and She began to wake.

The bedroom was dark, save for a zebra pattern cast on the bedspread by the soft streetlights of East Greater Heaven filtering through the couple's Venetian blinds. God was sitting by the window, holding apart two slats of the blinds and peering out into the street below. Mrs. God couldn't see His face, but His shoulders were slumped and His head drooped as though He lacked the energy to hold it erect. He was whistling softly to Himself.

"Why dost Thou beith risen at such a late hour?" Mrs. God yawned voraciously, smacking Her lips, and arched Her feline back in a consummately satisfying stretch.

God turned just enough to bring Mrs. God into His doleful gaze, but said nothing. He stopped whistling and let go of the blinds guiltily. He strained for a smile, but His eyes betrayed Him as anxious. Mrs. God hated seeing Her husband depressed and it was a rare enough occurrence to alarm Her. Suddenly awake, She scooted into a sitting position and turned back the sheets on God's side of the bed, temporarily disrupting the zebra stripes that had settled over them.

"Speaketh to Me, O God!" Mrs. God cried. She tried to inject severity into Her gaze, but was incapable of ever truly speaking harshly to Her husband.

"I'm sorry if I woke You up, doll face," God said, standing and shuffling to Mrs. God. He put a hand on Her head and wove Her golden hair between His earthen brown fingers. As She looked up to Him with Her chill blue eyes, He wanted nothing more than to keep Her from ever having to see anything that wasn't beautiful. "Troubles, baby," He continued, "weigh on My tired old mind, but don't let that bungle Your beauty sleep."

Mrs. God joined Her hand to His and brought Her cheek to His chest. "Thou weareth not Thine slippers," She said. "Thou shalt catcheth pneumonia."

Silence descended over the Gods' bedroom as They held one another, each comforted by the other's close physical presence. On Earth, the night was quiet, cloudy, and starless.

After several hours, God finally slid back into bed, though His omniscient eyes remained wide open. Mrs. God softly began to say what had been on Her mind since She had woken to find Her husband troubled by something.

"God," She said, "I love Thee. Thou knowest that. But there beith no need for You to play John Wayne all the time. I'm as powerful as You and I can help You. But I can'teth help Thee without absolute truth. For six hundred years Thou hast doneth nothing but smoketh the doobie and liveth the high life. Now something beith up. I wasn't begat yesterday. Why didst Thou smiteth the space shuttle? What is bummething Thee out so completely?"

"It's a cruel world, angel."

"Telleth Me. I command Thee."

God observed the sincerity in His wife's eyes. She had always trusted Him. The people of Earth used to trust Him, too. A handful still did. He considered what He had seen while looking out the bedroom window. A gas fire was burning in one of the factories near the Greater Heaven Dockside and had been for decades. Even from the suburbs in the thick of night, the smoldering ruins of the gargantuan factory could be seen. Police sirens and gunshots were probably piercing the still evening air in the inner city. Lazy spumes of toxic runoff from the business district were corrupting the potable water supplies. Millions were hungry and yet couldn't die from starvation. Millions were frostbitten and yet couldn't die from the cold. Millions were asthmatic from the poisonous air and yet couldn't die from asphyxiation. Over the past six hundred years, Greater Heaven had become a veritable hellhole.

Dark tears suddenly spilled over God's face. Mrs. God had never seen Him look so old.

"I'm all washed up, honey-pie," God said, weeping into His wife's shoulder.

"Shhhhhh. Thou beith retired. All the world's ills now beith the doings of fucked up humankind."

"No." The tearstorm dwindled to a light drizzle, but the ferocity of God's remorse was no less. "I've been drop dead dull in the noggin."

"For the love of You, what hath happened?"

"I fear that Our good friend Vince has fallen into the clutches of some bad eggs and is in considerable danger."

Mrs. God gasped. Life in Greater Heaven was lonely. During the vast majority of God's retirement, time had seemed to crawl by. Mrs. God could vividly remember the time before God had ceased His active involvement in the world below, but everything since had been a foggy haze until Vince had come along, through his prayers, to revitalize Them. When he had first journeyed up to Greater Heaven as a child to ask for his first bicycle, God and Mrs. God had taken to him immediately, finding that he, in his generous heart and sly smile, resembled Them uncannily. Both God and Mrs. God had begun to think of him almost as a son. At the word "danger," Mrs. God's heart began to thud loudly in Her ears.

"Well," Mrs. God said, jumping out of bed, "something needeth to be done. Thou shalt not mopeth. Thou must act, for goodness's sake!" She hurriedly lashed a robe over Her body and grabbed God's fedora from its place atop the dresser. She tossed it to Him in bed like a Frisbee.

God caught His hat and perched it on His head. He admired His wife. He always tried to be strong in the face of problems, but, in a pinch, it was always Mrs. God who was first to act. She never fell to doubting Her own abilities. She saw a problem and believed that She could solve it. With a deep breath, God resolved to take a lesson from His wife. He leaped out of bed, rushed to Mrs. God, and captured Her lips in a deep, passionate kiss.

Finally pulling His mouth away from His wife's, God grinned and yelled, "Baby! You're right, damn it! I'm coming out of retirement! Now, where's My houndstooth jacket?"

The Prophecy

Arlo was finding it hard to sleep as well. Every time he espied an opportunity to shuffle off to bed, a new howl from the basement brought him grumbling back down the creaky wooden steps to his new friend's hiding place. Amanda was asleep. Arlo had brought the head home earlier in the day, making sure to carry it by the sides of its helmet so that his hands didn't get anywhere near the bloody stump that used to be the spaceman's neck. He had been quite thankful to find Amanda in an incoherent state when he arrived back at the farmhouse. When she saw the head, she emitted a delighted squeal in her girlish voice and told Arlo that their baby was getting bigger every day. She dug up an unused bassinet from the basement, put the head in it, and spent the better part of the evening playing peek-a-boo with the severed space head, utterly unconscious of its coarse insults and macabre visage. Arlo, glad to avoid the traumatic scene he had envisioned, bit back his anger at hearing the head refer to his wife as a "freight-assed whaling ship" and allowed Amanda's delusions to continue. After she had gone to bed, he had moved the head – bassinet and all – into a far corner of the basement, hoping that Amanda, when she returned to a more lucid state, would not come across it.

Now, having given up on sleep, Arlo sat in the unlit kitchen, holding a mug of stale coffee in his trembling hands. The Texas night had turned quite blustery and the high shriek of gusty winds ripped through every crack and crevice of the old house. The sealant on the kitchen window had long since hardened and grown porous, now admitting drafts of the frigid February air. Arlo, draped in a musty afghan, held the warm mug close to his face. The coffee was thin and tasted of water mixed with old cigarettes. Regardless, it was Arlo's sole point of warmth in his chilly, shadowy kitchen.

Underneath the high-pitched whine of the wind, Arlo could hear a low, growly summons from the basement. "Serving biiiiiitch! Where the fuck is my serving bitch?" The head had recently decided that Arlo was not worthy of being addressed by his Christian name.

Ignoring the stubborn protests of his stiff back, Arlo got up from the table and felt his way to the basement steps. He did not want to turn any lights on because he did not want to wake Amanda; besides that, he had no desire to see the grinning, eyeless face of the decapitated head any more than he needed to.

As he stepped carefully down the stairs, the cries of the head got louder. "Step to it, Methuselah!"

"Sir," Arlo stammered in a low tone, "I wish you wouldn't raise such kind of fuss. I know Missus is hard of hearing, but that ain't no call to...."

"Ah, fuck that fossilized ostrich turd."

Arlo had reached the cold cement basement floor. The air was damper beneath ground and the stifling smell of thick mold hung obstinately in Arlo's nose. He imagined that he could faintly perceive the stench of the sulfurous swamps that lined his property. Utter darkness blinded him, but he knew that a bloodied head with thick, purple lips and patchy blond hair taunted him from a nearby bassinet. Arlo drew the afghan more tightly around his shoulders, feeling the scratchy wool on the back of his neck.

"What is it you want of me, sir?" Arlo asked. "I don't mean no disrespect, but maybe it'd be best if we could just get on to bed, you know?"

"I don't know anything," said the head, "unless you address me by my proper name." Earlier that evening, the head had been very explicit about his preferred title.

"Mr. Pimp Daddy, sir..." Arlo began, feeling rather foolish. "Don't you think you might be able to let me get some shuteye? I ain't so young as I been."

Pimp Daddy took a moment to consider Arlo's request, but when his voice returned from the dark void of the basement, it trembled with rage. "You think that after that mess of a dinner I choked down and that putrid coffee you inflicted on me, I owe you a favor? Takes some nerve, you indigent flea flask! You're lucky I haven't zapped your puckered ass to Hell's Kitchen Culinary College."

"Please, Mr. Pimp Daddy, sir, I think we can all do without no more zapping."

"Then make yourself useful, Old Faithful. Massage my temples while I prophesize."

"Prophesize, sir?" Revulsion churned in Arlo's gut. Pimp Daddy had asked to be shampooed earlier and so Arlo had been forced to remove the space helmet and touch the leering head underneath. Pimp Daddy's skin was tough, but was covered with a fine film of slippery slime whose origin Arlo could not determine. Pimp Daddy's skull was lumpy and irregular. It felt as though he had tumors, which pulsed fitfully beneath his skin. Arlo's fingers were already tingling at the idea of coming into contact once again with the repulsive head.

"What did you expect, you luminary? I'm a goddamn soothsayer. A fucking oracle of truth, if you will. What did you think I was, you cripple-hearted manifestation of flatulence? An interior decorator? Now get over here and massage me, because I've got a bevy of badass prophecies to bust out before dawn."

Feeling his way along the dusty cardboard boxes and defunct furniture that littered his basement, Arlo groped blindly towards the head. His fingers brushed against the metal rim of the bassinet and he carefully felt for Pimp Daddy. Arlo took extra care to ensure that his fingers stayed far away from the empty eye sockets. He had no desire to feel whatever lay within. Walking his fingers cautiously along Pimp Daddy's slippery scalp, Arlo found his temples and began to rub as vigorously as his arthritic fingers would allow. The meat under Arlo's fingers was cold and disgustingly malleable. He continued pushing deeper and deeper until his fingers were almost entirely enveloped in Pimp Daddy's gooey temples; the head then let out a long, contented sigh.

"That's the stuff, pisspot. It's been a long day. Don't be shy – get your whole hand in there, if you can."

Arlo issued a silent prayer of thankfulness that he had not eaten since morning as he exerted more pressure on the head. He felt his hands slipping into the necrotic flesh as deep as his wrists. Pimp Daddy exhaled gleefully.

"All right. I've got three prophesies for tonight and, I have to say, they're fucking sweet. First of all, cougar season's coming early this year. That's all you get. It's vague, so make of it what you will. It doesn't concern you anyway. Secondly, I think a patsy somewhere's gonna wise up, but it's gonna be too late. He'll come by here tomorrow, I imagine. If you help him, I'll rip off your testicles, paint 'em like eyeballs, and stick 'em in my head. If you don't, then I'll make good on prophesy number three – your wife Slutbucket, or whatever her name is, will be ten years younger by tomorrow night."

Arlo heard all of this with great confusion. He knew nothing about cougars and, aside from the guys at the general store in Longview, he didn't know that many people. He went through the roster of his acquaintances and couldn't think of anybody who qualified as a "patsy." Nonetheless, he believed the head. Arlo didn't need to be reminded of the painful jolt he had received in his fields when he disobeyed Pimp Daddy. He didn't have much use for his testicles these days, but he liked them fine where they were, thank you very much.

Sensing that the head had finished prophesying, Arlo pulled his hands out of Pimp Daddy's temples with a sickening thwock. He discreetly wiped the lingering goo from his fingers onto the afghan on his shoulders. "Mr. Pimp Daddy, sir? May I please sleep now?" he asked.

Pimp Daddy let out a crackling smoker's laugh. Arlo pictured Pimp Daddy's yellow teeth and greenish, gangrenous tongue and felt ill. "Yes," said the head. "Go rest those osteoporosis-riddled bones of yours, because we've got some work to do. First thing tomorrow I want you in the fields looking for something we can fashion a pair of legs out of. The Pimp Daddy's meeting his daddy soon, and we want to be presentable for Pimp Granddaddy, don't we?"

"Pimp Granddaddy, sir?"

The head emitted another phlegmatic guffaw and spoke through peals of laughter, "What do you think, you noisome nobody? Everybody's created by someone else. Fuck yeah, I have a daddy – and, let me tell you, when Pimp Daddy and Pimp Daddy's daddy team up, we're gonna make it hot for that Heavenly Daddy of All. Now you better scurry along, you lame excuse for a mammal, before I change my mind about letting you sleep."

***

The campsite was dark, but almost nobody was asleep. Flares, flashlights, and headlamps were all strictly prohibited by the NASA regulations, so setting up the tents had been irritating and difficult. Moreover, the night had gone from cold to colder, with strong winds whipping through the trees and ruffling the flimsy canvas of the crew's government-issued tents. Ana had decided to set up camp in the first clearing the crew had come across, about a mile and a half off the highway; on all sides, a dense mat of interweaving vines, brambly shrubs, and dead tree branches enclosed the Las Cruces crew.

Juliet was huddled in her sleeping bag, listening to the branches rattling outside her tent. Robin had driven them in a circuitous route all over Longview before stopping in front of an anonymous field; he had hiked them by flashlight through the forest until Ana had found a campsite she pronounced acceptable. Once the crew was settled in, Robin had hiked back in the direction of the highway and presumably driven off, leaving the eight firefighters alone for the night. Juliet was troubled by the secrecy permeating the operation and the fact that she hadn't seen anybody from any other crew. She stared into the darkness, listening to Ana snore lightly beside her, and trying fruitlessly to relax. She had no idea how Ana had fallen asleep so easily in a cold, uncomfortable tent on the edge of nowhere.

Bracing herself against the frigid air, Juliet wriggled out of her sleeping bag and slipped out of the tent into the night. The sky was utterly starless and Juliet could only just barely perceive the silhouettes of the nearby black trees jutting from the earth as tangled shadows. The wind tousled her hair and sang plaintively in her ears.

"Who's that?" a male voice whispered several feet behind her.

Juliet, startled, turned to face the voice. "Juliet," she hissed. "Who's there?"

"It's Roger," the voice replied. He stepped closer to Juliet and she could discern his hulking frame. She wanted, for some reason, to run into his arms and cleave to his powerful, protective body. However, she swallowed her instincts and stayed where she was, burying her hands into her pockets for warmth. "Can't sleep?" Roger asked.

"How could anybody?"

Roger shrugged. "Takeshi's out like a light. But I kept rolling over in my sleeping bag. Trying to sleep, you know? Didn't want to bug him. Came out here." Roger had never spoken much to Juliet before. He liked her, but had always received the vague impression that she didn't like him; plus, he thought her friend Chris was an overdramatic nut job. He wasn't sure how to address Juliet, so he spoke haltingly, fearing that any wrong word on his part would send her back into her tent in a huff.

"Where are Francis and Scott?" Juliet asked.

"Asleep, I think. Went by their tent. Didn't hear anyone talking inside. Didn't want to wake them. Kind of a lonely neck of the woods, though. You know?"

"It's a bitch of a cold night, too."

"Yeah. Can't believe they wouldn't let us have more clothes. I'm wearing both pairs of socks."

Juliet laughed. "Me, too." She had always classed Roger with Francis and Scott as a dumb jock, but it hadn't escaped her that he possessed a more acute sensitivity than his friends. She remembered the loneliness that she had been feeling earlier and hoped that maybe Roger would be her ally during the mission. She was itching to ask him what he thought of the crew's assignment and the odd secrecy with which they had been conveyed to the Search Sector, but she didn't want to appear apprehensive. Instead, she dug her hands into her back pockets and tried to dredge up some confidence. "But whatever," she said, wondering if she sounded as cowardly as she felt. "We're not here for pleasure."

"Yeah. Killer." Roger nodded. He wanted to ask what Juliet did think they were there for, but worried that his uncertainty would look too weak. True, Juliet was a pretty girl, but Roger found the brazenness with which she stood up to Ana rather gutsy and he imagined that Juliet would not waste her time talking to men who weren't as tough as she. However, in the absence of voicing his concerns about the mission, he found that he had nothing else to say to Juliet. Deciding that saying nothing was better than saying something inane, he dug the toe of his boot into the moist Texas soil and said, "Well, I guess I'll try to go to sleep."

"Yeah, me, too."

For a minute, neither made any motion to leave. Both looked silently into the night, feeling cold and scared. They looked everywhere except at one another. Roger was the one who finally broke the moment by retreating wordlessly into his tent. Wishing for some reason that she could shatter night's solitude with a scream, Juliet squared her shoulders, bit her lip, and marched silently back to the tent she was sharing with Ana.

***

Vince was scared of Chris. No sooner had the two pitched their tent than Chris knelt in the dirt and blindly, frantically began to scratch figures into the mud with his fingers. It was too dark for Vince to see what Chris was drawing and he figured that it was probably too dark for even Chris to see what, exactly, his pictures looked like. The obsession with which Chris scraped up the dirt worried Vince. Without saying anything to Chris, he retreated into the tent, knelt on the rubbery floor, and closed his eyes to pray.

As Vince knelt in the middle of the tent, however, with the ferocious winds caterwauling about him, he received a second fright. Usually all Vince had to do to pray was kneel and shut his eyes and he would immediately find himself raised up to Greater Heaven to meet with God and Mrs. God. Tonight, though, without his cross, he found that he was going nowhere. He took a deep breath and tried to concentrate. He pictured God and Mrs. God and Their suburban home. He pictured Their leopard-print bedding, Their paisley carpet, and the Mondrians covering Their walls. He tried to smell Mrs. God's incense or the faint odor of cigars and Old Spice that always lingered in God's bathroom. He strained to hear the busy roar of Greater Heaven's traffic and the clamor of street gangs and derelicts, but only heard the still Texas emptiness, devoid even of crickets. The more frustrated Vince became over his inability to connect with the Gods, the less able he was to will his mind into a prayerful state. For the first time in his life, Vince simply could not pray.

The flap of the tent rustled abruptly as Chris pawed his way inside. Breathing heavily, he crawled into his sleeping bag and proceeded to dig the dirt out from beneath his fingernails. He was conscious of Vince's warm body beside him. Even in the darkness, he knew that Vince was looking at him. Chris wanted to say something, but wasn't sure what.

"Chris," Vince said softly.

Chris didn't reply. Vince had never directly addressed him before.

"What were you drawing?"

Vince heard Chris's vaporous breath, but received nothing more. He wanted to just get into his sleeping bag and try to sleep, but he knew that he wouldn't be able to find any peace unless he had first spoken to God. Something was wrong in Greater Heaven, or on Earth, or perhaps both, and Chris's silence made him profoundly uneasy. Chris's fear of parting with his sketchbook still rang oddly in Vince's memory. For some reason, he felt that Chris was inextricably tied up in his feelings of dread.

"I just draw what I'm thinking of," Chris finally replied.

"What were you thinking of tonight?"

Silence hung awkwardly in the tent. When Chris finally replied, he sounded quiet and uncertain. "What are you most scared of, Vince?"

Vince considered. He could only think of one thing.

"Evil. Why do you ask?" Chris didn't answer. "What scares you?"

Chris took so long to reply to Vince's question that Vince assumed he had fallen asleep. After several minutes, however, Chris's voice came shakily out of the dark, "You'll find out soon."

Vince shuddered. He could think of nothing to say in response, so he lay down in his sleeping bag, shut his eyes, and began the long wait for morning.

***

God and Mrs. God walked briskly into the great hall of Greater Heaven Central Station, a busy depot for commuter trains into the downtown. Even in the dead of night, the sprawling, glass-walled station was filled with people, all elbowing one another for a spot on one of the bi-hourly monorails that made the three-hour journey from Greater Heaven Central in the far west, through Heaven Proper, into Central Heaven, and out into the eastern suburbs before terminating at the East Heaven Depot. Greater Heaven was a particularly affluent suburb and so its central station was free of the musty urine and sour cheese odor that pervaded many of the outlying stations. No rats wended their ways among the legs of harried commuters in Greater Heaven, no homeless derelicts yelled incoherent profanities over the necks of their beloved bourbon bottles, and no fuzzy mildew crept steadfastly along the edges of the station floor's pearly white tiles. Despite the crowds and the roaring clamor of an infinity of footsteps, the station maintained the pristine gleam of ivory and marble. Busts of God and Mrs. God looked down over the teeming crowd from atop high fluted pillars. An immaculately Windexed glass ceiling revealed the night sky above. Long wooden benches with cottony clouds for cushions lined the walls. At the north end of the great hall, an enormous golden clock face protruded from the wall. As the Gods moved towards Track 554, the clock read midnight.

"Keep on Your toes, sexpot," God cautioned His wife. "Petty thieves and pickpockets slip through these haunts like Jack Daniels down the throat of a hustler."

God, however, had no need for concern. The populace of Greater Heaven generally loved the Divine Couple. Anybody who had met the two could not deny the warmth and protection they felt in Their presence. As They made Their way to Their train, a respectful bubble of space emerged around Them as people scrambled to step out of Their way. Though it was not so unusual for people in this area to see the Gods on Their occasional excursions, the sight of the Almighties never failed to inspire wonder and love in Their beholders. The Gods had grown used to the deference of Greater Heaven's citizens.

"Thank You, God, for the life You've given me!" shouted one red-faced man in a black bowler as he hurried to his train.

"I love the haircut, Mrs. God!" said another passing commuter, touching her own flat red hair with self-consciousness.

The Gods smiled fondly at all the compliments, but could not stop today to acknowledge Their fans. The 12:10 express train to the Central Heaven Terminal was in the final stages of boarding and the Gods needed to catch this train in order to be at the terminal in time for the 1:30 non-stop comet to Earth.

God and His wife darted onto the platform and squeezed into the train just as the polished steel doors slid noiselessly shut. The train car was packed with people. God found His face distastefully wedged into the armpit of a fat, elderly man with long grey hair and a black "Dog Is My Copilot" T-shirt. Mrs. God pressed close to Her husband but couldn't help noticing that the head of a gawky prepubescent boy in thick glasses was pressed unavoidably to Her cleavage. The body heat made the poorly ventilated train car like an antique oven.

The train jerked forward and quickly began to accelerate. God grasped the slimy metal bar running along the ceiling of the car to steady Himself. A short woman in a black velvet hat with an elaborate floral arrangement sprouting from it took hold abruptly of the closest available anchor – God's knee, dangerously close to His crotch.

"Watch it, toots!" God said through the side of His mouth. "A dame with such quick fingers spells 'danger' with a capital 'D' to a man like Me. You've got a knock-em-dead smile, but if you round the bases too fast, this umpire's calling foul ball!"

The offending woman flushed in embarrassment. "Oh, God! I'm so sorry," she stammered. "I didn't even see it was You." With burning cheeks, she smiled meekly.

"Tut, broad." God leaned over and, as best as He was able in the jerkily advancing train car, planted a kiss on the woman's forehead. "You're a sweet kid and I like the cut of your jib, but I've got to answer to the old ball and chain here."

"Oh, shut Thine damnable mouth," Mrs. God said, rolling Her eyes.

"Jealousy!" said God. "Intrigue! The numerous petty fears born of woman's passion! What crime of the heart could My darling dove be imagining in Her heart of hearts?"

"As though I could haveth any suspicion of You beingith untrue to Me," Mrs. God said with a yawn. "In the millions of years I've knownethed You, Thou hast not once beeneth unfaithful."

God, however, ignored His wife's complacence and continued speaking. "Suspicions and rumors thrive in this train car like mold on a week-old bagel! Falsely accused, Babs! I have been falsely accused, and if You weren't as beautiful a bird as ever strutted in these parts, I'd walk You out to the morgue to see the last squawking dame that thought she'd raise her voice against this old ace!"

In order to lend greater emphasis to His declamation, God released His grip on the handlebar and flailed His arms as dramatically as He was able within His confined space. This disrupted His balance when the train suddenly braked upon its arrival at the Central Heaven Terminal and sent Him careening into a middle-aged man with a harelip. The man glowered until he saw that it was God who had jostled him; a sloppy smile then suddenly emerged on his gloomy face.

"Good to see You, God!" the man gargled through his deformed lips.

"Hang in there, Joe! This town needs more right chaps such as yourself!" God called as He followed Mrs. God out of the train. "Joe" was His name for every anonymous man in Heaven.

Stepping out into the Central Heaven Terminal, the Gods were faced with quite a different image than that which They were used to at Greater Heaven Central Station. The floors were not white marble, but unadorned asphalt studded with vibrant bouquets of fluorescent vomit. The tile walls were chipped and cracked. Black water dripped incessantly from the exposed piping on the ceiling. Though the station felt less crowded than Greater Heaven's, this was largely because the crowds were not blustering about one another, trying frantically to catch their trains; on the contrary, the people at the Central Heaven Terminal were largely inert, sprawled out on benches, lazily swiping at passing flies, and raking their fingers along the ground in search of pennies, bottle caps, or any other small treasures. The denizens of the Central Heaven Terminal were mostly unwashed, unshaved, and unhinged. Some fingered knives – others, assault rifles. Many had scars from past brawls – in Heaven, of course, death was an impossibility and so people fought fearlessly. Between the supine positions and mangled appearances of the thousands of derelicts who called the Central Heaven Terminal home, the place more resembled a convalescent home than a busy depot.

God had not set foot in Central Heaven in months and always found the scene at the terminal unsettling and depressing. Mrs. God clutched His arm tightly as They picked Their way around prone bodies whose arms groped drunkenly at the Heavenly Couple in tortured supplication. Even in the inner city, everybody held a reverent view of the Gods. Although many saw God's abandonment of the people of Heaven as the root of the city's social ills, nothing was to be gained by challenging God. He was indestructible, at least by means of the crude weapons available in Heaven, and, moreover, anybody setting out with intentions to harm Him would find that, as soon as he looked into the face of God, he was so inexplicably filled with love and respect for Him that even the direst indignation would fade away.

The 1:30 redeye comet was departing for Earth from Gate 28 on the north end of the station. God, clutching His wallet, and Mrs. God, clutching Her husband, raced to the gate. The express comets could only accommodate five people at most, but the Gods knew that They took priority. Tonight, however, there was no need to bump anybody. The only other passenger on the comet was a smiling elderly woman who said that she was heading to Seattle to look down on her granddaughter's wedding. The Gods sat down beside the woman and buckled Their seatbelts.

The station attendant, a rat-faced redhead with puffy cheeks, emerged from in front of the comet and said, "It's going to be just two minutes, folks. I've gotta check the tail on this guy. Been making a funny noise, last few trips. But don't you worry. We'll be off in no time." With that, he disappeared down a spiral staircase adjoining the comet. The passengers could hear him swearing below as he fiddled with the comet's blasters.

Suddenly, a voice cut through the air.

"God! Don't go down to Earth!"

God and Mrs. God turned to find the source of the voice – a very short, unkempt young man in a stained dress shirt and a rumpled tie was running across the main hall to the gate. He was waving his arms wildly; his eyes flashed with crazed frenzy. He was tripping over the bodies of sleeping recluses, causing them to raise their heads blearily before sinking down again into drunken slumber.

"It's a trap, God! It's a trap!" the man shouted.

An icy fear shuddered through God's head; Mrs. God, too, felt Her heart leap at the man's warning. However, God patted Mrs. God's knee and muttered to Her, "Loons and kooks stroll these shady streets this time of night. Don't You listen to this madman's mumbo jumbo."

At that moment, the station attendant emerged and leapt onto the comet, joining the three passengers. "Off we go!" he shouted, as the comet exploded out of the gate, leaving a shimmering trail of translucent sparkles in its wake. God peered over the edge of the comet back towards Heaven as He was jetted away from His home. Within minutes, He could see the lights and skyscrapers of Heaven disappearing into the bright center of a galactic whorl. The comet leapt along into the dark void of space, leaving Heaven further behind with every passing minute. God sighed and took the hand of His wife. "Don't worry, angel-pie," He said, pointing to Himself "Things will be just fine, as long as You stick with this hepcat."

"I knoweth, baby. I knoweth."

Mrs. God reclined Her head on God's shoulder and watched the blackness of the mortal universe expand before Her. Cuddled up next to God, She tried to rest; They would be in the northern hemisphere of Earth by daybreak.

***

Had God had more time before the comet departed, He might have recognized the crazed stranger at the terminal as Ross Tucker – in life, the chief engineer of NASA's Daedalus mission. Had God correctly identified Ross, He might have realized that Ross was in a position to know far more about the dangers of His imminent journey than He Himself. Had God realized this, He might have immediately unstrapped Himself from the comet, prompted His wife to do the same, and rethought His entire plan of action. However, this list of contingencies was not fulfilled and so, as the comet blasted towards Earth on a tail of red and yellow luminescence, Ross Tucker stood agitated in the afterglow of the comet's departure, bouncing with nervous energy, and racking his astute brain for the answer to this question: what to do now?

***

Dreams. Fleeting fragments of a half-lived life. Brightest oasis points in the deadest hours of a jet black night. Guarded receptacles of the most secret desires, the most paralyzing fears. Loosening of self-control. Allowing oneself to be buffeted by tempestuous flashes of untidy worlds. Freefalling into the imaginative unknown.

Takeshi finds himself blown onto the shores of his own Hawaii. The glimmer of a white sail from a boat some distance away. His father's Asiatic face. The smell of his mother's suntan oil. The susurration of surf on fine-grained sand. Sun.

Roger on his family's farm. Wheat unusually blue. Warm summer rain blasts from a cloudless sky. Shirtless. Shoeless. Breezy. A clapboard church by the side of a lonely dirt road. Peppered with rain as he looks inside. Empty pews. Wooden altar. Stale odor of incense. Silence and solitude. Water dripping from his hair into his eyes.

Juliet materializes in Paris. Everything in English. Walking down tidy streets. Potted flowers in front of romantic cafés. Who is the man next to her? Friendly. Asks her if she knows the way to the Seine. She does. Over the mountain, past the Grand Canyon, nestled in the valley glistening with sunflowers. She's going that way herself. Should they go together? He is gone.

Ana in a blizzard. Snow blind. Not scared. Voices nearby. Soft ones. "Let's make a fire!" Crackling of logs. Ash billows from invisible fire, spirals into air as a dusty cyclone. Amidst the ash, a face. Dead father alive. Surprise. Embrace.

Robin floating in outer space. No space suit. Touches Jupiter. Feels smooth, like a marble. The moon! Small enough to hold in his fist. Passes spaceship. Waves hello. Spacemen wave back. Inside spaceship. Becomes captain. Sits at console. Touches red button. A voice: "Abort mission." Suddenly dark. Flashing red light. Panic. Firefighters running past, disappearing into space's vortex. Robin's own voice: "Stop!" Surroundings spin fiercely. Uncontrollably.

Arlo – smooth hands, young voice, short black hair. Sits by brook. Knees operable. Spine aligned. Chirping birds on birch branches. Amanda. Long blonde hair. Removes stockings. She stands in the brook. Beckons Arlo. Rises. Smell of spring grass and thyme. Dives headfirst into brook. Amanda catches him. Underwater embrace.

Amanda sees herself in bed. Floating. An angel at her side. Muscular and handsome. The wings of a bird. He whispers, "It will be our secret."

Chris has never been here before. Cold, dark room. Concrete floor. Stacks of yellowing newspapers. Old tools covered in rust. Someone watching him. Sees nobody. Stare from somewhere makes him shiver. Low voice from nowhere. "Take a good look at this." Can't concentrate. Something feels familiar. The voice. "Put your mind to work, Chris." Whose voice? Where is he? Terrified.

Francis and Scott together. See one another with surprise. "Why are you here?" Both look around. Jungle. East Texas. Dread. Silence. A sudden flash of red. The dream ends.

***

Vince couldn't sleep. Chris writhed next to him in an agitated dream, muttering something. Vince tried to make out what Chris was saying, but it was unintelligible. He had tried praying again after Chris had fallen asleep, but to no avail. Soon thereafter the heavy winds tapered off, leaving an utter absence of noise in the wilderness. Vince felt trapped. The silence of the night unsettled him. It seemed that there should be raccoons or squirrels or at least crickets. He couldn't shake the feeling that something was going terribly wrong.

A little before dawn, Vince heard a soft rustle and a few animalistic grunts not far from the tent. "Thank God," he thought, smiling for the first time that night. "There is some life out here after all." The noise soon disappeared, but it had alleviated enough of Vince's anxiety to allow him to shut his eyes and wait calmly for sunrise to rouse his crewmates.

The Fauna

Robin rose early the next morning, feeling far from rested. He didn't remember any of his dreams, but he knew that they had been tiring and a little upsetting. However, as he ambled to his murky kitchen, feeling the grit of his unswept floor under his bare feet, his primary concern was downing a cup of coffee. He had slept with his two-way radio on the nightstand, but hadn't heard a word from the Las Cruces crew during the night. He was gratified to think that no problems had arisen on his watch; he looked forward to tying in with the crew at his leisure this afternoon.

Robin sat down at his tiny kitchen table and stirred a spoonful of coffee crystals into a mug of hot water. The crystals collected together in a sludgy mass at the bottom of his mug; regardless, Robin gulped down the concoction in two swigs. The warm coffee temporarily allayed the apartment's chill. Robin was watching his expenses and didn't want to turn on the heat unless it proved strictly necessary. He figured that he spent so little time in the apartment that it made no sense to bother regulating its temperature. Once he got a promotion, though, he would move someplace more comfortable. His current apartment was small and the ceiling was too thin to keep out the noise of his upstairs neighbors' three children. His bedroom window looked out on an interstate exit and he had only recently put up black masking to prevent the glare from the headlights from keeping him awake at night. In short, Robin welcomed every opportunity to get out of the apartment.

Now, in the chill, dry morning, with the honking of commuters on the highway outside leaking into the kitchen and the first light of dawn shining a pale green through Robin's dirt begrimed windows, a hollow knock sounded on the door. It was still before 7:00 and Robin couldn't guess who might be calling at such an early hour. He crossed the kitchen to the front door, swatting at a slow-moving spider on the way, and unlatched the door's hook from its eye. Opening the door, he discovered a well-shaven blonde man in a spotless white dress shirt and heavy brown slacks carrying a leather briefcase. The two men shook hands across the threshold, the stranger in his neatly pressed clothing, Robin in his threadbare cotton bathrobe.

"Hello, Mr. Rodriguez," the man began. "I'm Jimmy Hawdon. I live next door. I apologize for how early I'm coming around, but I heard you puttering around in there and I figured, well, I'd never come by before to introduce myself proper. I'm a man that keeps early hours myself, because mine is work that can't be done in darkness, and, from what I know of you, the morning is not your usual haunt. Therefore, here I am on this atypical day. Hope it's no inconvenience to you."

Jimmy spoke confidently, though not quickly. He shaped his words gently in his mouth, as though each one were a precious gem that he needed to polish before he was willing to expose it to the world. His eyes worked with the same precision; Robin felt that, having once surveyed the room, Jimmy had surely already discovered his entire personal history and psychological makeup. Jimmy, Robin couldn't help thinking, would be an excellent candidate for a PR job.

"Sorry not to invite you in," Robin said, "but we're facing quite a heavy load at work these days and I have to head out as soon as I'm dressed."

"No apologies necessary." A brilliant PR smile gleamed on Jimmy's boyish face. "I should apologize for bothering you at the crack of dawn. However, one question before I get out of your hair. I'll run the risk of taking up just five minutes of your time, if I may, since a mere five minutes can mean an eternity in matters such as this. Well, in the interest of time, I'll put it to you bluntly: do you believe in God, Mr. Rodriguez?"

"I'm sorry?" Robin did not, in fact, believe in God – nor did he disbelieve. God was the same thing to Robin as telekinesis or Atlantis – a vaguely plausible legend whose veracity or lack thereof could have but little effect on his own life. Robin knew that he could expect to wake up every morning, see a sunrise, live a day like every other day, and go to sleep again in darkness; whether or not this routine could be attributed to someone named "God" made no difference.

"Let me put it this way," Jimmy said, undeterred by Robin's lack of responsiveness. "That hair on your head. Is that the same hair you had when you were a baby?"

"No."

"How about your teeth?"

"No."

"How about all those skin cells you've got flaking off your body by the millions? What about those blood cells that are tirelessly dying, dividing, and regenerating? Hang on, Mr. Rodriguez, I'll answer for you. There isn't a single cell in your body that has lived through the entire course of your life alongside you."

"Is that true?" Robin was fairly certain that it was not, but he saw no reason to argue.

"True as I'm standing here. But – what do you think – this wad of cells you call yourself master of is not the same wad of cells you owned four years ago, but aren't you the same man, Mr. Rodriguez? Don't you act on the same memories? The same conscience? The same likes and dislikes? Aren't you, in some way, still the Mr. Rodriguez of your childhood, prey to the same quirks and habits, the same prejudices and predilections?"

Robin was too confused to be irritated. He had never seen Jimmy Hawdon before and found it incomprehensible that a man could be so earnest and self-assured upon first introduction. He found himself staring impolitely. Thankfully, Mr. Hawdon seemed to have no problem with yet again responding to his own questions.

"Yes," Jimmy continued, "you are precisely the same man. What can we learn from this, Mr. Rodriguez? Can we trust this illusive physical world? Or must we not admit to ourselves that there's just a smidge more to life than the things we can lay our hands on? Somewhere over our heads there's a whole other world, my friend, no less real than ours. Think on that, Mr. Rodriguez." Coming to a natural pause in his argument, Jimmy extracted a thin book from his briefcase. The cover was made of blue-pebbled leather and boasted a simple cross wrought in gold filigree. "Trust me, Mr. Rodriguez. This is a topic that can't be crammed into five minutes before work. Where is it you work, again?"

Robin served out the first answer that sprang to his head. "I build spaceships."

"Ah. Earth-shattering. Well, I don't want to make you late, so I'm going to leave this Bible with you. Feel free to shove it in your drawer and forget about it. We've just had the first of what I expect to be a fair number of chitchats, Mr. Rodriguez. May God grant you a beautiful day, my friend!"

Jimmy smiled sharply, revealing an immaculate row of lupine teeth, and extended the book to Robin. Robin took the Bible and ran his hand over its unblemished skin. It was a nice, new book; the edges of the pages shone with a dusting of gold. It seemed almost too tidy an artifact to plumb the spiritual depths to which Jimmy had referred. As Robin was looking over the book, Jimmy saw himself out, shutting the door noiselessly behind him. Now alone, Robin dropped the Bible onto the kitchen table, rinsed out his coffee mug, and returned to his bedroom to get dressed and see if the fire crew had tried to radio him.

Still, no noise issued from Robin's radio. He had to admit to himself that he was surprised and even a little anxious. Though he tried to convince himself that the silence was an indication that the crew hadn't run into any problems, he remained wary. Better safe than sorry, he thought, as he made the decision to radio the crew. His memo had gravely cautioned him against radioing the crew before it had radioed him. It cited such a transgression as a "threat to the security of the NASA program" and unnecessary, besides. However, Robin figured that nobody at the top would ever find out – and that a little bit of working outside the rules right now would certainly be excusable if the crew was, indeed, in danger.

Robin picked up the radio and pressed the button on the side. He selected the frequency for the Las Cruces crew and, though he knew it to be unnecessary, couldn't help glancing over his shoulder before he began speaking.

"Las Cruces, this is R Star – do you copy me?"

An excruciating silence ensued. Robin, with a somewhat shakier hand, tried again.

"Las Cruces, this is R Star – do you copy me?"

Again, Robin heard nothing but the low rumbling of static. He could feel his hands growing unsteady. He pictured what might become of him if anything had happened to the crew left in his charge. He'd be unemployed and, worse, NASA would ensure that he was unemployable. He'd have to give up the apartment and move home. No more company car, no more government health benefits, no more writing his Christmas cards on NASA letterhead, and a lifetime of moral guilt and regret, besides.

"Las Cruces, this is R Star – do you copy me?"

Nothing.

With arduously maintained patience, Robin cycled through each frequency the radio was capable of receiving, in the hopes that Ana had programmed the wrong frequency on her handset. Not one of them yielded a response.

Robin checked the batteries on his handset, although the radio was lit up and the batteries were clearly not dead. At a loss, he pulled the batteries out from the base of the radio and blew on the exposed anodes. At this moment, Robin discovered something that sent a jolt to his heart and caused a wave of paranoia to crash over him. He suddenly felt as though he weren't alone in the room. The noise from the highway below and the pounding of juvenile feet on the ceiling above him oppressed him in a way they never had before. He felt completely enclosed and invaded.

Somebody had neatly cut the wire connecting the mouthpiece to the transmitter. His crew had been abandoned in the Texas wilderness.

***

"R Star! Come in, R Star! This is Las Cruces with a Class A emergency! Do you read me, for the love of God?" Ana, ashen faced, cried into the mouthpiece of her radio one more time. For fifteen minutes, she had been trying to reach Robin. At first, she had kept a tight lid on her feelings of panic and had astounded the crew with the calm and even-voiced manner in which she had radioed for help. However, by this point, her coolness had atrophied and she was now shrieking with a frayed voice that threatened to dissolve into incoherent bawling at any moment.

The crew was assembled in a tight knot around her. The morning sun was rising, casting swaths of gossamer pink and effervescent ribbons of yellow over the dark, gnarly treetops and slowly baking the chilly morning air. Birds chirruped together in idle morning chatter, the sound of buzzing insects underlined the dawn with the throbbing pulse of an electrical current, and leaf litter and dried pine needles crackled gaily under the feet of darting chipmunks. The firefighters, however, were not enjoying the brisk February morning. They were gathered a small distance away from the shreds of bloodied flesh that had formerly been Scott and Francis.

***

Takeshi had been the first to discover the bodies. He had stepped out of his tent an hour or so before dawn and had noticed that one of the four tents had collapsed in the night. When he drew closer, he saw that the sides of the tent had been torn open in long, jagged gashes. Within the rent fabric of the tent lay the rent bodies of its inhabitants. One of Scott's thin legs had been partially ripped off at the knee and his chest had been scratched into near oblivion. Francis had fared worse. Virtually every square inch of his body had been rendered unrecognizable. Large chunks of his thighs and midsection had been bitten off; one eye and half a cheek were all that remained of his face. While anybody else might have gone into shock at the image and been unable to voice so much as a gasp, Takeshi – whose voice had not been heard once since the crew left for Texas – emitted a scream of such deep-bellied ferocity that the ground itself could be felt to vibrate with the resonance of his roar.

After the silence of the previous night, Takeshi's sudden, explosive noise startled the crew out of its dreams. Ana, as usual, was the first on the scene and, although the only available light was the murky greenish glow of predawn, swiftly determined what had occurred. As others raced towards Takeshi, Ana held them off with her voice. "Do not come any nearer than I am. There is nothing you need to see. There is absolutely nothing that you need to see." The crew, in near panic, naturally wanted to see what had elicited Takeshi's response, but the underlying horror in Ana's tone made everyone trust that, whatever the catastrophe was, it was not something pleasant to behold.

Only Juliet pushed ahead towards the tent, drawn by her fear, but Ana slapped one of her bulky arms across Juliet's midsection and held her tight, preventing her from reaching the gory scene. This exacerbated Juliet's frenzy and she struggled against Ana's grasp, shrieking, "What happened? Just fucking tell us!"

"Calm down," Ana commanded. Her voice wasn't loud, but it was level and direct and it was through its force, rather than its volume, that it interrupted Juliet's hysteria and caused all eyes except Takeshi's to turn fearfully and expectantly to Ana for explanation. For his part, Takeshi was still staring unblinkingly at the tent. He seemed to be frozen in an absolutely immobile, grotesque still life. If one were to look carefully, however, one could see a slight spastic quiver in his left hand, as though he had jammed all of his fear into that one tiny corner of his body.

By this point, the crew had figured out that Scott and Francis were absent and that something awful had undoubtedly happened to them. This certainty careened into Roger with the force of a freight train and he sank onto the ground as though he had just been smashed in the solar plexus. "Dear God," he whispered just at the level of audibility. His voice was strained and he looked pitiful as he sat like a child amidst the frost-tipped pine needles on the frozen ground. "Ana, tell us."

Ana's mind went back to the day her father had died. She had been twenty-one and just out of college. It was a beautiful spring day, and she had been out with some friends at a baseball game. When she came back later than expected – the game had gone into extra innings – she found her mother a twitching wreck in the kitchen. Ana's father had been in a terrible car crash and had died immediately. Her mother was wild with grief; Ana hadn't even had time to feel the sting of her own shock before she found herself remembering her father's old adage that "tears don't make heroes" and going to her mother's side. She was the pillar of support for her mother that day and throughout the following months.

Ana fortified herself with the memory of her past strength and selflessness and began to speak to the crew, "Please listen," she said, more to buy time than for any other reason. Nobody seemed to have any intention of failing to listen. Even Juliet, having spent the totality of her first rush of panic, was now hanging limply in exhaustion in Ana's firm arms. "It seems that the wildlife in this area has been more active than any of us have expected." The distant baying of a coyote punctuated her understatement in a way that Ana felt was almost cruelly derisive. "In short, Scott and Francis have passed on."

Though everybody had made that assumption by this point, Ana's final pronouncement sent a collective jolt through the crew. Chris felt his heart constrict sharply. Juliet buried herself further into Ana's restraining grasp, which she found surprisingly comforting. Badly hidden tears began to drip from Roger's face. Vince placed a hand on Roger's shoulder and squeezed tightly. Takeshi remained still, his left hand trembling faster and faster.

"I knew them when...," Roger choked out, feeling for some reason that nothing would be worse at such a moment than silence. However, a lump in his throat prevented him from completing his thought. Vince squatted beside him and draped an arm around his shoulders. Silently, Vince tried again to pray. God, he thought, if there is ever going to be a time I need You with us, this must be it. However, there was no response.

"I understand this is hard to take," Ana said, after she felt that a suitable period of time had passed. Her eyes glistened with tears, but none of them had escaped onto her face. "We need a plan of action, nonetheless. Clearly, we are in no condition to continue with the assignment – at least, not immediately. I need the five of you to hang tight, okay? I'm going to radio the folks at NASA and have them pick us up." She paused. "I'll also make sure somebody gets out here to take care of the bodies."

Ana's statement triggered something in Roger; he shook off Vince's arm, stumbled to his feet, and began walking towards the site of the massacre.

Ana stopped him with the same quiet, direct voice she had used to calm Juliet, "Where are you going?" She put one of her hands to his chest; although her touch was light, it somehow expressed the latent threat that she would exercise more force, if necessary, to hold him back.

"I...," Roger began. He sniffled, blinked, shook his head, and continued, "... Gotta say goodbye."

"Okay," Ana said, taking Roger by the hand. "I think it's better that you not do that, all right? There's nothing to see there. Just bodies. They're not your friends anymore. Your friends have gone someplace else."

"Is it really that bad?" Roger asked, nervously scanning the mangled tent in the near distance before looking at Ana with pleading eyes.

Ana took a moment before she replied. "There's nothing to see," she repeated, but with such firmness that there was no possibility of challenging her. Ana, now holding on to both Juliet and Roger, maneuvered them back to Chris and Vince. Takeshi, finally emerging from his hypnotized preoccupation with the destruction, staggered to a nearby tree and sat down beneath it, staring vacantly at an invisible point in front of him, as though he were a shell-shocked soldier just home from war.

Ana pulled out her radio and spoke with professional efficiency. "R Star, this is Las Cruces. Come in, please. We have an emergency." When nobody replied to her first message, Ana's misgivings began to stir.

***

Now, having been speaking into the radio with increasing urgency for a quarter of an hour, Ana was on the edge of panic. The crew had clustered together near her and was watching her quickly deteriorating self-control with marked apprehension. To have two crew members killed violently in the night was an unspeakable horror; to then find their one link with the safety of civilization rendered impotent transformed tragedy into nightmare; to have this happen and then to see Ana Jenkins, the unshakeable colossus of the crew's collective esteem, fall into desperation was utterly unfathomable. Therefore, when Ana became so frustrated that she screamed in furious exasperation and hurled the radio to the ground, Juliet, who had managed to steady herself over the past fifteen minutes, dissolved into tears again.

Seeing that Ana was temporarily incapable of taking charge, Vince felt a stirring inside him. He had never made much of an effort to assert his own role within the crew before, but he remembered that the Gods had foretold trouble. He felt for some reason that They were relying on him, and that he had the power necessary to lead his crew out of danger. With a nervous glance at Ana, he cleared his throat and spoke. "Guys," he said softly, picking up the radio and brushing the dirt from it, "we're going to have to walk back to the highway. I don't think we have another option."

The crew looked at Vince with surprise. Nobody would have thought him desirous of addressing the entire group, but the strength with which he put forward his suggestion caused Ana to come back to her senses.

"Exactly," she said. "I know it was dark when we hiked in last night, but the forest is thick, so our tracks should be easy to follow. I think that we can find our way back to the highway. It's only a mile and a half." She stopped to listen for any cars, but could hear nothing over the clamor of Nature. The sun was fully up by this point and the woods resonated with a symphony of wildlife noises. Frogs croaked. Grasshoppers leapt noisily from leaf to leaf. Low-flying birds stirred the air as they flapped among the trees. A mass of flies buzzed around Scott and Francis's tent. Somewhere quite far off, Ana could hear a low, bestial growl. She shuddered.

"What about Scott and Francis?" Roger asked. He had not yet moved from his place on the ground, but his tears had stopped. He, like Takeshi, was simply staring vacantly into the air. "We can't leave them here. If we go for help, I mean."

Ana tried with difficulty to keep from getting angry. She was still furious that the radio would not work, sickened by the glimpse she had caught of Scott and Francis's bodies, and scared of whatever had killed them. She just wanted to get the hell out of the woods and to do it as soon as possible; however, she needed the entire crew on board. A crew boss, even in times of crisis – especially in times of crisis – was responsible for the protection of everybody.

To Ana's great relief, Vince stepped in again. He spoke quietly but earnestly. "Roger. I don't want to shake you up, but it seems we're in danger. I don't like the idea that we have to leave them, either. But we do have to leave them. We'll come back as soon as we can, but to stay here any longer than we need to would be a bad idea."

For a moment, Roger made no indication that he had heard Vince. Then, he shook his head slowly and said, still staring into space, "You guys go back. I'll stay."

"Roger," Ana snapped, before being silently shushed by Vince.

"Hey, Roger," Juliet said, crouching to bring her face onto Roger's eye level. "Hold my hand." She took one of his limp hands in hers and pressed his palm with her thumb. He looked at her vaguely. "Please come with us, okay?" She paused before repeating, "Please?"

Slowly, Juliet helped Roger to his feet. He had his arm over her shoulders and couldn't take the majority of his own weight, but Juliet was heartened by her success. She even thought that she might have caught Ana giving her a thankful smile.

"Let's go," Ana said. "Where's Chris?"

Chris had silently slipped back to his tent several minutes ago. Ana had been too tied up with the radio to notice his absence; Juliet, Vince, and Takeshi had all seen Chris go, but had figured that he needed to be left alone and hadn't said anything.

"I'll get him," Vince volunteered. He walked back to the tent he shared with Chris, but found that Chris hadn't gone inside. He was standing in front of the mouth of the tent, staring down at the ground.

"Chris," Vince said gently. "We can't get through to headquarters on the radio, so we're going to try finding our way back to the highway. Let's pack up camp, if you're ready, okay?"

Chris looked up with fear in his eyes. "Thanks, Vince."

Vince waited for Chris to move, but all of the motion in Chris's body seemed to be going on behind his eyes. He seemed as though he wanted to say something, but felt constrained.

As for Chris, he felt all the power of Vince's compassionate gaze and wished that he could be a worthier object of it. He felt full of something heavy and loathsome; he felt as though he had another self living somewhere in his chest. When he closed his eyes, he saw a large white room, full of machinery, with himself in the center. For some reason, this image terrified him, so he opened his eyes, focused on Vince, and decided to speak. For a moment, however, he couldn't find any words. "Thanks, Vince," he repeated. He wanted to say how much he respected Vince and how much he envied Vince's peace of mind and silent self-assurance. However, Chris felt profoundly uncomfortable with such sincerity and imagined that Vince, too, would be uncomfortable with it. Finally, he spoke,"Vince…do you ever, like, hate yourself a little?"

Vince was seized with the same fear of Chris that he had felt the previous night in the tent. "Why do you hate yourself, Chris?"

Chris toed the dirt in silence for a moment before shrugging and shaking his head. "Never mind. I don't want to hold up the crew." With that, he grabbed his backpack and walked past Vince back towards the remainder of the crew.

Vince moved to begin breaking down the tent, but his attention was arrested before he could begin doing so. On the ground, where Chris had just been staring, were Chris's rudimentary drawings of the previous night. Even though they were crudely rendered, their intent was clear enough to cause a chill to pass over Vince. The drawing consisted of six stick figures, seemingly modeled after members of the crew – one figure was extremely tall with long hair, one was short with long hair, one was medium height with a cross around its neck, one was short and skinny with an X for its mouth, one was tall and lanky, and the last was short and holding what could have been a book. Each of the figures, however, seemed to have suffered a recent death. One had crude waves carved above its head and bubbles streaming from its mouth. One was waist-deep in something and had a tortured O for a mouth. One was clearly decapitated. It wasn't too clear what had happened to the other three – some hasty lines had been dug out around them, but not to form any immediately identifiable image. There had originally been more to the drawing than just the six figures, but the rest had been completely obliterated by pawprints. Vince felt sick.

"God," he said aloud. "Please. Where are You?" He listened attentively, but received no answer; instead, he heard a hungry animal's growl echoing through the woods not too far away.

***

Amanda woke.

Arlo was already gone, but his side of the bed was still warm, so he couldn't have been up and about for very long. Amanda could hear him moving around the kitchen. He was probably getting dinner ready for the baby. Dinner? No, breakfast, rather. The sun was only just rising, after all.

Amanda frowned when she remembered the baby. Something seemed wrong. Was there any baby at all? Wasn't she too old to have had a baby? How old was she? With sadness, she realized that she couldn't remember. She dragged herself out of bed. Looking at her liverspotted feet on the bedroom's wooden floor, she thought, Looks as though I am getting on in years, after all. Her back cracked loudly. Feels that way, too.

Arlo was being noisy in the kitchen. It sounded as though he were scraping twigs along the floor. What was he doing in there? It was Amanda's job to make breakfast. It was Arlo's job to eat it. That's the way it had always been since their wedding – however many years ago that was. He was probably hungry.

Amanda felt like getting dressed up. She opened her antique wardrobe and pulled out a long, white skirt with lace embroidery. Where would she have gotten such an impractical skirt? Regardless, she should wear it – Father was taking her to the horse show today. Although... hadn't Father died? Unsure, Amanda stepped with effort into the skirt and caught sight of her gnarled hands. That's right, she suddenly remembered. Of course, Father's been dead for some time now. I'm getting right old. I've just been letting my imagination gallop off without me.

Having put on a denim blouse with red embroidery, Amanda felt her way down the hall. With her cataracts, she had some trouble seeing, though she knew her house so well that this never posed a problem. Even when her mind deserted her, her body was so used to performing her morning ritual of waking up, getting dressed, and making the breakfast that the process had become second nature to her.

When she got to the kitchen, she was surprised to see Arlo sitting at the kitchen table, scraping away at some logs with a long knife.

"What'd you be doing, dear?" Amanda asked. The familiar feminine sound of her voice caused him to raise his head. He smiled fondly at his wife; she certainly didn't look any younger, but, then again, Pimp Daddy had promised nothing until after the "patsy" had been repelled.

"Just making some knickknacks, angel. Too cold to get out there and look over the land; besides, I got my cough acting up nowadays." In actuality, the morning was not especially cold – it was warmer than the previous morning had been. Arlo had simply wanted an excuse to remain at home to look out for patsies. Right now, he was working on a pair of legs for Pimp Daddy. He had gone down to the basement early in the morning, hoping to examine the head while it was asleep. He wasn't sure why he had assumed that the head would need sleep, but his assumption was wrong. Pimp Daddy had been as energetic as ever and had made Arlo's task of figuring out where to attach a pair of legs more difficult than Arlo had expected it to be. In the end, Arlo had found a quarter-sized hole on the base of the neck, through which Pimp Daddy's spinal cord must have formerly run. Arlo was now trying his best to construct a set of legs upon which he could plant the head. He had no idea how to approximate the knee joint, so he was just carving the legs as solid blocks and hoping that Pimp Daddy would not mind. Of course, the odds of Pimp Daddy not minding, by Arlo's reckoning, were quite slim.

"I never knew you to be a craftsman," Amanda said with self doubt. Was she wrong? Hadn't Arlo built a crib for the baby? Amanda decided that she would watch Arlo's reaction to what she had just said; if he seemed puzzled, she would know that he was a craftsman after all.

"Idle hands, Amanda. Idle hands." Arlo winked at his wife and hoped that she couldn't pick up on the uncertainty in his eyes. "You're all dressed up pretty."

Amanda, surprised, looked at herself. She was wearing a denim blouse and a white skirt. She didn't know she had such clothing. Was it even hers? Suddenly, she remembered. "Oh, yes. Father's taking me to the horse show." She had the feeling that she was saying something foolish, but she couldn't figure out what was foolish about it. Shaking off the uncomfortable feeling, she remembered that she was supposed to be making breakfast. Once again relying upon her muscular memory, she began opening cabinets and gathering together everything she would need for pancakes.

Arlo smiled. He knew that his wife could whip up a hearty breakfast with her eyes closed. He was at his happiest when Amanda was at her happiest – and Amanda was at her happiest when she was of use. Arlo was perfectly capable of cooking for himself, but he liked listening to his wife's tuneless humming and watching the self-satisfied smile that lit up her face whenever she became master of the kitchen. Today, however, he had to deny himself the pleasure of watching Amanda cook; now that he had roughly cut the logs into oblong shapes from which he could craft legs, he thought he should take his work outside so as not to get wood chips all over Amanda's kitchen.

Arlo rose and kissed his wife lightly on her wrinkled cheek. "I'm gonna haul my bones outside to work, angel. You just come get me if you need anything."

"Okay, Robin," Amanda replied. She saw a dark sadness come over her husband's eyes and wasn't sure why. "What's wrong, honey?"

"Nothing's wrong, little lady. You just get on with our breakfast." Arlo once more kissed his wife and hauled his logs out with him to the back porch.

Amanda continued her preparation of the meal. As she dexterously sifted the flour, she allowed her mind to wander. She thought about the angel who had visited her in her sleep last night. She hoped that her husband would not find out that the angel came to her every night; he might be jealous. Even when she couldn't quite make sense of the waking world, she could remember the angel in great detail. He had begun visiting three nights ago. Young, handsome, and clean-shaven, he whispered the sort of loving platitudes that Amanda hadn't heard since Arlo had begun courting her. Amanda didn't know her angel's name, but she trusted him. He told her that she was just as beautiful as she had been when she was younger; he told her that it wasn't too late to have children; he told her that he would never stop loving her. Sometimes Amanda told him to get lost and that she was spoken for. Other times, however, she couldn't help blushing over the inexplicable affections of such a charming youth.

Amanda was brought back to the present moment when her hands discovered an obstacle to the completion of their usual task – there were no more preserves in the cupboard. "Where do you keep the extra preserves in this house?" Amanda asked aloud. When nobody responded, she realized that she was the only one in the kitchen. Where had Robin gone? Had he left for the horse show without her? Amanda grew frustrated with herself. She knew that Robin was the wrong name, but she couldn't for the life of her recall the name of her husband. She also couldn't remember where the preserves were, but she knew that she had made at least fifty jars in the fall. With an irritated click of the tongue, she decided to set off in search of the extra preserves.

Amanda wandered into the den. The only furniture was a sagging, moth-eaten sofa, a tiny television set, and an uneven bookcase that housed a collection of yellowed women's journals. This was clearly not the right room. Backtracking, Amanda found a low door in the hall, behind which were the stairs to the cellar. Women usually kept their preserves in the basement to keep them cool, right? Amanda believed that this must be true. She clutched the splintering banister with both hands and slowly made her way down the creaky staircase to the concrete floor.

The basement was dark by anybody's standards, but Amanda's cataracts made it virtually black to her eyes. Though she could make out the general shapes of the things in the room, she had to feel her way clumsily around piles of rusty shovels, boxed-up fabrics, and retired, deteriorating appliances. As she continued to look for the preserves – Amanda was certain that this was where her son had put them – she heard something that sounded like heavy breathing. Much as Amanda's other senses had deteriorated, she had retained her sharp hearing and now stopped to listen more carefully. Something was definitely breathing slowly and steadily. A wave of adrenaline rushed to Amanda's head. She could hear an ocean of blood roaring through the veins in her ears. Where was the staircase back to the safety of daylight? She couldn't quite remember which way she had come.

"Oh, calm down, you twittering old fuckwad." Pimp Daddy's derisive voice shot suddenly from the darkness. Immediately, Amanda's mind was jarred back into proper operation. Arlo was her husband, Robin was the liar who had come by three days ago, the horse show was sixty years ago, she had no children, the preserves were indeed in the cellar, she was alone, and a familiar yet terrifying voice was taunting her.

"Please come out of the darkness," she said with a quaver in her voice.

"What are you talking about, you bat-faced pupa? I'm stuck right where I am until your rectum of a husband fetches me my goddamn legs."

"Who are you?" Amanda began backing towards the staircase in terror.

"No need to run away, you vaginal cyst. If I were going to blast your brains out, I'd have done it by now. Relax – stress isn't good for old fishwives like yourself."

"What do you want, you awful critter?" Amanda knew that she recognized the voice from somewhere, but she couldn't place it. In spite of the voice's assurance that she was quite safe, she wanted to get upstairs as soon as possible.

"What do I want, you brazen harpy? I believe you're the one who came down here looking for me."

"I was just looking for my preserves...," Amanda trailed off. Her hand hit the banister. She began backing up the stairs.

"Ha! Preserves aren't going to do you a damn bit of good, you spoiled tuna salad sandwich. Once the rot's begun, the rot can't be undone! That's my mantra on aging, and once I get out of this fucking root cellar and into the public eye, I'm going to have it printed up on buttons and sold across the country as profundity. Once the rot's begun, the rot can't be undone! Clever, huh?"

Amanda didn't respond, but turned and loped up the stairs as quickly as possible. When she had almost reached the top, however, the head called out to her one last time, "Hey, Shitcicle! Where's your damn sense of humor? I'm just having a little fun with you; you're my friend, you know. Your ass might be puckered, but you're consummately fuckable under all those wrinkles. And I'll tell you what. Pimp Daddy – that's me, by the way – is gonna be in charge of your makeover. We start tonight. Ten years younger by sundown or your money back. How does that sound, chump?"

Amanda was shaking. She wished she were back in her dream with her angel. She just wanted the awful disembodied voice to stop speaking, so she hollered, "Yes, that'll be fine," into the darkness below. She waited anxiously to see if the voice would reply.

After a moment, the head said, "I can see you want to go. Well, I won't keep you. You've got to rest up, after all." Pimp Daddy suddenly cracked a toothless smile. "Won't be too much longer before you're giving birth to your beautiful baby son."

***

Unfortunately for the Gods, comets – while the speediest form of transportation available from Heaven to Earth – were also the least accurate. They invariably shot with such velocity from the Central Heaven Terminal that the conductors were hard pressed to steer them to any real effect. As the express comet to North America blasted through the Earth's atmosphere, the conductor had to grasp it by its tail and shove his own weight backwards against the comet's forward momentum. It was tense, arduous work and few in Heaven were equal to it. The conductor tried as faithfully as possible to accommodate the Gods' desire to wind up in East Texas, but strong headwinds forced the comet drastically further west than anticipated. The comet careened towards

Earth and the Gods realized with dismay that They were going to end up somewhere closer to Santa Fe than to Longview.

"Jump!" screamed the conductor when the comet was roughly five hundred feet above the desert landscape. This was the usual landing procedure for comets – because celestial technology had not yet allowed for the deceleration of comets prior to their collision with the Earth, the only way to land gently was to jettison oneself from the comet and allow one's buoyancy of spirit to reduce one's speed of descent.

"Thanks, ace!" God shouted, as He jumped from the comet, one hand on His fedora and the other around the waist of His wife.

The conductor and the other passenger jumped as well, waving to the Gods as they floated lightly towards the ground. The conductor would have to find a geyser or volcano that was ripe for explosion in order to ferry himself back to Heaven. Because these phenomena were so rare, the Earth was heavily populated by stranded spirits who came to Earth for a pleasure visit but ended up at the end of a long waiting list for transportation back to Heaven. Comet conductors and the Gods, of course, were on the priority list for volcanic transit, but, even so, a conductor could expect an average of a twenty-five year holding period before returning home. The Gods Themselves could expect to wait at least three years.

"Take a good look around, toots, because We'll be here a while," God whispered to His wife as the New Mexico landscape slowly grew larger beneath Them. The mesas, streaked with pink and orange sediment, glowed in the warm morning sun. The Gods could see jagged red mountains in the distance, ferociously ripping through the delicate desert sand. Lonely roads crisscrossed the expanses beneath the Heavenly Couple. In the near distance, the low skyline of Santa Fe was visible.

"Let's aimeth for Santa Fe Airport," Mrs. God suggested. Because of the slow rate of Their descent, the Gods could navigate easily. Mrs. God held on to Her husband with one arm and held out Her skirt with the other as a crude sort of wing. About two hundred feet from Earth, the Gods espied the command tower of the Santa Fe airport and directed Their descent so that They landed just a quarter of a mile from the departures terminal.

The impact with the ground was very light, as though the Gods had fallen with invisible parachutes attached to Their backs. Though it was February, the morning sun was not obscured by clouds and it burned brightly, heating up the asphalt streets of Santa Fe. The streets were clogged with commuter traffic, the dusty storefronts all still said, "Sorry,

We're Closed," and the noise of departing and arriving jet planes tore the air overhead.

"Stick close to Me, doll face," God said, sucking in a deep breath of Earth's notoriously lousy oxygen. "Here's the plan: hitch a plane to Texas, take a walk in the woods, find Our man, and have him home in time for happy hour. Margaritas are on Me."

"God," said Mrs. God. "Thou knoweth that I appreciate Your optimism, but I can't shaketh this damn feeling that something downright awful beith about to goeth down on this Usforsaken planet. You never even toldeth Me why You're so convincedethed that Vince beith in danger in the first place."

God kissed His wife on the forehead as the noise of the nearby interstate roared beside Them. "Forget it, babe," He said. "We've got a job to do, and We can't let the heebie-jeebies jinx Us before We even get rolling. Danger or no danger, God and His honey are hot on the trail of Their man. Now let's go hop a jet, because the sooner We snag Vince, the sooner tequila time rolls around in Texas!"

***

Ross Tucker was about to do something unprecedented in the history of Greater Heaven. After his warnings had failed to prevent the Heavenly Couple from heading to Earth, he had racked his brains for a way to keep Them away from the danger that awaited Them. Only recently arrived in Heaven, Ross had not yet adjusted his mind to the new parameters by which being dead bound him. His first idea had been to go down to Earth himself, but he quickly realized that he would be invisible to the living and useless to the Gods unless he could communicate with the heads at NASA. He had then considered making a quick jaunt to Earth, just to pick up as much information as he could before immediately returning to Heaven. He had almost bought his comet ticket before remembering that, if he were to travel to Earth, he would be unable to return to Heaven for decades. Given the fact that the Gods had, at most, a few days before disaster was bound to strike, this Plan B was also unacceptable. Therefore, he had lit upon his current plan after almost an hour of careful meditation. Ross felt profoundly uncomfortable about his Plan C, but he also recognized that the end, in this case, would likely justify the means.

Ross now stood outside the Gods' Greater Heaven residence, fingering the lock pick he had bought from a man at a black market home security store in Central Heaven. The Gods' house was far from the multistory Versailles that most people on Earth pictured. In fact, it was a simple two-story bungalow with a small herb garden in front and a faded welcome mat on the deteriorating wooden porch. The paint job – pure white, with gold highlights – was beginning to flake off the wooden siding. One of the Gods' quirks was that, whenever They moved, They would bring Their beloved home with Them. God usually hated to think of Himself as sentimental, but He had no trouble admitting that, when it came to the house, He would never want to live anywhere else.

Ross stood by the enormous tin mailbox, which was stuffed with unopened prayers. Ross couldn't help glancing at the envelopes. Some were so old that they were addressed to "Zeus." That was a name God had abandoned long ago as sounding too austere. These days, He was trying to decide between a number of names, all of which sounded perfectly acceptable. It was a decision He fretted much about, until His wife had finally confronted Him about it, saying, "Why dost Thou obsessetheth over this so damn much? " Mrs. God sometimes over-"eth"ed when She was fed up. "Spies generally haveth many aliases. Why canst not Thou?" From that point forward, God had relished His many names. Nothing could have gotten Him more excited about the prospect of multiple identities than thinking of Himself as a spy. Sometimes, when He received a prayer for "Yahweh" or "Jesus" or "Allah," He would wink at His wife, smile secretly, and announce, "Sounds like a job for You-Know-Who!"

Now, however, Ross did not have time to consider God's old mail. He had a job to do, and time was of the essence. As he stepped up onto the warped porch, Ross glanced around to make sure that he was not being seen; thankfully for him, the idea of anybody breaking into the Gods' house was so far from anybody's imagination that nobody looked twice at him. "God," Ross whispered as he jimmied the lock, "forgive me my trespasses." With a satisfying click, the lock popped open. Ross took a deep breath and crossed himself in humility as he opened the door and took his first step into the house of the Gods.

The Flora

Lucinda "Mad-Dog" Bruin was known among her NASA coworkers as "The Wall." Though standing a mere five foot two and weighing in at under one hundred and fifteen pounds, Lucinda was the impenetrable moat with which the upper echelon of NASA bureaucracy surrounded itself. Although she was technically at the same level of security clearance as Robin, she was, for all intents and purposes, his superior. She was in charge of withholding any information from Robin that NASA deemed worthy of withholding; the fact that she herself was not privy to any of this secret information was, to her, irrelevant. She enjoyed the power she had over her coworkers.

Today, The Wall was dressed in a cute navy power suit. Her outrageously blonde hair had been pulled into a ponytail and was held in place with a sparkly orange scrunchie. On her desk sat a blue-haired troll doll, a copy of Sun Tzu, and a gargantuan bottle of water that seemed to be about half her size. She was perusing the daily memo from the Higher-Ups through pink, horn-rimmed reading glasses. Like every other memo, it was incomprehensible.

"18 February 2008- Day one of Daedalus search mission. All crews recalled. Abort mission. Notify PR rep. Robin Rodriguez of demobilization of Las Cruces wildland crew. All sent back to home states. Repeat: mission aborted. New option for fulfillment of NASA goal statement. Further report unnecessary. End memo."

Lucinda had been aware of the search mission, but was utterly nonplussed by its cancellation. She had been working for the Feds long enough to know that, for one thing, 80% of the memo most likely consisted of lies and, for another, that the Higher-Ups would never do anything that jeopardized the aims of NASA. In truth, Lucinda wasn't particularly sure what the aims of NASA were, but she was certain that they were in some way beneficial to the majority of mankind.

Having considered the memo, she then turned to her correspondence. Around twenty requests from various people and agencies for information had been placed in her inbox. Today she needed to respond to every one of them, explaining in each case why it was "absolutely impossible" for her to provide the desired statistics. She began typing out a response to a defense contractor in Virginia. "Thank you for your inquiry regarding the results of our test of 05 November 2002 on the permeability of the isotopic barium shield. To our regret, it is absolutely impossible for us to divulge...."

The Wall was interrupted in her typing by the slam of a door and the noise of footsteps in the hall. She looked up just in time to see Robin Rodriguez breathlessly rush into her office. Rodriguez, she knew, was much valued among the Higher-Ups for the innate trustfulness and slightly disingenuous charm that qualified him so well for a top position in PR. Though he knew nothing of it, he had been hand picked by NASA authorities as the central PR representative for the Daedalus search and rescue operation. Lucinda knew that she currently wielded more power than Rodriguez ever would, but she couldn't help feeling slightly jealous nevertheless; she couldn't see why such a buffoonish patsy ought to receive special consideration. She peered at Robin coldly over her pink-framed glasses and waited for him to catch his breath.

"May I help you?" she asked, injecting a note of severity into her voice for no particular reason. She remembered that Robin had been mentioned specifically in her memo. It was quite rare that employees were ever referred to by name in official correspondence, so Lucinda knew that she would have to take extra care in dealing with Robin. I am The Wall, she thought as she grasped her enormous water bottle with both hands and took a long swig.

"Lucinda, I need authorization to speak with a Level Six employee. There has been an emergency with my search crew."

Lucinda blinked noncommittally. "There absolutely has not."

"Lucinda, what are you talking about?" Robin hated Lucinda. He felt that she occupied her position of privilege with far more smugness than such a low-level employee was entitled to.

"I mean," Lucinda said, slowly and distinctly, "that there absolutely has not been an emergency with your search crew."

"Somebody cut the wire on my radio."

"Perhaps." Lucinda took another swig of water and glanced back down at her paperwork. She said nothing as she squared the papers on her desk, realigned her pens, and wiped a greasy smudge off her computer screen. Finally, she continued, "Your crew has been recalled, and the search mission has been aborted."

Robin felt the floor falling out from underneath his feet. He felt himself catapulted into confusion. After such extensive planning and huge expense, the largest mobilization in NASA history was being called off after little more than twenty-four hours. It was absolutely inconceivable and Robin was, therefore, immediately suspicious.

"Lucinda," he said, "that is a lie."

The Wall looked at him with incredulous eyes. Lucinda had no doubt that it was a lie, to be sure, but exposure was not the name of the game at NASA. If it was a lie, it was a lie that had been instated to serve the greater good and it was therefore to everybody's advantage to assume that the lie was the truth. Robin – still green, Lucinda reminded herself – clearly knew nothing about the propriety of form. "Robin," she said, "it is absolutely not a lie."

"Lucinda…." Robin was at a loss. He felt his pulse begin to race, and he had to consciously slow his breathing; this was no time to lose his head. "You don't understand how dangerous this is. At least eight people are stranded in the middle of the wilderness. They could be in danger. They have no way of finding their way back to us. If they are still out there, it is your responsibility as a human being to get me in touch with somebody who can tell me what the hell is going on."

Lucinda considered the situation before her. Essentially, the problem boiled down to this: should she trust the philanthropic organization that had paid her salary for the past four years and had, moreover, put a man on the moon, or should she trust a twenty-something PR man wearing a suit that was not as expensive as he wanted it to appear? In spite of Robin's sincerity, Lucinda had trouble believing that he was anything more than an overdramatic neophyte. With a sigh that said, Give it up, Lucinda pronounced her final judgment on the matter, "All of the crews have been demobilized from the search detail. That is the absolute truth. The reason you have had difficulty contacting your crew is that it has been sent back to its headquarters. It is not in the forest, nor is it in any danger. You will receive your next assignment shortly." Lucinda pre-empted any objections that Robin might have had by immediately bowing her head once again over her correspondence and beginning to type diligently.

Robin, however, having assumed from the start that he would be unlikely to gain anything from speaking to The Wall, had already devised an alternative plan. He was going to have to go back over the search area and try to track down his crew. For the first time, Robin began to doubt the organization for which he was working. Was it really of no concern that somebody had cut the wires in his radio? Did they really assume that he would believe that the search had been called off? Had the search been called off? Riddled with questions, Robin decided that he would stop by his desk before setting off in search of the crew, so that he could see if anybody had left a message for him.

Indeed, a sheaf of papers was waiting for Robin on his desk. Picking up the documents, Robin perused them with considerable surprise. They were demobilization papers for the Las Cruces crew, with all the appropriate signatures. Apparently, federal health and safety officials had cracked down on the mission as too dangerous to justify. First thing in the morning, while Robin had been listening to Jimmy Hawdon talk about the immutability of the human soul, NASA staff had been tracking down the search crews at their campsites before they had the opportunity to stray too far. The crews had all been ferried back to headquarters, put through the appropriate bureaucratic processes, and released. Robin quickly checked the signature by Ana's name on the demobilization paper against the one he had on file for her; it proved authentic.

The buzz of panic in Robin's head began to slow. He sat down at his desk, allowing himself the first moment of peace since he had discovered the sliced wire in his radio. If Ana had been around to sign the demobilization paper for the Las Cruces crew, the crew must have returned from the field. If the crew had returned from the field, they were safe. Though Robin remained puzzled as to why NASA had initiated such an enormous operation without first ensuring that it passed federal work regulations, his puzzlement was a far more welcome sensation than his fear. Everything was fine; Robin could happily lay to rest the odd adventure he had been having for the past several days.

***

Unfortunately, from the perspective of the Las Cruces crew, everything was far from fine. The six remaining crew members had been walking throughout the morning and, as the sun neared its zenith, they each began singly to come to the conclusion that they were getting no nearer to the highway. Ana was leading the way, with Vince at her shoulder to chime in with his muddled recollection of the route they had taken the previous night. Juliet was walking with Roger, keeping a close watch on his emotional state; now that he was engaged in a physical task, his recent grief was temporarily allayed, but Juliet wanted to be alerted to his first signal of any retreat back into hysteria. Takeshi followed close behind, eyes roving the woods for any beasts that might come to feed on the crew, and Chris hung to the rear. At first, the crew had stopped every fifteen minutes or so to listen for any highway sounds, but each time nobody could hear anything but the chatter of wildlife. Now, without any words having been exchanged, the crew was pushing onwards blindly.

The vegetation in this area was dense, and the crew members found themselves frequently hung up in the brambles and shrubbery that were entangled into thick mats. Sometimes, the crew would face such formidable snarls of tree branches, grown over with hanging mosses and ropes of thorny vines, that nobody could see the next person over. Slowly and arduously, the crew proceeded. Vicious needles snagged clothing and ripped into the flesh of the Las Cruces crew as they forced themselves through the resistant wall of jungle. All around, animals could be heard, though, whenever anybody stopped to look around, none could be sighted.

Four and a half hours passed in this way. Finally, when he felt that it might be near noon, Chris hollered out to Vince and Ana at the head of the group, "Can we stop and eat something?"

Chris could see Takeshi in front of him, but the forest was too thick for him to see all the way up to Ana. After a moment, however, her voice came back to him. "No. We've got to push on. We can't be far from the highway."

Chris wanted to point out that they should have reached the highway four hours ago and that the odds were great that they were further away from civilization than they had been when they had begun walking in the morning. However, like the others, he was in no rush to voice his uncertainty. Instead, he simply shouted, "Can we just take five minutes, please?" A long pause followed, and Chris assumed that his request had been simply ignored. Finally, though, Ana shouted back that they could have five minutes once they reached the next clearing. Chris suspected that Vince had urged Ana's change of heart.

About ten minutes later, the crew pushed into a small open area and everybody sat down on his or her backpack. On all sides, solid fences of unmanageable wilderness contained the group. The clearing itself was overgrown with weeds and low-lying shrubs and was so small that the six crew members were sitting nearly shoulder to shoulder. Chris could see only intermittent snatches of blue sky between the tree branches that cluttered the space overhead. The forest had been particularly rough to the crew throughout the morning – brutal red scratches crisscrossed Juliet's face, and a long, jagged rip had been torn into Takeshi's pant leg. Chris somehow had the sudden certainty that he would never see New Mexico again. He wanted to weep from fatigue and emotional strain, but he didn't.

For a while, nobody said anything; nobody even seemed able to look at anybody else. Chris and Takeshi pulled granola bars from their packs and began to chomp on them silently. Roger stared vacantly at the forest surrounding him, tears once again coming to his eyes. Juliet put a limp hand on Roger's knee; she wanted to be reassuring somehow, but didn't feel particularly secure herself. Ana was counting noiselessly to herself. She did not intend for the break to take any longer than the allotted five minutes. The longer the crew was allowed to sit, the harder it was going to be to get them up and moving again. Ana knew that the hike was wearing on the group, but they had to keep pushing ahead. For some reason, she felt that, if she spent one more night in the forest, she would never make it out. In Ana's mind, then, they needed to find the highway by nightfall or all was lost.

Vince fished out the last of his granola bars from his pocket and considered whether or not to eat it. Absently, he remarked, "We should have thought to take the things out of Scott and Francis's bags."

Immediately, everybody's eyes were upon him and Vince had the awful sensation of having said precisely the wrong thing. For a moment, he hoped that nobody would remark, but, sure enough, Juliet opened her mouth and continued the thread of conversation that everybody had tried so hard to prevent.

"Why? How much longer do you think we'll be out here?"

The sacred seal of silence had been broken and there was nothing for Vince to do but reply. "I don't know."

"Guys," said Ana, standing up, "Let's go." However, everybody else remained seated.

"We're not going to survive, are we?" The plainness with which Juliet put forward the question, as though she were honestly expecting an answer, brought a chill to Vince's heart. In the brief ensuing silence, he noticed that the sounds of the forest, markedly noisy just ten minutes ago, had dwindled and that all he could now hear was a lone pair of twittering birds.

Chris spoke before Vince could reply. "No," he said, with downcast eyes. "We will not survive." His voice conveyed the utmost certainty.

The fatalism of the crew terrified Ana, largely because she felt a strong urge to join it. "Guys!" she said, a little more loudly than she had intended, "Get up right now and get moving."

"Yeah, she's right," Vince said. He wanted very badly to mitigate any of the damage he had inflicted on the group's morale with his unintentional comment. He picked up his bag and stood beside Ana; however, Roger, Takeshi, Chris, and Juliet made no move to join him.

The passing time weighed on Ana; she felt, quite literally, under pressure. She could feel the sunlight bleeding between the heavy branches and thick vines that enclosed the clearing and casting mottled afternoon shadows across the faces of her crew members. Ana's forehead began to sweat. "Right now, guys! This is ridiculous," she screamed.

What happened next stunned the entire group. Takeshi, who, until this time, had allowed only his trembling left hand to feel the trauma of all that had happened, abruptly leapt to his feet and, screaming something incomprehensible, ran to the edge of the clearing and began trying to claw his way through the foliage. He moved with such rapidity that he had pushed himself through at least ten meters of forest before Ana could crawl in after him, grab his waist, and drag him back to the clearing. She threw him to the forest floor and pinned his right arm and leg. Vince, acting on a nod from Ana, seized his left arm and leg. As Takeshi writhed under the grasps of his two strongest crewmates, the remainder of the crew gathered around him. His brief but frenzied jaunt into the forest had left him a bit worse for the wear; the rip in his pants had been snagged and stretched further, new tears had appeared in the fabric of his shirt, and three deep gashes, almost resembling claw marks, cut jaggedly across his cheek.

Some part of his brain now realizing that the crew couldn't understand him, Takeshi's screams, with no pause in tempo or rhythm, suddenly became more articulated, "I can't more! I can't more! I can't more! I can't more!"

Ana positioned herself so that one of her knees was holding down his leg; this freed up one of her hands, with which she tried to get a grasp on Takeshi's chin. However, whenever her hand neared his face, Takeshi would whip his head violently about and bite tigrishly at Ana's fingers, all while continuing to scream without pause, "I can't more! I can't more! I can't more!"

Vince remembered the time his father had taken him to a revival meeting; a woman there had had cancer, and the preacher lay magic hands on her to call down the Holy Spirit. She had then gone into an epileptic seizure, much like Takeshi's. At the time, Vince had suspected the woman of play-acting. When he had asked God about it later, God put a fatherly arm around Vince's shoulders and said, "That's an easy one, champ. When you believe in something, the believing makes it reality. When you're so full of belief, it just takes over you sometimes, until you bounce around like a slickster hopped up on pep pills." Vince asked if God hadn't entered her after all, to which God replied, "I'd never enter another woman without permission from the Missus."

"Which Thou ain'teth ever gonna getteth," Mrs. God had replied from another room.

If the woman at the revival had been full of belief in a divine presence, however, Takeshi's belief was surely in his own imminent doom. The woman's eyes had rolled back in her head in sublime ecstasy; Takeshi's darted frantically, as though he were searching for an exit from his own mind. Belief, it seemed to Vince, had subsumed Takeshi's rational mind.

Ana was at a loss. With the crew looking at her expectantly, a hysterical wreck writhing under the weight of her body, and the sun beginning its slow downward descent, Ana lost her control.

"Snap out of it!" she screamed and swiped a broad palm across Takeshi's bleeding cheek. Rather than jarring him into reality, however, this blow caused Takeshi to howl in pain and redouble his efforts to free himself from Vince and Ana's grasps. Ana screamed again, and once again slapped Takeshi to no greater effect.

"Calm down!" Juliet screamed, knowing that adding her own panic to the situation would not be helpful, but finding herself unable to keep silent.

Before five seconds had passed, each member of the group was screaming. Juliet and Roger tried to help Ana and Vince in holding down Takeshi; everybody had an order for somebody else. The volume rose. Everyone grabbed an arm, a leg, a handful of flesh. Tears ran down faces. A fist connected with an abdomen. As the cacophony grew, everybody screamed louder to get his or her words across. "Get a hold on yourselves!" An elbow slammed into a nose, drawing out a trickle of blood. "Stop it!" Somebody's knee against somebody's forehead.

At the height of this confusion of noise and violence, the deafening roar of an animal suddenly ripped into the clearing.

The tangle of arms and legs stopped moving. Immediately still and quiet, each member of the group waited, listening, with tensed muscles and trembling hands.

Again, the loud, hungry growl. Very, very close.

With an awful feeling of nausea, Vince realized that Chris was nowhere to be seen.

***

"Don't get your hackles up, pussycat," God said to the red-faced woman behind the counter at the Santa Fe Airport. The Gods had been having difficulty. Their last trip to Earth had been an excursion to Colombia, and They had not thought to change Their money out of pesetos. Now They didn't have quite enough dollars on hand to book a flight to Texas. The customer service representative, whose nametag revealed her to be called "Sharon," seemed unwilling to orchestrate a compromise.

"I would appreciate it if you would refrain from calling me 'pussycat,'" Sharon said, with a particularly feline scowl. She had not been able to sleep the previous night, and she was growing tired of this obnoxious schizo, who seemed to think he had come straight out of *Shaft*, and his peroxided trophy wife.

That Trophy Wife, who had remained silent until this point, suddenly interjected, "Doest thou knoweth to Whom thou speakesteth?"

"I'm sorry, Miss," Sharon said, somewhat agog at Mrs. God's odd speech pattern, "but rules are rules. You can't fly to Longview if you're not going to pay."

"I beithetheth the wife of God!" Mrs. God was utterly aghast at Sharon's rudeness. The Gods generally kept a low profile whenever They traveled to Earth, but Mrs. God had simply assumed that, if anybody knew about Their true identities, They would be welcomed in a manner befitting Their divine status.

Sharon's patience was growing thin. "Listen, lady, I don't care if you're God's wet-nurse; you're not entitled to jack shit unless you've got $367 for me."

Mrs. God's ordinarily pale skin was quickly suffused with an irritated red glow. She opened Her mouth to yell at Sharon, but, thinking better of it, spread Her lips into a superior smirk and turned instead to Her husband, "Zap her, honey."

God "tsk"-ed lightly before kissing His wife lightly on the forehead. "You know I'm no Frank Zappa, baby. Save such tough stuff for the rabble and roughnecks. You catch more flies with honey than with vinegar, and I've never met a young chippie yet who can resist My sugar." God blew a kiss at Sharon, as He slid a fistful of pesetos and a baggie of cannabis to her across the counter. "Take it, toots, and, moreover, I'll promise you a cushy penthouse in Heaven's poshest district when you kick the bucket."

Sharon, however, was not tempted. A headache pounded between her temples; she felt she should turn these nutsos in to security, but she thought about the sheaths of paperwork and hours of testimony that would entail. Gritting her teeth, she said, "I will cut you the favor of your life and pretend that I haven't seen this." She slid the baggie of drugs back into God's hands. "Now get your schizophrenic ass out of here before I reconsider."

Mrs. God was absolutely livid. "If Thou chooseth not to zappeth this brazen hussy," She hissed to Her husband, "I shall taketh it upon Myself." At heart, Mrs. God was every bit as pacifistic as Her husband, so She allowed only a very small electric charge to build up in Her fingers –

just enough to startle Sharon into obedience without harming her. However, as She flicked Her fingertips towards the surly airport employee before Her, expecting the familiar lightning burst of energy to flow effortlessly from Her hands, She received a scare.

Absolutely nothing happened.

Mrs. God's eyes widened. Never, in the infinity of Her recollection, had She been unable to exercise Her powers. She was so wrapped up in Her feelings of shock and puzzlement that She didn't notice the sad manner in which Her husband shook His head or the irritated sigh that Sharon heaved. God put a tender hand on Mrs. God's back, hoping that She wouldn't be too upset by what He had already suspected – that coming to Earth had this time, for some reason, stripped Them of Their powers.

Mrs. God's shock at Her unexpected impotence suddenly transformed into embarrassed irritation. She grabbed Her husband's hand. "Cometh on-eth, honeyeth!" She cried, agitated to the point of blind "eth"-ing. The airport was fairly quiet, and so only a few other people were hanging around the Customer Service desk. Mrs. God's loud remark drew everybody's attention to Her and Her husband. Unconsciously inflating Her exit for the audience, Mrs. God took Her husband's arm, wheeled about on Her heel, and, as She marched God out to the taxi stand, yelled, "It seemeth that Southwest Airlines considerethths itself to be greater than God! Well, fine! The Gods are not too high and mighty to take Greyhound, if it comes to that!"

The couple stepped out to the curb, where God hailed the first cab He saw. Opening the door for His wife before climbing inside Himself, He shouted to the cabbie, "Santa Fe bus station, Joe – and step on it! We've got a friend to save!"

***

There was no denying it. The resemblance was simply astonishing. The boy in the picture had God's rich black skin, Mrs. God's finely sculpted jaw, God's muscular physique, and Mrs. God's diminutive mouth. "Could the Gods have had a son?" Ross Tucker asked himself as he examined the pictures on the Gods' mantel. Although he had suspected something of the sort, Ross was unprepared to have the hard visual evidence in front of his face. However, it made so much sense, given what he knew about the ill-fated Daedalus mission. If They've got a son down there, Ross thought to himself, then They are in far more trouble than I could have imagined.

Ross's astute mind had already constructed the entire chain of events from space shuttle crash to the present moment. The family photographs had answered the one uncertainty he had been wrestling with since he had seen the Gods leaving town – namely, what was the bait drawing Them to Earth? However, an imperiled son was clearly enough to tempt any reasonable couple into danger; all that now remained for Ross was to figure out how to notify the Gods that They were being lured into an enormous trap.

Ross attempted to keep his anxiety from controlling him. The best thing to do, he thought, is to organize a systematic search of the house, in order to unearth any available clues about how to contact the Gods. This cannot be haphazard. True to his plan, Ross steadied himself and, biting back any twinges of regret at his sacrilege, calmly began to pick through every drawer and closet in the house, starting from the upstairs bedroom. In God's drawers, Ross discovered cigars, about twenty pairs of sunglasses, and some tiger-striped briefs; Mrs. God's drawers primarily contained lingerie, pearls, and roach clips. None of this proved useful.

Ross moved into the master bathroom. Most of the white tiles on the wall were chipped, and a tarnished cast-iron bathtub stood atop four clawed feet in the center of the room. Aside from God's musk-scented aftershave, Mrs. God's hyacinth massage oil, and a few other toiletries, the countertops were bare. The drawers were equally unenlightening, although Ross couldn't help being impressed by the quantity of dental floss that the Heavenly Couple kept in stock.

Beginning to grow discouraged, Ross descended the misshapen wooden stairway to the ground floor, passed through the living room where he had seen the photographs, and entered God's home office. Ross was simply floored by the image before him. If God's mailbox had been stuffed to overflowing, His office seemed to have been struck by a veritable cyclone of paperwork. Prayers in all languages were tacked to the wall with multicolored pushpins, the desk was hidden under a two-foot blanket of loose papers, documents were strewn across the floor, crammed into the closets, and piled on every available surface. The drawers bulged with unanswered correspondence. A series of enormous bins lined the far wall. Ross glanced at a few of the labels: "Thighbones," "Hearts of Virgins," and "Incense" were among the most easily accessible. Ross took a peek inside one of the bins. True enough, God, the grudging sentimentalist, was saving all of the offerings that had ever been made to Him.

Ross was in despair. He had hoped for information, but there was no way he was going to be able to sift through this enormous wealth of paperwork in time to find anything of immediate use. After all, even God, who had been retired for the past few centuries, was still facing a backlog. Ross picked up one yellowing, handwritten prayer from the top of the desk, "4 October 1915-Please stop the war!" Ross grunted in exasperation; this was utterly useless. He tried once again to keep himself calm. If this were a mission, and something had gone wrong, he would think logically and systematically until the appropriate answer had reached him. One thing that Ross had learned at NASA was that a problem without a solution was an impossibility; sometimes deriving the solution took a good deal of creativity and willpower, but every question was inevitably answerable.

As Ross's mind churned, his eyes strayed about the room. It was just then that he noticed something interesting. On God's desk, beneath a stack of old mimeographs and next to an orange ceramic ashtray, was a telephone. Ross hadn't been in Heaven very long, but he knew that telephone communication was unheard of; people, once they had died, realized that almost everybody was endowed with a weak telepathy and, after a couple weeks of practice, could hone it well enough to communicate within the Heaven Metropolitan Area. Telephones were only used to send messages long distances – generally, to Earth.

Unburying God's telephone, Ross was heartened by what he saw. Rather than the usual numbered buttons, the telephone boasted only one large button – red, round, and labeled "For Emergency Use Only." Ross, of course, wasn't sure what the button would do or to whom the telephone would connect him, but, taking a deep, steady breath, he thought, Well, if ever there was an emergency…and proceeded to depress the button.

***

Robin, much as he hated PR work, hated some varieties of PR work more than others. Compared with his current project, going door-to-door to notify ranchers of NASA's intention of trespassing had been downright thrilling. After Robin had filed the demobilization orders and had finished his final report on the search and rescue mission, he had received a memo regarding his next assignment. He was to devise a presentation for area grade schools, wherein he taught them how to build model solar systems, using peas, marbles, ping-pong balls, and an orange. Robin was now sitting at his desk, reading over an illustrated pamphlet entitled "Mission: Learn!" and cursing his lackluster collegiate grade-point average.

As Robin agonizingly watched the hands of his watch move from 2:42 to 2:43, he heard his telephone ring with an odd, tinny noise that he had never heard before. I've got to have them replace this damn Stone Age phone, Robin thought, as he picked up the receiver and said, "Hello? National Aeronautics and Space Administration, Personal Relations Division. Robin Rodriguez speaking."

However, there was nobody on the other end; the ringing continued. Puzzled, Robin replaced the receiver and looked around. He couldn't place the source of the noise, though it was coming from quite nearby. Now intrigued, Robin listened closely. The ringing sounded muffled, as though it were coming from inside one of his desk drawers. He opened his top drawer and saw nothing to explain the phenomenon. He opened his bottom drawer and was about to shut it again, when something caught his eye – the bin of confiscated materials from the search crew. Two thoughts simultaneously entered his brain: firstly, he tried to remember if he had confiscated anybody's cell phone; secondly, and more pressingly, he wondered why the confiscated items had not been returned to their rightful owners after the mission had been called off.

Robin pulled out the bin – the ringing was definitely emanating from within – and dumped the contents onto his desk. There, amidst the porn and the extra shirts and the watches, was the article responsible for the sound. The crucifix that Robin had taken from one of the guys on the Las Cruces crew was glowing and emitting a shrill, intermittent ringing noise.

Robin picked up the crucifix and put it to his ear. Not knowing what to do, he allowed habit to take over. "Hello? National Aeronautics and Space Administration, Personal Relations Div...."

However, before Robin could finish his pre-scripted greeting, he found himself bodily whisked up to Heaven to meet Ross Tucker.

***

Robin, of course, did not realize from the beginning that he was in Heaven. He was simply too flummoxed to posit any hypotheses as to his whereabouts. All he knew was that he had, for some reason, materialized in a cluttered office with beige shag carpeting. In his confusion, Robin attached his attention immediately to the sole point of familiarity in the room – a middle-aged man who, although not smiling, was looking at Robin with curiously sensitive eyes. Robin had, of course, met Ross Tucker in life and, had he been thinking more calmly, surely would have recognized the man; as it was, Robin simply stared in stupid incomprehension.

"I'm sorry, but who are you?" asked Ross. He didn't know what he had been expecting, but, whatever it was, it hadn't taken the form of Robin Rodriguez in his imagination. He supposed that he was hoping the phone would have called God back to Heaven or at least put him in contact with God's son on Earth. Instead, it had caused a nervous young man with a stubbly chin and a cheap wristwatch to be belched out from the floorboards in considerable confusion.

"Hello?" Robin said to himself, ignoring Ross's question. He pinched himself, as if to ascertain that he was, in fact, standing in this strange environment. "Am I awake?" he asked Ross.

"I hope so." Ross didn't want to waste any time; however, he wanted to make sure he knew who this fellow in front of him was, before senselessly placing trust in him. "Who are you? Please answer my questions as thoroughly as possible. I am working under a considerable time constraint. I will tell you where you are and, to the best of my knowledge, why you are here, but I require your absolute cooperation."

Robin, as anybody might when thrust into a foreign situation, immediately put his trust in the man who was speaking to him in a familiar manner. Inspired by the promise that he would be told where the hell he was, Robin eagerly replied, "I'm Robin Rodriguez, and I'm the brains behind NASA's latest search and rescue operation."

Unfortunately for Robin, he had picked a bad time for a self-inflating lie. Ross heard Robin's assertion with a falling heart; however, Ross's disappointment was quickly replaced with burning anger. "You shameless twat!" Ross screamed, in utter despair. "You've even hijacked God's private phone line?"

Robin's expression of surprise immediately betrayed that he knew nothing of what Ross was talking about. "God's private phone line?" he muttered to himself.

However, Ross was so upset that he didn't immediately realize that Robin was clearly not who he claimed to be. He leapt onto Robin and began pummeling him with his fists. Though Ross was small, he had the benefit of surprise; Robin fell easily, too taken aback by the inexplicable events of the past three minutes to even consider the option of self-defense. All Robin could manage was a faint "What on earth?" before Ross's fist slammed into his jaw. Robin felt his head going light; he was vaguely aware that the man on top of him was yelling something, but couldn't focus his attention on what it might have been. Robin pulled all of his energy into willing himself into consciousness. His face hurt; that was a start. Focusing as much as possible on the sensation of pain, Robin tried to feel his back on the floor. Another punch landed forcefully on his abdomen. Robin could feel the wind rush out of him. He felt nauseated. Blinking hard, Robin tried once again to focus on his crumpled abdomen to keep from blacking out. The man brought his face close to Robin's and, suddenly, something clicked in Robin's mind.

"Holy shit!" Robin exclaimed weakly but, nonetheless, with genuine amazement. "Ross Tucker!"

Ross, having heard his name spoken, leapt to his feet. "What's it to you?"

"Ross Tucker," Robin repeated, haltingly mustering up the strength to transform his thoughts into sentences. "Ross Tucker...why did you beat me up? Ross Tucker...uh...didn't you die?"

Ross looked down the bridge of his nose at Robin and sighed. "You're not actually the brains behind the search and rescue, are you?" Robin feebly shook his head. "Well, I apologize for the thrashing I've given you, in that case, although maybe it will have the unexpected benefit of encouraging you to be more honest in the future." Ross extended a hand to Robin and helped him to his feet. Aside from a split lip and a bruised belly, Robin was fairly unharmed; Ross's sudden attack had been more violent in its speed than in its force.

"Sit down, Robin," Ross said, indicating a musty green armchair with an enormous gash on the seat. "Robin is your real name, by the way?" Robin nodded feebly. "Excellent. I would offer you some cognac, but, unfortunately, it is not mine to offer. I'm an uninvited guest in this house, but I suppose we will reach that fact in due time. Before I dispense the promised explanations, I'll need, as I said, your perfect frankness. So you're not who you claim to be. Who, then, are you? Please know, Robin, that the fate of the cosmos could depend on the quality of your honesty with me."

Robin, settling into the old armchair, instinctually wanted to spin another lie. However, Ross's barrage had given him a headache, he was disoriented and a little scared, and, moreover, he was quite certain that Ross was supposed to be dead. Maybe in such strange circumstances honesty really was the best policy. "I'm in PR with NASA. I started as an intern pretty recently."

"Mm-hmm." Ross nodded. His limber mind was already attempting to fit all the jumbled pieces together into a coherent story. "And why are you here?"

"I don't know. Where is 'here?'"

"What do you remember having happened last, immediately before you found yourself in this room?"

"I heard a ringing noise. It was coming from a cross I took from a rescue worker. I picked up the cross. Now I'm here."

A sudden spark lit Ross's eyes, although no other reaction registered on his face. He darted out of the room and immediately darted back in, carrying a framed photograph. The photograph displayed God and His son in the kitchen, dyeing Easter eggs together. "Is this the man from whom you took the cross?" Ross shoved the picture in front of Robin's face and indicated the son.

"Yeah, that's him."

"Then it's as bad as I thought…He's got a son down there." Ross seemed to suddenly disappear into his own mind. His attention strayed from Robin, dwelling instead on the scenario he was beginning to construct in his imagination.

Robin called him back to the present moment. "So you're not dead?"

"Sorry?" Ross was startled. "Oh, yes, yes, I'm dead. I have much to tell you, Robin, so I may as well get the ball rolling. As I asked you to be frank with me, I will be frank with you. I need your help back on Earth." Robin's eyes went a bit wide at the implication that, wherever he was, he was not currently on the planet he was accustomed to, but Ross continued without noticing. He spoke with a hurried efficiency that allowed for no interruption. "It is my hope that, when you have learned of the situation's magnitude, you will agree to be of use and not hold my recent fit of passion against me. You will agree that, had you been who you said you were, my attack would have been completely justified.

"This is as good a place to begin as any. Right now, you are seated in Heaven. Well, technically, you're in Greater Heaven, which is an upscale suburb, but that's irrelevant. I don't know if you are a religious person, but, if you're not, get over it. God exists, so does His wife, and so does His liquor cabinet.

"Those are the basics, Robin. Now for the meat. On Earth, I was an utter patsy. I always thought that I was towards the top of the NASA executive ladder…"

"I thought you were, too," Robin interrupted.

Ross glared at him. "No time for interruptions. If you're talking, you're not listening, and I need your full attention right now. So, the truth of the matter is this – no matter how far I pushed forward in the hierarchy, there always remained a level above me. I was always following orders sent anonymously from on high.

"Last year, I was asked to design a mission – to the American public, this was supposed to appear as just another research voyage; however, I was entrusted with what I thought was its real purpose. Those anonymous men at the top had received ambiguous evidence that God might, in fact, be more than myth. We were picking up neutrinos from an utterly inexplicable cosmic energy source – an energy source from which an unprecedented amount of capsule emission 4-beta ions were streaming as well. You learned about this in Astrophysics 101, no doubt, so I won't belabor the significance of these data; suffice it to say, I was convinced that, if we didn't have Heaven on our hands, we at least had something worth further exploration.

"As I designed the mission, I knew that NASA's secret aim was to ascertain whether or not God was, in fact, in existence – and, if so, to develop some sort of amicable contact with Him. However, as I said, I was a patsy, and, in hindsight, I can confess that I was a fool not to realize it. NASA, as I now know, has known of God's existence since 1969. The professed mission of Apollo 11 was, of course, the moon landing – a huge bone to throw the salivating media. With a poor-quality sci-fi short shot by some NYU graduates in a Hollywood backroom, NASA was able to convince the entire world that Americans were happily traipsing on the moon, when, in reality, the astronauts were on the other end of the universe, giving the boys back in Houston something to chew on. 'It's true! It's true! We've spotted Him with our high-frequency telescopes!'

"So, forty years later, when I went to design a mission that I thought would be a fact-finding voyage, I didn't realize that the Higher-Ups were about fifty steps ahead of me. Not only did they know God existed, but they had plans for what to do with Him. I inadvertently designed the mission in which NASA's most qualified hit-men hoped to bump off the Man Upstairs."

"Why?" Robin couldn't help interjecting.

Ross waved his hand in exasperation. "Why does anybody want to destroy that which is higher than them? Don't feign ignorance. It's the destructive impulse…or the creative impulse. In any event, impulses are impulses.

"So, to make a long story short, God got wind of NASA's goal and swatted down the ship. However, NASA outsmarted God. They had a contingency plan in place – a large, inefficient, utterly ridiculous contingency plan. God, you see, has a son on Earth. I didn't find this out until today, but I'm fairly sure of it now. This son is the man from whom you took the cross. In any event, son or not – and, given the family resemblance, I think it's a safe deduction to make – he clearly has some sort of special communion with God, facilitated by the cross through which you found yourself here. Somehow or other, NASA knew about this son, got him on payroll, and have lured him into a situation so dangerous that God had to go find him. That's how it's played out; now God and His wife are down on Earth, looking for this kid… and you have to find Them. They're walking right into a trap. You have to get Them to abandon Their son. Otherwise, They'll be killed, and we'll be faced with a Godless universe. Now, unless you have any questions…"

Robin, in fact, had quite a large number of questions, but all of them were tempered by the fact that he simply did not believe a word of Ross's lengthy monologue. The utter implausibility of the entire scenario, the senselessness of NASA's evil, and the fact that he was most likely just trapped in a dream all prevented Robin from having any desire to help the late Ross Tucker.

"They called off the search," Robin said. "I saw the demobilization papers myself." The thunderstruck expression on Ross's face made Robin feel as though he had just said something terribly inane.

When Ross spoke, he had to fight to maintain his composure. "We are talking about an organization that is capable of brainwashing an entire planet, and this guy worries about some signatures! Tell you what, Robin – those papers were forgeries, and you are a patsy. God! Leave it to humanity – we'll put our trust in anything except our own instincts. I was the same way. After the space shuttle crashed, I received a memo from the Higher-Ups, coming clean about the goal of the mission and asking me to help them put their wretched contingency plan into action."

"And you killed yourself."

"And I killed myself. Because I trusted that their power was superior to my own and thought there was no way around their blasphemous intentions. But maybe there was. Maybe I could have fought against them, but I simply didn't have enough faith." Ross paused. Robin felt that Ross was expecting him to say something, but he wasn't sure what, if anything, he ought to say. He still felt that he was being lied to, either by Ross or by his own senses.

"Robin," Ross continued. He pointed at the telephone. "I dialed this, not knowing what would happen. I've been given you. Like it or not, you're the answer to the problem. You have to save the Gods. It is simply your responsibility."

Robin's brain still teemed with questions, but he asked none. He wanted to get out of this strange place as quickly as possible and to begin forgetting what he had heard. Ross must have sensed Robin's uncertainty, but he also sensed the need to waste no time.

"Remember," Ross repeated. "It is your responsibility." Suddenly, he replaced the phone on its receiver and Robin was gone.

Meanwhile, on Earth, Robin materialized, dumbfounded, at his desk, as though he had never left. He was holding a cross. A sketchbook and some pornos lay in front of him. Oddly, he felt that his ribs were still hurt where Ross had been beating him. Robin rolled up his shirt to survey the damage. An enormous bruise was spread across his side. Ross had really just beaten him up. Robin had really just spent ten minutes in Heaven.

Robin's head span and he fainted.

***

Another growl, closer than before, rent the air. The Las Cruces crew was frozen, listening for any indication as to where the danger was.

Roger, his forehead creased with agonized wrinkles, whispered frantically, "Let's bolt."

Ana grabbed Roger's arm and hissed back, "It's better if we stay here, where it's open."

By this point, everybody had noticed that Chris was not among the group. Nobody could remember having seen him slink off, but he must have done so while the others were in their mass hysteria. Nobody quite knew what to make of his absence. Juliet assumed that he had just wandered off somewhere to pee, whereas Ana was terrified that he had deliberately separated from the group, trying to find his own way back to the highway. Roger desperately hoped that maybe if the cougar, or whatever it was, had snacked on Chris, then it wouldn't be hungry for the rest of the crew; he then hated himself for having hoped this and thought – without truly believing it – that, after such selfish thoughts, he should be the one eaten. Vince alone had the sensation that Chris was in some way intimately related to these terrible roars.

At that moment, another roar issued from the other edge of the clearing. Either the beast was pacing circles around the crew, or another animal had come to join the first. This uncertainty was immediately resolved when another roar answered from the initial position, soon followed by a more distant roar from a third location. The crew was surrounded.

Juliet was certain that she was going to die. It seemed that she had seen death in everything since she had left for Texas, in the sunsets, in the sunrises, in the craggy trees and ferocious brambles, in the haunting wind, and in the moments of silence. When the crew had been unable to find its way to the highway that morning, the certainty that she would not live until nighttime was cemented in her mind. If asked, she couldn't explain the origin of this assurance, but she had simply come to know it. Her fear was strong. Juliet had not had much experience with death; she only knew of it through movies. When she was growing up, her life had been sweet and easy, as far as lives go. Her mother was proud of her and achievement came effortlessly. She had been at the top of her class in high school, and all the boys nursed enormous crushes on her. She hated to think that she led her admirers on, but there could be no doubt that she did. She found empowerment in jilting the boys – not cruelly, but gently, so that their love for her never transformed into indignation. Juliet was not power-hungry, but she liked to exercise control over her own life.

Death was, to her, simply an enormous buzzkill that could be skirted around by living with unapologetic flirtation in her eyes, by holding opinions and speaking them loudly, and by refusing to relinquish her claim on her own existence. Death was weakness and failure, but Juliet had never quite seen it as inevitable until this moment. Now, however, Juliet felt that she had been an idiot her entire life. Even if her instincts were wrong, she thought, and she survived the day, and even the day after, she might kick on for another few decades or so, but, at the end of it all, she would still be faced with the same awful, unavoidable sensation that she was currently feeling – the sensation that death lay in wait somewhere close by and that, no matter how strong her will to live, it would pounce of its own accord.

Chris, a short string of brambles clutching on to his pants leg, suddenly burst into the clearing. "Guys!" he shouted. "We're safe for now, but we have to go."

Nobody could comprehend him at first, but, sure enough, the menacing roars had ceased. Chris was not waiting for the rest of the crew; he was already clawing his way into the thick foliage at the opposite end of the clearing. Vince was troubled – he was convinced that Chris knew far more than he was saying, and yet Chris's fear was so genuine that he appeared just as helpless as the other members of the crew.

Roger followed Chris, and Juliet hurried close behind Roger. Ana and Vince looked at each other. Vince had never seen Ana's face so pale before. She always used to be the first to initiate any group movements, but since morning her reaction time had been slowing. Now she seemed utterly uncertain as to what to do – half her crew had already followed Chris, and the power of authority she had fought so hard to maintain had dissipated at the first sign of danger. For the first time since Vince had known her, Ana looked weak.

"Go on with them," she said softly to Vince. "I'll stay here with Takeshi."

Though the rest of the crew had been jolted out of their panic when they had heard the roars, Takeshi had merely grown quiet; his hysteria had cooled into a motionless trance. He was now lying on the forest floor, eyes frozen open in terrified fixity, and, aside from the soft gusts of breath that occasionally escaped his mouth, seeming in every way as though he had died. Vince lightly prodded Takeshi's abdomen; no change registered on Takeshi's face. Though Takeshi's body was still alive, his spirit had clearly fled to a safer haven.

"Ana," Vince said. "What I'm going to say is going to be hard for you, but I need you to take me seriously. We have to leave him, and stick with the crew."

Ana had seen this coming and was prepared to respond immediately. "Absolutely not. You may follow the others, but I can't abandon a member of my crew."

"I know, but Ana...," Vince was uncertain how to proceed, largely because he was, for the first time, profoundly morally uncertain. In the past, whenever he had been in a morally ambiguous situation, he had been able to ask God for advice. Now, however, God was absent and the future was unclear. After all, God could have told Vince whether or not Takeshi was going to snap out of his coma. Vince was now reduced to working from his instincts – and he thought that, given Takeshi's regression from hysterical seizure to deathlike trance, the odds of Takeshi reviving were not high enough to justify self-sacrifice.

"Vince," Ana said. "Go catch up with the rest of the crew. There is no reason for us both to stay. It is my responsibility, not yours. It sounds incredibly stupid to me – though maybe it won't to you – but, ever since I got up this morning, I've had the terrible feeling that I won't live until tomorrow." Ana tried to disguise the fact that her jaw was trembling by speaking through her teeth, but it was evident nonetheless. "If I am going to die, I would prefer my death to be...," Ana searched for the right word to finish her sentence. Her first instinct was "respectable," but she felt that to be too condescending. "Noble" was too antiquated. With a shudder, Ana felt that she didn't want to die. She had known it all along, certainly, but had been able to distract herself by visualizing her own death. Of course, when you watch yourself die in your imagination, you do so from a safe, third-party perspective. Nobody ever imagines death from the point of view of the one dying, because nobody can. Now that it fell to Ana to describe the image that she held of her own demise, she realized that she couldn't find any words to describe how the moment might appear from her own perspective. The awful sensation of having left her sentence incomplete terrified her.

Vince sensed her uncertainty and espied an opportunity to sway Ana's typically unwavering opinion. "Ana." He gently led her towards the edge of the clearing by her shoulders. "You know I trust impressions, and so if you feel that you will die today, I won't argue with you – but maybe you're meant to do so in another situation. I don't think there's anything we can do for Takeshi." Vince glanced at Takeshi once more. The man's mouth, which had always remained so firmly clamped when he had been conscious, was hanging open in a stupid gape. A small puddle of drool was slowly spreading over his chin. "Look at him, Ana. Staying is senseless."

Ana could not think clearly, and her speech came out in jumbled fragments. "But if it were you…all alone, to wake up…with nobody… and…if you were scared…I just…it can't be right, Vince." Having settled on a comfortable anchor, Ana repeated, "It just can't be right."

"Ana, I can't talk you out of it, if you're determined to stay. But if you wait here, you're going to wish you had somebody to talk to. So if you stay with Takeshi, I'll stay with Takeshi, too."

"Can we just wait for one more hour to see if he wakes up? If he's still unconscious, then will you go find the rest of the group?"

"If we wait another hour, Ana, the rest of the group will be so far ahead of me that I will not be able to find them. Decide for both of us, then."

Ana felt trapped. She could not abandon Takeshi, and yet she could not drag Vince into what was essentially a suicide mission. At the same time, Ana could simply not shake her urge towards self-preservation. "If we go, though," she said, looking at Takeshi, "we can't just leave him to wake up. Do you think we should…?"

"What?" Vince felt the urgency of time; the rest of the crew was already far ahead of them by now. However, he couldn't display his anxiety. He needed to collect all of his calm in order to soothe Ana out of her stubbornness.

"Would it be right to…?" Ana could not believe she was about to voice such a thought. Rather than speak, then, she knelt next to Takeshi's body and put her hands lightly around his neck. Shuddering, she looked up at Vince to make sure he understood her meaning.

Vince was horrified – and yet he couldn't fault Ana for such a suggestion. Maybe it was the best thing, after all? If Takeshi did wake up, the terror he would feel at finding himself alone in the woods with hungry animals prowling about would be far worse than being strangled quietly in his insensibility. What would God do? However, for the first time, a voice from deep in Vince's subconscious answered the question, "What the hell does it matter, Vince? God isn't here, and you are. If God cared about a single thing you did, He'd make the answer clear to you. Seems the ball is in your court, bub." Vince went white at the sound of this voice somewhere in his soul; nonetheless, he could not argue with it. Ana was still looking at him expectantly, though she had come away from Takeshi's body. Vince felt the necessity to speak and he could feel that blood was rushing to his face and the tips of his ears.

"Ana," he said, "I think we shouldn't. It's not our decision." Vince tried not to belie his uncertainty. Although he remembered having heard somewhere about "sins of omission," it was far easier for him to resolve to inaction than to action. To kill seemed like a debasement; to let die seemed somehow different.

Ana scowled. She hated herself for having even thought to make the suggestion. Vince was right, of course. She thought sadly about her collapsed authority. Over the course of a single morning, she had lost control of the crew, but, worse, she had lost her own ability to make a decision with conviction. She felt that she was going to die in utter disgrace, and wanted nothing more than to be fifty miles away from herself. What's the point in having self-control, if it only deserts you under pressure? she inwardly berated herself. Anybody can be bossy when the stakes are low, but it takes a true leader to respond with bravery when half her crew is dead and the rest are lost in the jungle. Ana knew that, if she wanted to maintain the discipline she had fought for her entire life, she would need to make a firm decision, one way or the other.

Ana didn't know what she was going to say until the words were out of her mouth. "Okay, Vince. We need to go after the rest of the crew. Follow me." Hearing her own decision as though it had issued from someone else, Ana realized that they would need to move swiftly. She turned to the edge of the clearing and quickly started clambering into the forest.

Before following Ana, Vince knelt over Takeshi's body, made the sign of the cross, and issued a brief prayer to God that Takeshi's passing would be swift. God didn't respond, but Vince was no longer surprised. In fact, a sudden bolt of fury prodded Vince's heart. He could not deny it to himself – he was growing angry with God.

Trying as much as possible to deny his frustration, Vince pulled Takeshi's eyelids shut, stood up, and followed Ana out of the clearing.

***

There was something scary in the cellar.

Amanda flipped a pancake over on the griddle and tried as hard as she could to recall what had happened to fill her with such fear. She remembered having come out of the cellar in a panic. She had gone outside. Someone had been whittling; he had looked at Amanda as though she were someone he knew. He had asked what was wrong. Then, another big gap was rent into Amanda's memory.

By this point, a modest stack of pancakes was piled up on a plate next to Amanda. When she had come back into the kitchen, she had seen a job half-completed. Since she felt safe in the kitchen, she had decided to continue the breakfast that she had, she assumed, stopped in the midst of preparing. As she continued spooning batter onto the griddle and watching it bubble, she felt disoriented. She knew that these were actions she performed frequently, and her muscles carried her through with no problem; however, she wasn't sure why she was doing what she was doing. Primarily, she wondered for whom she was cooking. That man out back? she wondered. She knew that she ought to know, but, try as she might, she simply couldn't remember who he was.

Therefore, as Amanda finished making the pancakes with the aid of her muscular autopilot, she tried to deduce as much as she could about her present situation. First thing, she thought, I know I ain't wanting to head down the cellar. Second, I've got some nice clothes on me today, so it must be some important day. Third, it's cold outside, so it ain't summertime. Fourth, there's a man out there what seems to live here. Fifth, I'm pretty familiar with this kitchen, so I guess I live here, too. Sixth, this seems here to be a ring on my finger. So, put four, five, and six together, and I guess that man's my husband. Amanda was pleased that she had been able to draw a conclusion – and just in time, too, since she was already flipping the last pancake onto the serving plate.

"Sweet!" she called out to the backyard. "I put breakfast on the table! Leave off your whittling for just a minute, then."

Arlo came inside, wiping some stray curls of wood from his jeans onto the fading linoleum floor. Amanda's momentary pleasure at having guessed his relationship to her disappeared. Now, she was simply faced with the sickening realization that the man she had presumably chosen to spend the rest of her life with appeared as a stranger to her; she couldn't even call his name to mind. Though she tried to mask her uncertainty with a smile, it was obvious that looking at her made the man sad; this further fuelled Amanda's own sadness.

In truth, Arlo was actually more nervous than sad. He had been outside working on Pimp Daddy's legs earlier when Amanda had come out to him in incoherent terror. She had been shuddering and nearly crying, but she wouldn't let him come to comfort her; it had been clear that she didn't recognize him. All Arlo had been able to do was to tell her that there was nothing to be scared of, and to try distracting her with pleasant chatter. After almost three hours, he had been able to lead her back to the kitchen, in the hopes that the resumption of her interrupted routine would soothe her into forgetfulness, although it had already been well past noon. Now, as he sat down at the kitchen table and grabbed a couple of pancakes from the stack, he was wondering what Pimp Daddy had said to Amanda and how it would affect her. Even though she seemed to have pulled herself together, Arlo knew that stray memories had a way of seizing Amanda's mind at unexpected moments. If she chanced to remember Pimp Daddy, she would undoubtedly launch once again into terror.

"These are great, honey," Arlo said, through a mouthful of pancakes. "You know how your Arlo loves your cooking." He had taken to referring to himself in the third person lately, in order to subtly send a reminder of his name to Amanda without shaming her. "I'm the luckiest husband on God's green earth." He was pretty sure that she recognized him as her husband, but he was better safe than sorry.

"Want some preserves?" Amanda moved to the cupboard.

"No, ma'am," Arlo hastened to say. "I don't need a thing. These are fine just as is. What I want is for you to come eat with me, little lady, and get off them feet of yours."

Amanda smiled sweetly. "Alrighty, Arlo." She sat in the chair across from Arlo and helped herself to a small pancake. She wasn't very hungry, but she wanted to obey her husband. "You seem to be right busy out there," she said. "What're you carving?"

"Just something."

Amanda hesitated. She wasn't sure whether or not she was supposed to know already, but she eventually couldn't help asking, "What kinda something?"

"Just something for a friend."

A friend. The thought raced through Amanda's mind. She had heard that before recently, but from whom? "Hey, Shitcicle! Where's your damn sense of humor? I'm just having a little fun with you; you're my friend, you know." Somebody had said that to her. Who could have used such crass language? Had it really been her friend? Amanda had the strong sensation that it had been said to her mockingly, by somebody with whom she did not want to be friends. Had she been in the cellar when she heard this?

The minute Amanda's whirling mind lit upon the cellar, she felt a sudden jolt of fear. Something awful was lurking down there. She had to know what. "Dear," she began, already angry with herself – she had just heard her husband's name, and yet she had already forgotten it. "Dear, what'd we be keeping down in the cellar?"

Arlo could see Amanda's eyes squint, as though in an effort to help her remember. He wished he could say to her, "Don't remember, angel, for your own good." However, he knew that such a response would scare her more than even the truth, the imagination, when left to itself, can always come up with something more troubling than reality. Instead, he dished out a plausible lie. "You don't want to go down to the cellar, baby; there's rats what live down there." He hated lying to his wife, even when he felt that it was justified.

Thankfully for Arlo, he didn't have to keep up his lie for very long; his conversation with his wife was interrupted by a knock at the front door. Is this the patsy I'm expecting? Arlo thought as he rose from the table and opened the door. For her part, Amanda welcomed the opportunity to slip her pancake, untasted, back into the stack.

At the door, Arlo discovered a clean-shaven twenty-something man with dark hair and tan skin. Constellations of sweat stood out on the man's brow and he appeared profoundly uncomfortable in his rumpled suit. The man awkwardly stuck out a meaty hand, which Arlo grasped and shook. "My name is Robin Rodriguez," the man said, "and I'm from the NASA Personal Relations Division."

In spite of his nervousness, Robin was thankful that the husband, rather than the wife, had come to the door. He remained acutely aware of the gross deception he had visited on Amanda three days ago by claiming to be her son. He wasn't sure that he would be able to look her in the eyes again, although he hadn't, of course, ever planned on returning to her house.

Robin's decision to come back to the Saunders' had come very quickly after he had passed through his brief fainting spell. He was still uncertain as to how much of Ross's story to accept, but one thing had been absolutely clear – the demobilization papers filed for the Las Cruces crew were indeed forgeries; upon closer inspection, the signature of "Ana Jenkins" authorizing the demobilization of her crew was clearly a photocopy – and a poor one at that. Further spurred by the obvious evidence that the confiscated materials had not yet been returned, Robin had been fully convinced that, God or no God, NASA was lying to him.

The Las Cruces firefighters were still out somewhere in the jungles of Texas and somebody didn't want him to know that. In the absence of any other ideas, Robin decided to put "Mission: Learn!" on hold and return to the homes of the ranchers he had talked to near the Las Cruces crew's search path, in order to find out whether or not anybody had seen any trace of the crew.

Now, Robin was faced with a bent old man with so many wrinkles in his face that it looked like a fingerprint. A couple tufts of dusty hair crept around the circumference of the man's otherwise bald head. A pair of faded overalls hung off the man's body; perhaps they had once fit, but the man had grown so thin that they were now ridiculously oversized. The house, as it had on his previous visit, reeked of mothballs and mold, and the oily smell of something recently fried hit Robin's nostrils as well. Consciously assuming an expression of dignity and self-importance, Robin proceeded, "Sorry to bother you this afternoon, sir, but I'm from NASA. We are currently undertaking a vital search and rescue operation for a mission that was recently tragically lost in this area. As you may or may not have been notified, your property happens to fall within…"

Robin continued to speak so quickly that spit was collecting in the corners of his lips; periodically, he would wipe his mouth with the back of his sleeve, as a child might. He kept shifting his weight from foot to foot, but kept his gaze locked onto Arlo. Arlo, however, was no longer listening. Looking at the nervousness in Robin's eyes, the forced formality of his speech, and the discomfort with which his young body fidgeted within his suit, one thing was clear to Arlo – Robin Rodriguez was a patsy and, what's more, an easily deflected patsy.

"… So, have you seen any unknown men or women around your property in the past day?" Robin concluded.

Arlo looked at Robin with regret. He looked like a nice kid, and Arlo wished that he could help. However, he valued his own life, waning though it might be, too much to tell Robin about the head in the basement. "I'm sorry, sir," he said, "but I'm afraid I just can't help you."

"Sir, please think very hard about absolutely anything you might have seen – footprints, for example, or even a stray granola bar wrapper or a scrap of fabric."

"I'm sorry," Arlo repeated. "There just ain't nothing I can tell you."

Just then, Amanda wandered out from the kitchen. Robin was completely taken aback. Though the woman before him was clearly the same one he had spoken with three days ago, a marked change had come over her. Her white hair, which had previously been unsullied, now contained a few streaks of blonde. Her wrinkled skin seemed to be pulled slightly more taut over her body, which itself seemed to have grown a bit more muscular. The gauzy cataracts over her eyes were now slightly less opaque, and, most noticeably of all, the beginnings of a healthy pink blush seemed to be lurking just beneath the surface of her previously pale face. It was almost as though she had grown five or ten years younger during the past three days.

"Can we help you, young man?" she asked, almost with a twinkle in her droopy eyes. Robin was once again stunned. Though Amanda had undergone an inexplicable physical change for the better, the one quality Robin had previously remarked as standing out about her – her clear, mellifluous, and almost girlish voice – had deteriorated. Her voice was now by no means repellant, but it sounded as though she had suddenly taken upon herself a ten-year smoking habit. Her voice was lower and raspier, which startled Arlo as much as it startled Robin.

"Please keep your eyes open for unknown men and women," Robin said, now wanting to get out of the house as quickly as possible. Something about Amanda troubled him, and he had no desire to wait around until she recognized him as the man who had lied to her.

"Only unknown man around here," Amanda said with a smile that could almost be described as coy, "is you, stranger."

Arlo looked at his wife in astonishment. There was no doubt in his mind that, indeed, Pimp Daddy's prophesy had come to pass. Arlo had rebuffed the patsy, and his wife was now ten years younger. What's more, she spoke with more confidence than she ever had before. Although her voice had taken a turn for the worse, she gave no indication that she was struggling with her usual confusion. She seemed certain of who she was, where she was, and with whom she was speaking.

"As I said, sir," Arlo said, "we ain't able to help you here."

"I understand. Thank you for your time," Robin said. He started to shut the door, but was arrested by Amanda's voice.

"By the way, stranger," she said. "I remember you well. You came 'round here just the other day, spinning your yarns of deceit. Now don't hold it against me if I say that maybe it'd be best for you to stay out of the homes of honest folk. Life's too short to live in lies."

At that, Robin shut the door behind himself and shivered in the crisp afternoon air. However, he had no time to process what had just occurred – he had a crew to find, and sunset was growing closer with every passing minute.

***

It wasn't until evening that the bus containing God and Mrs. God finally clattered to a stop in front of the Longview Greyhound depot. The area around the bus station reminded the Gods emphatically of the Central Heaven Terminal. Sleeping bodies were draped across the hard wooden benches in front of the depot, mounds of mashed cigarettes clogged the cracks in the sidewalk, and fungus festered in the tepid puddles at the bottoms of potholes. Grey dusk already lurked in the sky, but most of the streetlights were either shattered or burnt out. People drifted along the sidewalks, silhouetted like ghosts against the fluorescent glow of shop windows. As the Gods climbed out of the bus, God turned to His wife and remarked, "Stick close, honey bear. There's no telling what insanity lurks in the hearts of these Earth-born lunatics."

Now that They were in Longview, however, the Gods had no plan as to how to proceed. "If only We hadeth some kind of sign where to goeth from here," Mrs. God observed. She held Her husband's arm tightly as She looked around at the other people on the street with anxiety.

"Hallelujah!" God exclaimed, pointing across the street. "We've hit the jackpot, baby. Lady Luck must be winking at Me tonight!"

God was pointing at a tiny, ancient building with sagging eaves and dusty windows. A cardboard sign reading "All Welcome" hung on the heavy wooden door. In general, the building was far from noteworthy, but what had drawn God's attention was a discolored marquee overhanging the door, upon which "F iends of od" was spelled out in plastic letters. A "G" was hanging on just below the "od."

"Glory be to Us!" Mrs. God exclaimed. "Friends on Earth, and right near the bus station. Convenience hath been Ours!"

The Heavenly Couple crossed the street and went into the mission, causing a rusty bell attached to the door to emit a tinny clang upon Their entrance. The main room of the mission was empty, aside from a row of plastic chairs around the perimeter and a splintered wooden desk at the end of the room. The odor of cigar smoke hung thick in the air. God inhaled deeply and commented, "Cheap stuff," to His wife.

Two disheveled men in rags were sitting in the chairs and playing cards; neither man seemed to be enjoying the game and each eyed his opponent suspiciously and even murderously. A third man, dressed in an immaculate white shirt, was sitting behind the desk and busily sticking stamps and address labels onto a stack of glossy brochures. As God neared the desk, He caught a glimpse of the title on one of the pamphlets: "Ten Tips for Bringing God Into Your World."

Before God or Mrs. God could speak, the man at the desk raised his eyes with an earnest smile. "Hi there, folks," he said. "Jimmy Hawdon's the name here, and I'm pleased to have you." He stuck out his hand, which God and Mrs. God shook in turn. Since leaving Robin's apartment that morning after what he felt had been an enormously successful house call, Jimmy had gone directly to work, where he had remained until now. He tended to work long hours, especially in the winter months. Though he had joked about not being able to work after nightfall, he liked the idea that his mission was a bastion of warmth and light in the midst of the dark, chilly season. "You seeking salvation this blessed evening?" he asked.

"Salvation, sure," God said, "but not for Myself. I've got a little buddy running around out there in the woods, and I've got the sick sensation he's about to get into some serious scrapes. I'll let you in on a secret, ace, if you promise not to go stool pigeon on Me. I hate using My name in vain, but you claim to be a friend of Mine, and I don't stand on ceremony. So, you got some time to help out God? I'll make it worth your while," He said, about to reach for his baggie of hashish; Mrs. God stopped Her husband just in time with a severe glance.

For his part, Jimmy was so flabbergasted by the audacity of the Gods that he allowed an uncharacteristically untactful answer to slip through his lips, "Blaspheme!" He felt immediately embarrassed, knowing that the kooks standing in front of him probably meant no harm; they were undoubtedly crazy and not intentionally hoping to offend.

Mrs. God arched one eyebrow and leaned over the desk to Jimmy; She was quite conscious of Her seductive beauty and hoped that it worked as well on Earth as it did in Heaven. "Looketh here, mortal man. Our friend has falleneth into a bad spot, and We'd beith just ever so grateful if you helpedeth Us out."

"Ma'am!" Jimmy exclaimed. The two men playing cards looked up to see what had gotten him so riled up, but, finding the scene uninteresting, returned to their joyless game. "If you please, lady, I am your friend and will help you find the path, even in this rocky world of ours, but if you are in any way attempting to mock the Divine...."

"Listen, bub, I'm not mocking a thing – not even that square haircut of yours," God said, now with a bit of irritation. "You say you're a friend of God's. So, are you a friend of God's, or is that just lip service? We've got a fellow to save and if you're not going to help Us, just say so."

"Hey, now," Jimmy said, self-consciously running his hand over his new crew cut and forcing out a smile. Perhaps he could use this occasion as a teaching opportunity. "I'm in the business of helping out; that's my line of work precisely, so I'm happy to do it. Overjoyed, no less. But if I'm going to do what I can to help you, I think it's reasonable to ask you to play by my rules a little. That means no spitting, no swearing, no fighting, and a good, reverent attitude towards God."

One of the card players laughed at something the other had said under his breath.

"All right, partner," God began again. "You're treading on thin ice here."

Mrs. God could see that Her husband was about to berate Jimmy, and so She interrupted immediately in what She felt was a reasonable tone. "Thou beith a believer in God," She said soothingly to Jimmy. "So why doth it be so mysterious to you that He should appeareth if He so desireth to appeareth?"

"Oh, ma'am, God is revealed to us every day through His works, and I have no doubt that He is as real as you or me."

"So isn'teth it reasonable that My husband should be God?" She asked.

"No," Jimmy said, his patience nearing its end, "it isn't at all reasonable. I'm afraid you're misunderstanding something. God does not walk about in fedoras and poorly knotted ties. He transcends humanity. This is a hard concept to grasp, unless you're actually willing to grasp it." Jimmy opened one of the drawers in the desk and pulled out a leather-bound Bible like the one he had given to Robin. He hated to part with it to these lunatics, because he feared that they were too far gone to understand its significance; nonetheless, he felt that he would be remiss in failing altogether to counsel them. "Please," he continued, "read this book before you slide further down the slimy chute to eternal fire. I want to rejoice with you in Heaven when the day comes, and I want to be your friend on Earth, too. So, please, promise me you'll give it a good, thorough read. If you have any questions, we can talk them through."

"I read it already," God said. "Mostly good." He tugged on His wife's arm and hissed, "Let's blow this Good Humor stand, Babs; this kid's crazier than a California kookaburra."

"Mostly good?" Mrs. God said. "They lefteth Me out of the book entirely! Plus, they gotteth My dialect all wrong. They couldn't even 'eth' properly if I knockedeth out their front teeth and they lispethed for the rest of their lives."

"Don't mind the dame," God said to Jimmy as He led His irate wife towards the exit. "She's just sore that you didn't start giving your broads down here any shout-outs until the seventies. And I'm sorry if I got hot under the collar; it hasn't been an easy retirement." With that, the Gods went out of the mission, leaving Jimmy in a state of confusion. Jimmy felt that he ought to be offended, but the entire situation was simply too ludicrous. "Maybe I'll just close shop for the night," he thought, seeing that the two drifters had finished their card game and were preparing to leave as well. "It's a tough job, talking sense to these crackerjacks."

As the two card players left the mission, one muttered to the other, "The eagle has landed."

The second card player smiled subtly and replied, "With a vengeance."

Had Jimmy not been busy with his pamphlets that day, he might have noticed that the two men playing cards were the same two men that had come in the previous day in different outfits. Had he watched the men very carefully, he might have noticed that they seemed particularly alert, as though they were waiting for something very specific to happen. Had he spoken with them, he might have noticed the extremely tiny microphones that had been carefully and almost inconspicuously stitched into their tattered T-shirts. Of course, Jimmy had noticed none of these things and so he thought nothing of it when the two men packed up their cards and followed the Gods out into the street.

In turn, the Gods took no notice of the two men trailing Them at a distance of several blocks; nor could They have possibly been aware of the satellite that glided with sinister silence across the starry night sky and that was, at that moment, refining its focus on Them and beaming Their images and coordinates to the people at NASA headquarters.

The Storm

"I knock ten years off your withered wife, and you bring me these truncheons?" Pimp Daddy was dissatisfied with his legs. Arlo had carefully fitted them into the hole at the base of Pimp Daddy's neck and now they stuck out ridiculously. Pimp Daddy had been expecting fully functional prosthetic legs, complete with knee and ankle joints; instead, he was now simply a severed head with two chunks of crudely hewn cedar jutting out from beneath his chin. "Even you're not too stupid to realize that you're going to get zapped for this idiocy."

"Oh, no, Mr. Pimp Daddy, sir," Arlo stammered. He was tired and frightened. After seeing Robin off, he had continued working all day on the legs. He knew that his handiwork was bad, but he had done as well as he could. Amanda had already gone to bed by the time he had gathered up the courage to head downstairs and display his efforts for Pimp Daddy. "Please don't zap me, sir."

"Well, because you asked so nicely," Pimp Daddy began, "I'll only give you a little zap." With no greater ceremony, the head closed its eyelids over its hollow eye sockets and creased its forehead in concentration. Arlo felt as though his spine had suddenly snapped in two. He screamed in pain as electrical currents pulsed up from his tailbone and down from the base of his skull, meeting in an agonizing explosion in his lower back. His eyes crossed and his vision grew bleary. He felt his brain growing too big for his skull and momentarily felt as though his head might burst, sending a shower of cranial shards across the room like shrapnel. However, no explosion occurred and the pain melted away in a moment. Wheezing for breath, Arlo slumped down heavily onto the cold concrete floor.

"Next time I won't be so merciful, you uni-testicled dollop of dung," Pimp Daddy said. "Now what the hell do you imagine Pimp Granddaddy's going to think of me when he sees me wearing these ridiculous clubfeet?"

"I don't know, sir," Arlo managed to choke out between labored breaths.

"And how am I going to kick God in the cojones without any knees, you Nancy-pants nitwit? Are you trying to sabotage my Holy War?"

"No, sir."

"Well, then fix these things by tomorrow night." All of a sudden, Pimp Daddy's eye sockets opened wider than usual, and his slimy lips pursed into an excited O. Arlo was nervous; he hadn't yet seen the head quite so agitated.

"Prophecies, you barking bitch!" the head exclaimed. "Quick – make sure you get this shit! Today's are pure gold."

Arlo heaved himself to his feet and, feeling as though he had aged fifty years in the last three days, began massaging the repulsive head. It seemed as though the layer of slime had grown even thicker since yesterday. Arlo had to concentrate on not retching.

"Ahhh," moaned the head. "Those arthritic fingers can't build legs, but they can sure rub an old pimp like me the right way." He then allowed a blissful smile to creep across his lips. "Don't let that compliment go to your head, though, you distended dingbat."

"No, sir," Arlo whispered, afraid that if he allowed more volume to come out of his mouth, the afternoon's pancakes would come out alongside it. As he kneaded the elastic skin of Pimp Daddy's scalp, a sudden revolting image came to his mind; try as he could, he could not clear his head of the thought. Arlo, worn out by Pimp Daddy's demands, and still smarting from his recent zapping, saw himself exerting every last reserve of strength to put pressure on the head until it cracked open like an egg.

Pimp Daddy sighed contentedly once again, unaware of the murderous thoughts running through Arlo's head.

"He's at peace," Arlo thought. "I could pop him like a pimple before he realizes what's going on." Without making the conscious decision to do so, Arlo pressed harder on Pimp Daddy. Far from appearing to be in pain, however, the head let loose with a long, relaxed groan. This groan galled Arlo further and led him to squeeze the head even harder than he had thought possible. However, Pimp Daddy proved incredibly malleable; Arlo's violent efforts were for naught.

"Grandpa's been hitting the weight room!" Pimp Daddy exclaimed with satisfaction. "That's the way a massage is given, you fetid glob of sputum! I've got half a mind to zap you for holding out on me yesterday!"

Arlo couldn't avoid releasing an aggravated sigh as he eased off the pressure on the head. Pimp Daddy heard the sigh, guessed its intention, and chuckled.

"Oho, a little Judas Iscariot, eh?" Pimp Daddy laughed. "Thought you'd try and rid your cellar of pimps, you putrid protozoan? Well, sadly for you, only a pimp can kill a pimp, and you, gramps, are long past your pimping prime. However, I'll show you some mercy for your yellow-bellied treason and not zap you, but only because your assassination attempt proved to be the best goddamn massage I've had in decades.

"Anyway, three's a good number for prophesying, so I'm going to let loose with another triad of titillating testimonies that'll knock your rotten socks off. Firstly, I like the way your wench of a wife is filling out, so let's say I give her another twenty years of youth tomorrow; that, of course, is contingent on a better pair of legs and maybe some eyes, too. I don't expect brilliance out of you, because I myself am not a chowder-brained nincompoop, but I can't be dishing out miracles for free, now can I?"

As Arlo dejectedly continued to massage the cold meat of the severed head before him, he couldn't help agreeing in some regard – Amanda was beginning to look much better, and Arlo, in spite of the cost, was eager to see this trend continue.

"Secondly," moaned Pimp Daddy, as Arlo's hands worked over his flabby cheeks, "I'm counting on a big storm tonight. Keep your umbrella on hand, because, let me tell you, the world hasn't seen a downpour this fucking sweet since God fucked the world over in Bible times. Thirdly, speaking of God, our badass brawl is about to go down. My daddy should be rolling in here in two more days, which is convenient for me, because that's right about the time that Baby Pimp is due."

"Baby Pimp?" Arlo, struck by anxiety, stopped massaging the head. Between Pimp Daddy, Pimp Granddaddy, and Baby Pimp, he had no desire to see what was slated to occur at his house in two days. He wished for perhaps the thousandth time that he had never found this disgusting head.

"They don't teach you much in school these days, do they, you syphilitic cyst? If I'm Pimp Daddy, the logical conclusion is that I'm somebody's daddy. Can't have daddies without sons, now can we, Mr. Droopypants?" Pimp Daddy's lips suddenly twisted up into a tight, sarcastic grin. "So, verily, I say unto thee – prepare thyself for a bundle of goddamn joy."

***

Roger looked at Juliet across the campfire. The ripples of heat rising from the flames distorted her face eerily. Though the night had been clear, a cloud cover was beginning to creep in from the west. The rest of the crew had all gone back to their tents. Chris had made the proposal that they continue traveling through the night, but without any flashlights or headlamps it seemed that rest was going to be ultimately more beneficial than whatever small amount of ground they might have covered before sunrise. The crew had happened upon a promising clearing just as the sun was setting – they had stumbled upon an expansive field littered in snow-white wildflowers, painted rose and amber by reflected light from the sunset. Though everybody had silently wondered why such healthy flowers were sprouting in the middle of February, nobody saw any reason to say anything; the flowers were soft, and the crew had set up camp.

Juliet had volunteered to be the first watch. After the previous night's massacre, it seemed like a good idea to have somebody sit up to sound the alert in the event of imminent danger. Roger was sitting out the first half of her watch with her; now that Takeshi was gone, Roger had no tentmate, and he wasn't eager to surrender himself to the loneliness of the night. He picked a wildflower from near where he was sitting and gently tossed it into the fire. It burned with an almost noxiously sweet odor. He wanted to say something to Juliet, who was staring fixedly into the campfire, but he didn't want to interrupt the peaceful moment.

For her part, Juliet was trying to imagine herself anywhere but where she actually was. The feeling of doom that had been pressing on her ever since she had stepped out of the van in Texas was now so heavy that she had difficulty breathing. In the white-hot cone of luminescence that danced at the center of the fire before her, Juliet saw images. She saw her mother – a redheaded divorcee with an angelic singing voice and a hard-learned aphorism for every occasion. She saw her first nature hike in the White Mountains, with cool pines arching overhead in almost maternal protection and speckled hares bounding joyously through spring foliage. She saw her first lover – a summer fling on Martha's Vineyard with whom she had gone skinny dipping in the placid, silvery waters of the moonlit Cape. She saw her first wildfire – a sooty, breathtaking adventure that elicited all the heat, sweat, and adrenaline of her boundless youth.

She saw Takeshi's convulsing body, cut through with thorns and left to die.

Juliet grimaced and wished she could claw the image out of her brain. She closed her eyes and tried to conjure up another pleasant memory from her past.

"It's too bad about Takeshi," Roger said, just to say something, and little knowing that he was saying precisely the wrong thing.

Juliet's eyes flew open. She looked angrily at Roger, feeling the heat of the campfire on her face. "Don't."

"Sorry," Roger said. He pitched another flower into the blaze, watching it wither and dissolve into white ash. For a moment, the two sat in silence, the fire crackling between them with the aroma of scorched sap. "When I get back to Kansas, I'm not going to be sober another day of my life," Roger went on. "I'm going to sit on the porch with a cold bottle of beer. Forever. I'm going to sit out in the sun, sweating, and drinking, and watching kids ride by on their bikes. And then when it's winter, I'll switch to bourbon, but I don't think I'll go inside. Even if it's like ten feet of snow. I'll just put on a coat. But I won't go inside. At least, I probably won't...," Roger trailed off, conscious of having said something silly. Nonetheless, it felt good for him to hear his own voice – it allowed him to be certain that he was still alive.

"What will you do when you get home?" he asked Juliet. She continued staring into the fire, as though she hadn't heard him. Her silence continued for nearly three minutes, and Roger had given up on expecting an answer by the time she finally replied.

"I feel filthy," Juliet said, holding out her hand towards the fire. Dirt was caked across her knuckles and under her fingernails. Long scrapes from the brambles ran across her wrist. Her palm was callused from the weight training she had been doing at the bunkhouse back in New Mexico.

"First thing I will do," Juliet continued, "is take a long, hot shower. Then, when I'm sure that I have every last particle of dirt scrubbed off my body, I'm going to draw a bath and fill it with every sort of bubble-bath I can get my hands on. I want to smell like a fruit basket. I'll dry off with a white, fluffy towel, and my bathroom will be cozy and warm, because of the steam from the bath. I'll brush my teeth, and then I'll probably brush them again. I'll floss. I'll brush my hair. If I have knots, I won't yank them – I'll work them out gently. I'll put on perfume. Actually, I'll spritz on perfume. And then I'll get dressed. I'll wear a red dress and big hoop earrings. I won't wear heels, though. I'll wear slippers, or anything soft. And I'll blow a kiss to myself in the mirror and be happy to see myself looking so good. Actually, looking so knockout. I'll look utterly knockout. And after that, who knows? But that's where I'll start."

Although Juliet had clearly given thought to her fantasy, she spoke in a monotone, as though she were simply reciting a list that she had memorized. Her eyes never left the flickering point of white heat at the center of the fire. Roger had never seen her quite so listless. Looking at Juliet, he saw his own fear and dejection; he needed to fight against it.

"If nothing else, this will make a story to tell," Roger said. "I mean, you can't make this shit up."

Juliet looked up at Roger with tired eyes. "I'd like to do the rest of my watch alone, please." She was conscious that she was speaking rudely, but she couldn't bring herself to care. If she was going to survive, she needed to distance herself from her situation as much as possible; Roger was a blatant reminder of where she was and how little hope she could reasonably exercise.

"Okay." Roger stood up, hoping that Juliet would stop him; however, she said nothing. Already dreading the loneliness that awaited him in the tent, he stepped out of the fire's illumination and disappeared into the void of the now-cloudy night.

"Goodnight," Juliet said flatly.

Roger's voice came to Juliet out of the darkness, "Goodnight."

Will I ever see him again? Juliet wondered before she could stop herself. She was flooded with anger at herself for having such a thought, and she tried once again to force her mind onto something pleasant and distant. As she pushed an image of herself building a snow fort in her backyard with her best childhood friend into the forefront of her consciousness, she felt the first icy drop of rain graze the tip of her nose.

***

Chris clambered into his tent with dirt streaked across his hands and face. Flower stems and blades of grass clung to his arms. He brushed them off and crawled into his sleeping bag, next to Vince's.

Vince felt the same fearful sensation that he had the previous night. After leaving Takeshi, he and Ana had caught up easily with the rest of the crew. The others had run into an impenetrably dense stand of briars and had been edging through it almost gingerly. Ana and Vince had not said anything upon rejoining the group, but it had been clear to everybody what had happened in the clearing. It had also been clear that Ana was no longer the leader of the group, although nobody had moved in to replace her. They were now, simply, five people lost in the woods. They were no longer a crew.

As soon as they all decided to bunk down for the night, Chris had once again scrambled to draw in the dirt. He took a long time over his drawing tonight, and so Vince had already decided how to begin the necessary conversation by the time Chris came back into the tent.

Now, Vince allowed a minute for Chris to get comfortable in his sleeping bag before speaking. "Tell me your secret, Chris."

Chris stiffened. He possessed enough secrets to be left in uncertainty as to what Vince wanted to know. At this moment of fear, Chris's love for Vince seemed to swell. He was tempted to simply curl up in Vince's arms and allow his action to speak for itself. However, with a high, dizzy

110

laugh, Chris brought himself back to reality and asked, "What do you mean?"

"This afternoon," Vince said, "we were surrounded by animals. You disappeared and, when you came back, the animals were gone and you told us we were safe. Obviously, you know what's been going on here."

"That's far from obvious, actually."

"Chris, please." Vince was starting to get angry with Chris, but he knew that he couldn't allow that feeling to register in his tone; Chris seemed to be the type who needed to be coaxed gently into revealing anything. "We're in a lot of danger. You understand that, of course. So if you can tell me anything at all, you need to. I think you are capable of saving all of our lives."

"Vince," Chris said through a rigid jaw, "I think you believe I understand more than I do." Chris was more than a little embarrassed. While it was true that he had not been entirely honest with Vince, he felt that anything he could say would do more to confuse the situation than to clarify. He felt that if he shed one of his secrets, the rest would come tumbling out; though it certainly mattered little at this point whether or not Vince found out about Chris's feelings for him, Chris's pride would not allow him to say or do anything that might compromise himself.

"Please, Chris?" Vince tried not to sound desperate, though he knew that he did. Stubborn silence greeted him. After a minute, Vince reached out to Chris and touched his arm lightly. "Please," he repeated.

At Vince's touch, an army of shivers stampeded through Chris's body. Chris's heart felt that it might leap from his mouth and explode. He tried to figure out what to say, but his thoughts all seemed to puddle together into an incoherent mess. He had a sudden memory of himself strapped to a bed, hooked up to a million machines, with digital readouts on every available surface. He saw a syringe forcing its way into his veins. Finally, trembling at the images, he began to speak tentatively, "Vince, do you remember last night? You asked what scared me more than anything else in the world?"

"You told me I'd find out," Vince replied. "I'm still waiting to learn it."

Chris felt that his whole body was quivering; it was only with concentrated muscular effort that he could steady himself enough to get his words out in a normal voice. "I'm scared of myself."

Vince blinked. He hadn't been expecting this answer and yet it didn't surprise him. "Why are you scared of yourself?" Chris fell into another silence and Vince eventually had to repeat the question.

"I believe," Chris continued, "that you were right when you said I am the only one who can save us." Vince, though surprised, deliberately remained silent in order to compel Chris to go on.

"You're right that I got rid of the cougars this afternoon."

"How did you get rid of the cougars, Chris?"

"I…," Chris began, but fell silent again. He had long ago admitted his powers to himself, but he had never spoken about them to anybody else. He felt that talking about them would somehow validate them – if he voiced his suspicions, no more question would remain as to whether or not they were true.

"How did you get rid of the cougars, Chris?" Vince's voice was less calm than he wanted it to sound.

"I drew them," Chris said, suddenly feeling that he had imploded. He distantly remembered a white-coated technician looking at him in horror. He had spoken. The desire for suicide flashed through his head, but of course he had no means.

"Yes?" Vince's quiet response seemed odd to Chris against the enormity of his own reaction. "Go on," Vince prompted. "You drew them and they disappeared?"

"Yes." Chris groped for breath. He launched into an explanation, which, he found, calmed him as he proceeded. "I've always had an active imagination. I mean, when I was little, I created whole worlds in my head. It's a good thing, they say. Kids are supposed to be imaginative. We're supposed to make up stories that can't possibly be true; that's creativity. So, that's what I do. I imagine things. That's what we all do, I guess.

"But a few months ago – I don't know exactly when, and I have no idea why – little parts of my imaginary world started becoming true. I might see an open door in my mind, and then I'd see it in reality. Nothing major." The awful face of that technician flashed once again through Chris's mind. "But these visions came side by side with an urge – I felt an urge, a strong urge, to draw what I was seeing. This was the only way I could keep the images from leaving my mind. If I drew them, they didn't have to come true. In reality.

"But the more I drew, the more images kept springing to mind, and the more I had to draw. If I thought of a plane crash, and didn't draw it, there would be a plane crash. And so I just had to draw. And now…I haven't been drawing. Or, I've been drawing, but in the dirt, and my drawings get messed up. Or stepped on. Or something…."

Chris trailed off, and so Vince breathlessly picked up the thread, "And now the images in your mind are all coming true?"

After a moment, however, Chris said something unexpected, "No." He took a deep breath. "That's the whole problem. These images aren't coming from inside my mind. Somebody's putting them inside my mind. I don't know where they're coming from."

The ensuing silence was cut short by a magnificent clap of thunder.

***

The mist had rolled in silently, and now it was so thick that Robin's headlights simply reflected back to him off the airborne water droplets and did nothing to delve into the quickly settling darkness. As Robin rolled over the unpaved, one-lane Texas back roads in his mud-splattered truck, he peered in vain into the impenetrable haze surrounding him. Nobody he had talked to had seen any sign of his crew. It was as though the firefighters had simply vanished into the Texas wilderness. Though his rational mind told him that there was no way he would track down the crew in such a haphazard manner, Robin had decided to drive aimlessly through the search sector in the hopes that he might spot something. Of course, at the moment, the only thing he could spot was fog and dreary darkness; nonetheless, he couldn't just go home and go to sleep when his crew was still out in the woods, and he had no other plan than to drive randomly and hope for good luck.

The downpour began suddenly, as though the sky had been abruptly ripped open. Raindrops raced from the sky, creating an irregular cadence on the metal of Robin's truck. Robin flicked on his wipers, but they did nothing more than smear the water across his windshield in an opaque film. The radio station he had been listening to was rendered inaudible by the violent roar of the rushing rain.

"Damn," Robin growled in frustration. The day had been long and fruitless, he was scared for his crew, and he had never hated his job more than he did at that moment. Because he couldn't see where he was going, he had to ease off the gas pedal until the truck was merely inching blindly through the storm. Occasionally an arpeggio of loud raps would sound on the roof of the truck's cab – hail, it seemed, or perhaps falling pinecones. Robin's tires grew slick with water, and he found it difficult to control the course of his vehicle. Just as he thought that it might be best to simply key off the ignition and wait out the storm inside the truck, the truck ground to a halt of its own accord. Troubled, Robin cautiously toed the accelerator; the low grind of the revving engine whined in the air, but the truck went nowhere. With a little less patience, Robin put more pressure on the gas; again, the engine squealed, but the truck felt utterly motionless.

"Damn it," Robin said aloud, as he opened his door and, assaulted by rain, stepped out to glance at the tires. Sure enough, the storm had already turned the dirt road into a soupy river of mud. The truck's wheels were nestled into imposing ruts. Robin bent over in frustration and clawed at the mud around the tires, but as soon as he dragged away a fistful of dirt, a deeper, slicker layer of mud bubbled up to entrench his wheels more hopelessly. The water was rushing down from the sky at such an alarming velocity that the soil could not absorb it, and so muddy puddles soon mottled the road. Robin could feel the ground softening under his feet. Rain poured off his head and into his eyes. Icy trickles of water ran beneath his collar and between his shoulder blades. Dripping and shivering, he decided that he would have to wait out the storm.

Just as he was about to pull himself back into his truck, an earsplitting crack of thunder sounded in the waterlogged evening and a burst of lightning cleaved the darkness and allowed Robin a momentary glimpse into the world surrounding him. In that moment, his coldness was forgotten. In the near distance, caged in by silhouetted tree trunks and webs of brambles, lay a remarkable white object. Nearly five-hundred feet long, reflective, and gently contoured, it seemed to resemble an enormous Modernist refrigerator. It was engulfed once again by darkness before Robin could consider it more thoroughly.

Robin's heart stood still as he was peppered with raindrops. He could feel his feet slowly sinking in the muck. The mud was creeping up to his ankles. A sudden gust of wind whined a warning into his ears, but he remained still. He was not concerned with the mud or the rain; his mind was occupied by one sole consideration – what the hell had he seen?

After a moment, a brilliant flash once again illuminated the woods. This time, Robin's eyes were trained immediately on the object. Though the jolt of lightning had spent itself in a heartbeat, Robin had been able to make out a prominent blue, red, and white patch on the side of the object. Black letters were inscribed next to the colorful patch. Almost as soon as he had received the fleeting image, Robin had processed it.

The patch had been an American flag.

The writing, then, must have said "NASA."

Robin's heart pumped frenziedly as he realized that he had just happened upon the wreckage of the space shuttle.

***

Boris and Norris were undeterred by the rain. In their years with NASA, they had been required to trudge through the ice fields of Siberia, the torrential monsoons of northern Japan, and the scorching aridity of drought-stricken China. Each had taken a bullet – Boris's was still lodged in his right shoulder, whereas Norris's had been successfully removed from his left bicep – and they were trained to withstand the greatest physical torture without revealing so much as the name of the organization for which they worked. They were NASA's best espionage practitioners – "Eeeps," as they were called within the agency – and each boasted an extensive résumé of actor training from the best conservatories in New York and Paris, as well as NASA's own top secret acting program, nestled in a hollowed-out mountain in the New Mexico desert.

Now, as they followed the Gods out of the mission and onto the street, they inconspicuously changed their personas. They quietly shed their rags and ditched their deck of cards behind a trash can. Norris withdrew a collapsible umbrella seemingly from thin air, as Boris slipped on a fake mustache. The transformation was seamless and within five minutes they had become two young businessmen, huddling under a blue umbrella with yellow ducks printed on it. The umbrella did little to guard them against the rain, which was so savaged by the wind that it was blowing almost horizontally, but even as raindrops whipped into their eyes, they didn't blink. Their assignment was to keep on the trail of the Gods, and not even a nuclear holocaust would succeed in breaking their concentration.

As they followed the Gods, they hung back just far enough that there was no threat of the Gods' hearing their conversation.

"Norris," said Boris, in a flat, nondescript tone, "how will we..."

"Handle Them?" Norris picked up immediately. Norris and Boris had spent enough time together as professional partners that they knew one another's minds intimately. People often mistook them for brothers; though they certainly were not identical, they shared the same unremarkable brown hair, the same average build, the same dark eyes, and the same expressionless face. "I suggest we..."

"Keep Them away from Markham?"

"Keen. Just one day longer. Weaken Them."

"Crackerjacks," Boris assented. The men had been entrusted with the task of ensuring that God and Mrs. God eventually found Vince. However, they were instructed not to rush – the longer the Gods stayed away from Vince, the weaker his faith; the weaker Vince's faith, the weaker the Gods; the weaker the Gods, the easier the assassination.

Norris and Boris knew nothing of how the assassination was to occur, however; they knew that Gods cannot be destroyed by bullets alone, but, beyond that, they had not been granted access to the details of NASA's ultimate plan. They knew that the secret weapon on the Daedalus had done nothing to dent the Gods' power, but they trusted NASA and figured that, when the time was right, everything would be clear to them.

Boris and Norris simultaneously stepped into a puddle on the sidewalk. Icy water ran over the tops of their shoes and chilled their toes. "Ick," they both grunted, but did not break their stride. Rain continued to rush from the skies, muting the noises of the cars in the street.

"Boris," said Norris, as they followed the Gods around a corner and onto a bike path that led out of town, "did you close…"

"The windows?"

"In the car?"

"No. Didn't you?" Boris replied dryly. Thunder crackled very nearby. As the men walked, they could see that the buildings were spaced further and further apart. They were getting into the outskirts of town and would soon be in the forest.

"Double drats," said Norris. "The…"

"Upholstery!"

"Is going to be soaked." Norris shrugged. "Oh, well." Pellets of hail began bouncing off the umbrella as the wind screamed around the two men. God and Mrs. God became harder and harder to make out in the distance, but thankfully God's clearly visible fedora gave Norris and Boris an obvious target.

"Do you think we'll kill two birds with one stone out there?" Boris asked. In addition to the Gods, NASA was aiming for the extermination of the entity now calling itself Pimp Daddy.

"It's possible."

"Roger-dodger." The two men walked in silence for a moment before Boris continued. "You scared, Norris?"

"No." Norris spoke flatly, as usual, and quite honestly. Fear was an emotion he had long ago discarded as unproductive. One could not function effectively as a NASA Eeep if one was crippled by the debilitating insecurity of fear. "What about you, Boris?"

"Me neither." In the gray gloom, dense thickets of black trees became visible. The road that the Eeeps were walking along had narrowed from four lanes into two, and fewer structures were around to deflect the wind-lashed rain. They were on the edge of the forest. "Think we'll be killed?" Boris continued in an unwavering voice.

"It's possible. The Gods…"

"Would never do it. But that other one…"

"Might." Norris and Boris had never seen Pimp Daddy in his current form, but they were aware of his existence and of his ruthlessness. "Ready to enter…"

"The forest? Sure."

God and Mrs. God had just veered off the road and into the thick verdure of the forest. Norris and Boris exchanged glances. Each man solemnly removed his suit to reveal camouflaged gear beneath. Boris brought a small tin of olive green face paint from his pocket and smeared first his own face and then his partner's. Almost as soon as the paint had been applied, it began to streak off in the heavy rain. Norris produced two crowns of leaves and the men wreathed their heads. The entire transformation from businessmen into covert jungle prowlers occurred within the space of forty seconds. Nodding to one another, Norris and Boris followed the Gods into the forest. The roar of the storm crescendoed.

***

The Gods remained dry, in spite of the torrents of rain assailing the ground around Them. The radiative auras surrounding Them were strong enough to bend the paths of the raindrops and thereby deflect them. The slickness of the mud beneath Their feet, too, did little to deter Them. The Gods enjoyed excellent traction as a perk of Their divinity. Nonetheless, the sight of the storm raging around Them, sending dried pine needles skipping across the forest floor as if they were alive, and rattling the empty tree branches like oversized maracas, gave Them considerable unease. Throughout Their trek from the city of Longview, the Heavenly Couple had grown quieter and quieter, and now, as They squinted among the thick tangles of vines, trying to spot any sign of life, Mrs. God broke the long-brewing silence with a tearful sigh.

"What dost Thou thinketh, oh My Husband?" Thunder grumbled in the distance. Though it was fully night by now, the rain clouds trapped enough of the ambient light wafting up from Longview to cast a pallid illumination over the forest. All the trees, bathed in half-light, looked like silvery ghosts sending their twisted talons heavenwards. Between the rushing rain, the tormented wind, and the incessant thunder, Mrs. God doubted that She would be able to hear any sign of Vince or his crew.

"A pleasant night, if you're a minnow," God said, trying to deflect Mrs. God's trepidation. "Raging skies, sugar-pie, but We'll find our man nonetheless. Neither rain, nor sleet, nor dead of night is gonna keep this cat from swinging His groove-thing."

"I beith…," Mrs. God hesitated. She had questioned Her husband before, certainly. God did not always work in the most obvious ways, and sometimes His wisdom was not readily apparent. Nonetheless, She had always trusted God, even in the moments when She outright disagreed with Him. Now, though, Her feeling was different. She felt that Her husband was being willfully blind – and dangerously so, moreover. "I beith…," She said again, "not so sure about that."

"Come on, sugar plum," God said. "We're invincible."

"We're not."

God stopped so abruptly that His wife nearly walked right into Him. The look He cast back to His wife made Mrs. God tremble a little bit. Though God nearly always had a goofy grin on His face, His smiles had appeared more and more forced over the past few days. Now He wasn't even attempting to look carefree. His brow was creased with worry, His gaze appeared doleful, and, altogether, He looked older and wearier than Mrs. God had ever seen Him. A sudden fork of lightning blasted nearby, and in the moment of luminescence, the Gods looked one another in the eyes. Mrs. God's were fearful and full of tears; God's were bloodshot and worn.

"What nervy rat planted that piece of mumbo-jumbo in Your ear, sunshine?" God asked. "Gods and disco never die."

"I beith no idiot!" Mrs. God screamed, Her shrill voice rising above the monotonous pounding of the rain. "God, Thou knowest that I loveth Thee to no end, but You've gotteth to faceth up to the damn fact here – I beith no fuckething idiot."

God wanted to speak a million platitudes to comfort His wife, but He knew that She had now discovered Her own mortality and that anything He might now say would be nothing more than condescending lies. So, instead of saying anything, He wrapped His muscular arms around Mrs. God and gave Her a tender kiss on the cheek. As the Heavenly Couple stood together, a throbbing yellow glow emanated from Their embracing bodies. Rain struck the halo of illumination, but simply rolled off its surface. Safe in Their love for one another, the Gods were unconscious of the pounding storm outside. Finally, without raising His head from Mrs. God's shoulder, God murmured, "How did You find out?"

Mrs. God gave an exasperated sigh, but Her heart wasn't in it. She was no longer annoyed with Her husband, but now was only sad and scared. Her voice, when it finally emerged, seemed weak and flat. "Why didst Thou not telleth Me before? Why art You always tryething to protect Me?

I beith Thine wife, and I could have tried to help. I could have beeneth there for Thee. I beith no less brave, no less clever than You."

God said nothing, so Mrs. God continued.

"I beith not blind to the fact that Our powers beitheth less than they used to beitheth. We rode here on Greyhound, for cryething out loud! We possesseth not the power to do a damn thing down here, and how dost Thou not expecteth Me to know that without Vince's faith We will be impotent? Dost Thou thinketh that I remembereth not Our previous times of weakness? Dost Thou think that I believethed that Your retirement was voluntary? I remembereth sittething up in Heaven for six hundred years, smokething blunts and beithing absolutely incapable of doething anything. I remembereth as well as You how boring Our lives becameth when there was no faith or imagination on Earth to animateth Us. I may beith blonde, but I beith no fool. And now I beith scared, God, because You have never hiddeneth anything from Me before. Tell Me what was on the space shuttle that Thou smoteth – I commandeth Thee!"

"It's true, baby," God said. "Those NASA cats want Us pushing up daisies. They sent that shuttle up with their secret weapon to take Us down once and for all. But it was no match for Your Man. As long as this cat's got the faith of one good man behind Him, not a single thing that comes out of mankind's collective noggin can touch Him."

"But that iseth precisely what I feareth," Mrs. God pressed. "What if We lackest the faith of he who hath sustainethed Us?"

"In that case," God said, nervously fidgeting with His fedora, "I just don't know."

At that moment, God noticed something unusual in the swirling puddles of mud at His feet – in the midst of the mud was a hand. God reached down and grasped the hand. As He lifted it, He could feel that the body to which it was attached was submerged deep in the slick mud. Mrs. God bent over breathlessly and began scooping fistfuls of mud away from the dead body. After a few minutes, the Couple had freed the body enough to lift it out of the dirt. Unlike the Gods, the body was not immune to the weather, and as the Gods held it before Them, the rain caused rivulets of dirt to steak its face and exposed arms. God wiped the mud off the corpse's face, and recognition flooded Him immediately. He was holding Takeshi, whom He knew to have been a crewmate of Vince's. Takeshi had died soon after he had been abandoned, and once the storm had started, he had been quickly dragged underground by the suction of the mud. Now, his body was cold and damp, though his eyes and mouth remained wide-open.

God unceremoniously dropped Takeshi's body back into the pit of mud in which it had been mired. He spoke to His wife with gravity, "Okay, peach, We've got to save Our man pronto. Looks to Me like this sort of danger's nothing to sneeze at."

With that, the Gods continued their advance into the heart of the wilderness. The furious rain continued, quickly loosening the soil around Takeshi's body. As the Gods pushed onwards, Takeshi, abandoned once more, was sucked deeper and deeper towards the center of the Earth.

***

Rain pattered like machine gun fire against the warped windows of the Saunders' bedroom, but Amanda seemed to have no trouble sleeping in spite of the noise. Arlo looked down at her as she slept. He was absolutely exhausted – he had barely slept the previous night, it was already quite late, and he doubted that Pimp Daddy was going to let him sleep in the next morning – but Amanda, he had to admit, was improving rapidly. Her hair, mostly returned to its original buttercup color with only a few highlights of silver, was splashed about her head like a halo. The veins on her neck that used to be so prominent were now simply faint blue lines and, during a flash of lightning, Arlo observed a healthy pink glow in her usually pallid cheeks. True, the skin around her eyes remained saggy and the muscle tone had not yet returned to her legs and upper body, but it was quite clear that Amanda was no longer an eighty-six year-old; in fact, she no longer looked even seventy-six – she appeared to be in her fifties again.

Arlo was pleased in spite of his fatigue, and he climbed into bed with his heart swelling with love for his wife. Now that he lay beside her, he could hear her breathing. Her respiration was no longer irregular and labored; she was breathing deeply with ease and comfort. Arlo could feel a lump in his throat as he remembered how breathtaking Amanda had been when they first met, over sixty years ago. It struck him as cruel that such beautiful women ever had to age. It wasn't watching Amanda's beauty getting slowly gnawed over by time, however, that upset Arlo – by the time a man reached his age, he had no more use for aesthetics – it had been watching her react to her own aging. When Amanda had first started to notice herself growing saggy and frail, she had become despondent for a period of months. Arlo knew that it would do no good to tell her that he would love her, no matter what she looked like – her grief hadn't been for his love, which she knew enough not to doubt, but for her own mortality.

Now, however, such sad remembrances were banished from Arlo's mind, and he only saw his wife as she used to be, carefree in the starlight of her youth. Though she still looked middle-aged, Arlo knew that her spirit was being rejuvenated and he couldn't help looking forward to how she might feel in another day's time. Soothed by the noises of the storm outside, Arlo wrapped his arms around his wife. However, at her husband's touch, Amanda jerked in her sleep. With an expression that almost appeared angry, she twisted out of his embrace and turned her back to him. Arlo was puzzled. Amanda had never been a touchy sleeper before. Placidity seemed to have returned to her, though, so Arlo allowed his weariness and the rushing sound of the rain overflowing the gutters to carry him off into sleep.

***

Shreds of dreams. Feverish images piling one on top of another. Brief snatches of sleep amidst thunderclaps. The delirious uncertainty of half-slumber. Dream woven into reality. Reality side by side with fantasy. Thrumming rain melts into your dreams. Minutes telescope into hours. The night is four times longer than usual.

Ana's tent flaps noisily in the wailing wind. Ana inside, feels the uncertain earth moving beneath her. Lightning splits the night. She closes her eyes. Opens them. Night darker, voices whispering in wind. Indistinct. Shadows of bats cyclone about the tent. Is she asleep? Someone lying next to her, motionless. Does not want to look, but must. Scott's slashed body, oozing blood from lacerations. Face smashed open, slick and moist inside. A lizard slithers from his gaping abdomen. It winks? Ana blinks again. No corpse, no lizard. Alone in tent. Rain unceasing.

Roger shivers in a threadbare sleeping bag. Tent colder tonight without Takeshi. Suddenly back outside with Juliet, tending the campfire. Light flickers in sinister patterns across her face. More smoke than usual. Why? Move closer to get a better look. Suddenly, bubbling pain. Fire consuming him. Snapping, popping as flesh sears, fat melts. Try to extinguish self. Juliet watches impassively. Skin blackening, charred and brittle. Scream. Open eyes into blackness. Hear a noise. Crackling fire? No. Rain against the latex tent.

Arlo in sunshine. Strolls through a temperate spring day. His fields. Verdant. Springtime. Cows graze serenely, no bugs disturb them. By the well, Amanda fetching water. Her back to Arlo. Blonde curls. He will surprise her. Steals up behind her, dewy grass soothing on feet. Reach out to grab her, but she has already turned around. Where eyes should be, sockets. Where smile should be, sneer. Patchy, purplish skin. Bulging temples. She holds not a bucket, but a space helmet. "Who did you expect, you noxious nonentity?" Suddenly in bed, next to Amanda. Feel silly, but check to make sure her face is her own. Relief, but unable to shake the feeling that the head is in the room, watching.

Vince awake. Chris snoring beside him. Tent too cramped. Feels he must get up and stretch legs. Outside the tent, daylight. Child nailed to tree, still alive. Wails for help. Vince looks around, sees mother. "Your child! Help it!" Mother looks indifferently, sits, does nothing. Vince rushes to child. Hands and feet nailed to tree, screaming. Try to pry nails loose, but tear child's flesh. Slick blood streams over hands. Can't grasp the nails. "Where are you, God?" Earsplitting cries of pain. Back in tent, next to Chris. Still feel slippery blood on hands. No, it is sweat. Thunder.

Amanda sees herself sleep. Looking better and better. Cheeks rosier, skin smoother. Swooping up from beneath the bed – her angel. Beautiful blonde hair, lucid blue eyes. Wings of golden eagles' feathers. He carries a red-crested shield and a broadsword. Whispers in her ear, "It's yours now." Meaning unclear, but what does it matter? Repeats, "It's yours." The voice is familiar, but where from? Feels her stomach stir as the angel grasps her in tanned, muscular arms. Soaring out the window, see the Texas landscape beneath. Vast green fields studded with thickets of impenetrable forest. Here, a marsh. There, a lake. Angel speaks again. "It's yours, Amanda. The baby is yours now."

Chris tossing in agitation. Finds himself in the same place as last night's dream. Hard concrete beneath him, darkness all around. Vague outlines of objects – a rusty chainsaw, a garden hoe. Spider runs across his hand, bites him. Someone laughs. A voice he's heard before. Same voice as last night. "Like my fantasies?" Scared. Chris knows the voice. Whose? Voice again, "Put your mind to work." Crawls tremblingly along the dusty floor. Can't find an exit. "Put your mind to work." Lightning explodes in the darkness. The inside of the tent. Vince beside him, sleeping fitfully. Chris examines his own hands. There – a spider bite. In panic, realizes where he has heard the voice in the dream before. It is his own voice.

Juliet outside on lookout, sits by the soggy remains of the fire. Wrapped in a soaked sweatshirt, she shudders. Blinks. Sees a coffin sitting on the forest floor, filling with water. It is empty. Somebody shoves her from behind. She falls into the coffin. It is bottomless, bottomless. Wasn't she supposed to stay awake? Jolts to alertness. It is too late. Screams.

***

Ross Tucker did not leave the Gods' house after sending Robin back to Earth. Instead, he had continued to rummage through the Heavenly Couple's belongings, in the hope of finding some way to monitor situations down on Earth. The only communication link he had discovered was the telephone he had used to contact Robin, but hours had passed and Ross was growing anxious. He wanted to see what action Robin was taking to help the Gods, and whether or not he was achieving success. Now, Ross had been searching all day and had only managed to turn up more and more sheaves of unanswered correspondence in unexpected places – stuffed into the mattress, behind the bookshelves, and even crammed into the toilet tank.

On the verge of giving up, Ross turned now to the pantry. The shelves were poorly stocked. After all, Mrs. God was known throughout Greater Heaven as an abysmal cook, and the one time God tried to prepare the dinner, He started a fire that burnt down nearly a third of the subdivision. Suitably enough, the pantry primarily contained packets of Ramen noodles and economy-sized boxes of Wheaties. The bags of flour and cartons of Bisquick were open, but almost entirely full; either the Gods could replenish Their stock at will, or They simply didn't do much baking. However, one item in particular drew Ross's attention – a ceramic recipe box, adorned with a pink ribbon and prominently displayed. What use do the Gods have for a recipe box? Ross wondered. They eat frozen pizza for nearly every meal.

Ross cautiously opened the box. Inside was not recipes, but a series of Polaroids. Ross flipped through the pictures. The first was a copy of the picture of God, Mrs. God, and Vince that Ross had found on the Gods' mantel earlier. The second seemed to have been taken in a room with stone walls and velvet draperies. Three people were pictured – a young man in chain mail with a bowl-cut and an enormous, gem-studded crucifix, an older man with the same complexion and facial features as the younger man, shooting a thumbs-up to the photographer, and a beautiful lady with the young man's eyes and build.

Odd, thought Ross, as he continued.

The third photograph had been taken in an open field against the setting sun. Though the three figures in the picture were badly backlit, Ross could discern a man in flowing purple robes and blue face paint, an older man whose skin appeared to be painted entirely blue, and a woman who glowed orange, with bright red hair and jet black lips. The next photograph depicted a beautiful young woman wading in an enormous river with a basket of vegetables on her head and her eyes turned heavenwards. The other woman in the picture shared the first woman's olive skin and black hair; she was holding up two fingers behind the head of the man standing next to her.

All of the pictures, Ross soon discovered, followed the same format: three people, who all always vaguely resembled one another, stood comfortably with one another against backdrops of differing places and times. Ross flipped through the pictures again, and came to rest on the first – Vince, God, and Mrs. God dyeing Easter eggs. He fanned out the pictures before him and looked at them all together. Different people were shown in each picture, and yet Ross felt that there must be some obvious connection between them.

Ross turned one of the photographs over to see a caption penciled on the back, "Summer fun with the Holy Spirit, 1014." Intrigued, Ross examined more of the photographs. "Holy Spirit shows off hot new bod, 1322." "Middle East trip with Holy Spirit, 222." "Celebrating Easter with the Holy Spirit, 2000." Flipping the pictures back around to look at them once more, Ross was struck with the beginnings of a suspicion.

However, Ross was interrupted in his contemplation by something unusual – the walls around him suddenly became slightly transparent. Ross wrinkled his brow and examined the interior of the pantry. In fact, not just the walls, but everything had become less opaque, as though dissolving slowly into a gas. Ross stepped out of the pantry into the kitchen. He could see faintly through the walls of the Gods' house, and into the street. A woman with long red hair came tearing out of the front door of a house nearby, and raced down the street, screaming, "Not again!"

Without wasting a minute, Ross hurried out of the house and chased down the woman. He caught up to her quickly, next to a vacant lot. "Hey!" he shouted.

The woman turned to Ross in a frenzy.

"I'm new up here," Ross said. "What's going on?"

The woman's eyes grew wide. "You don't know?" she asked. "Heaven's going down the tubes!"

"What do you mean?"

"I mean," she said, huffing for breath, "that God's getting weak, and if He dies, this whole place is going to be up in smoke until someone comes in to take His place."

"Take His place?"

"Could take days, or it could take centuries...but there's no guarantee it'll be pretty."

"What won't be pretty?" Ross asked.

The woman rolled her eyes, exasperated at Ross's curiosity, and anxious to flee. "The birth of a new deity. It's not very common, but God dies from time to time. Shit happens – that's not the scary part. The scary part is who's birthing the next incarnation. God's not always good, you know; that's a Sunday school myth." Having recaptured her breath, the woman raced away before Ross could figure out what question he wanted to ask next.

Ross briefly considered rushing after her, but decided on another course of action. Returning to the Gods' house, Ross hoped that Robin had thought to keep Vince's crucifix with him.

***

Ana, for the second day in a row, was awakened by a scream. Images of yesterday's carnage flashed through her head as she sat up in her tent. Even in her panic, she couldn't help noticing that, due to the softening of the soil, her sleeping body had made a huge impression in the ground. She flung open the flap of her tent and leapt outside. The storm had only increased in intensity during the few hours that Ana had slept. The instant she was outside, bullets of rain fogged her vision and airborne twigs slapped into her face. As she moved towards the source of the scream, she struggled both against the wind and the tendency of her feet to sink into the soil. Every step was arduous; she had to muscle out of the gooey mire beneath her and strain into the howling wind that seemed intent on checking her every advance. She heard another scream – it was Juliet.

The sensation that had been brewing in Ana all day suddenly returned – she felt that the moment of her death was imminent. In a sense, she felt that by going after Juliet she was relinquishing control over what might happen next. She felt that somebody else was controlling her actions at this point and yet, surprisingly, this produced no fear in her. Instead, she felt an overwhelming placidity, as though all she had to do was relax and see where circumstances placed her.

As Ana came near to Juliet, her progress was slowed. She had come to the edge of what almost resembled a marsh. A wide expanse of water, whirlpooling in the storm, stretched as far as Ana could see. Several meters away, Juliet could be seen, up to her waist in mud and water, thrashing frantically. A stream of bubbles rose from the depths of the marsh, and Juliet got sucked down a couple of inches more. She screamed again.

Ana could hear Roger, Vince, and Chris running towards her. Without turning around, she screamed, "Stop!" The sound of the running ceased. Ana did not allow her eyes to stray from Juliet, who had spotted the crew and was waving her arms frantically. "Get up in that tree," Ana ordered the crew, indicating a tree that seemed relatively stable. Many of the smaller trees were being uprooted in the wind and whipping back towards the crew.

"But lightning…," Roger began.

"You'll be safe there," Ana screamed with authority. "Get up there." Without waiting to see whether or not her crew had heeded her instructions, Ana plowed ahead into the muck that threatened to engulf Juliet. With each step, her feet sank further and further into the mud. Juliet continued to gesticulate wildly. As Ana advanced, feeling the water slosh inside her fire boots, she realized that Juliet was not flailing aimlessly – she was attempting to caution Ana not to come any closer. "Fat chance," Ana thought, as she finally glanced back to see that the crew had secured itself safely in the tree she had indicated. "Nobody more is dying on my watch."

Ana was now close enough to hear Juliet's words distinctly over the hammering rain. "Get out of here! Get out of here!" Juliet's midsection had been all but devoured by the mud, but she kept her arms safely over her head. Ana could feel herself starting to sink as well. She couldn't lift her feet out of the mud, but instead had to shuffle through it as though she were treading water. When she was close enough, she thrashed out in a mad effort to grasp Juliet under the armpits. However, the rain had made Juliet's skin slippery, and Ana failed to get a good grasp. She was just barely able to maintain her balance and keep from plunging face-first into the ravenous sinkhole.

"Ana, what the fuck?" Juliet whimpered. When she had first woken to find herself entrapped, she had been in panic. Staining every muscle in her body, she had attempted to free herself, but discovered that any efforts only served to enmesh her further. Once she had realized that the situation was hopeless, she tried her hardest to shut off any part of her brain that responded with fear. Juliet did not want to go out in a flash of anger and resistance – if she was to be buried alive in the wilds of Texas, she wanted at least to be able to spend her final moments bidding farewell to the world she left behind and resigning herself to the uncertainty of the world to come. Now that Ana was on the scene playing hero, however, Juliet felt that her death could not be peaceful. "Ana," she screamed with sudden rage. "Get out of here!" She wanted to start kicking, but she could do nothing with her buried legs.

Had the sun been shining and the air not obscured by mist and rain, Ana might not have misunderstood – she would have been able to see the genuine pain in Juliet's eyes and to hear the pleading in her voice. As it was, however, the murky night air rendered Juliet's face a vague form and the noise of rain trickling off of dead branches and leaves overshadowed all the nuances in her words. Ana assumed that Juliet was resisting her solely because she felt uncomfortable accepting Ana's self-sacrifice. As rain bounced off the ground around the women, spraying muddy droplets into their eyes, Ana swiped once again towards Juliet. Once more, she missed, but this time she failed to regain her balance and toppled forward into the whirling puddle of mud. She threw out her hand just in time to catch herself, but her arm plunged into the mud as far as her elbow. Ana smiled humorlessly as she noticed that the mud was studded with the withered, uprooted bodies of the flowers that had formerly made the clearing appear so appealing. "Goddamn flowers," Ana couldn't help thinking. If she had had any thoughts of turning back, it was now too late – she was fully stuck and had nowhere to go but downwards.

Juliet watched with dread as Ana entrapped herself, splashing mud into the air and creating noise and disorder around Juliet's final moments. Juliet began to cry out once more, but she immediately realized that it was too late to talk Ana out of her final gesture – Ana was stuck and, ironically enough, Juliet was fated to die with the woman whom she felt had never understood her.

From their positions in the tree, the remaining crewmates observed a miracle through the still-frames exposed by periodic lightning blasts. First, they saw Ana and Juliet stuck near one another in the plain of mud. The next flash of lightning corresponded with Ana's loss of balance, and the crew could see only her head, shoulders, and one arm aboveground. Then, Ana was gone, but Juliet seemed to have risen a bit. After a moment, it became clear that Juliet was indeed freeing herself from the mud. A crack of lightning split the sky nearby, and in the brief moment of illumination the crew could see Juliet's prone body, almost entirely brown with mud, lying safely on a rock next to the sinkhole; Ana was nowhere to be seen.

Chris turned to Vince in amazement. "Did Ana save Juliet?"

"She must have dived into the mud and pushed her up from beneath," Vince replied. The crew watched Juliet; she lay motionless, aside from an occasional convulsive shiver due to the rain. Everybody felt that they should go to her, but nobody made the first move.

After several minutes, Roger whispered, "Look." Nobody had needed Roger to point out what was quickly becoming obvious – the storm was dwindling. The steady stream of rain had trickled down to a soft patter, and the previously monstrous thunder sounded further distant, as though it were a hungry animal who had passed the crew by and was now wandering elsewhere to satisfy its appetite. Concurrently, the first aura of dawn was beginning to gild the lowest branches of the trees on the edge of the clearing. In the low half-light of early morning, the men could see that the field in which they had been camping had been pitted and mutilated by the erosive effects of the heavy rains. Oblong puddles and mounds of mud now covered the field, and crumpled wildflowers lay everywhere like fallen soldiers. Rain sobbed from the branches of trees and cut across the ground in rivulets. Somewhere in the distance, a lone whippoorwill hooted.

Roger leapt from the tree and padded out to Juliet. He was careful to avoid any soil that appeared too soft. Juliet was draped lifelessly across a rock. Roger knelt to her level and whispered, "Juliet. You're safe."

For a moment, he thought that she wasn't going to reply, but she finally loosed a tortured moan.

"Juliet?"

Another pause hung in the air; Juliet moaned again, but quieter this time. She didn't move, but she allowed Roger to put his hand on her shoulder. Finally, in a low, flat voice, as though speaking to herself, she said, "I was the one who was supposed to go." Roger could not get her to say anything more than this.

Meanwhile, Chris stared dumbfounded at the site of Ana's death. He felt that everything had happened too quickly – between waking up to Juliet's scream, being ordered into a tree, and witnessing the death of one crewmate and the salvation of another, he knew that a long time must have passed, but the images of the evening seemed to collapse together in his mind with no sense of time or order. Vince, too, was struck by the ferocity with which Ana had been wrenched away from the crew. He also hadn't realized until this moment how badly he wanted to be the next to die. He felt that there was no possibility of his escaping alive, and all he wanted was that the torture should not be prolonged.

"Vince." Chris's voice brought Vince out of his reverie. "Look there." Chris indicated a small patch near their tent that had remained inexplicably dry. Four stick figures were carved into the ground, each with bubbles streaming from its mouth. Next to the figures was a sloppy puddle. "I drew five of us," Chris remarked, "but the rain destroyed one."

Vince looked at Chris, whose face seemed utterly drained of blood. "Ana had it easy," Vince remarked for some reason. "She had a moment of fear, maybe, and then...," Vince trailed off, unable to decide what death could be said to be.

"Maybe this is a stupid question," Chris said, his eyes hooked to Vince's face as though it were the world's only remaining oasis of certainty, "but do you really believe in life after death?"

"Chris," Vince said, watching the morning sun burn away the gray storm clouds of night. He was horrified by the sunrise, knowing that he could not predict where he might be when it next set. "I really don't know."

***

The interior of the space shuttle was every one of Robin's childhood fantasies come true. Multicolored buttons shone like gems on the expansive consoles. Brass gauges peeked out of every available surface. The cushioned leather seats seemed to be the most comfortable Robin had ever sat in. When Robin first got on board, he had sat down and pretended momentarily that he was blasting through space, whipping around treacherous asteroids and clusters of debris; had anybody been watching, Robin would have immediately turned red and smiled apologetically, but, with nobody there to ruin his fun, Robin became for a moment the same person who in his childhood had traveled to Mongolia with an ironing board for a horse and a spatula for a rifle.

Had Robin made his discovery under more appealing circumstances, he might have lost himself entirely in wonderment. However, he soon reminded himself that he had come out to the forest in the first place for a reason – he needed to get his crew back safely. After satisfying his lifelong curiosity as to whether or not a spaceship has a speedometer, Robin set immediately to a search of the premises. He wasn't sure what he expected to find or how it would help him, but he had a vague sense that, at the very least, he could investigate the truth of Ross Tucker's claims as to the purpose of NASA's mission.

The search proved surprisingly easy. The design of the space shuttle's interior reminded Robin of an exhibit he had once seen by Modernist Swedish furniture-makers – the walls were smooth, slick, and undulating, and no nooks, crannies, or corners existed in which to secret any materials. Robin felt almost as though he were on the inside of an enormous ball bearing. The entire spaceship seemed to have been built entirely without seams. Robin began systematically running his fingers up one section of wall and down another; however, he could find nothing but levers and switches of whose function he was ignorant. He supposed that on some level he had expected a logbook, or a flight recorder that would have given him all the information he desired. Though he was disappointed not to discover any such thing, he realized that his expectation had been somewhat foolish.

After he had examined the walls and the surfaces of the consoles, Robin turned his attention to the ship's most bizarre feature – sprouting from the center of the floor was an enormous protuberance. Like everything else in the ship, it was perfectly smooth and rounded, but, unlike the other surfaces, it was clear of readouts and gauges. It was simply a reflective black hemisphere with no apparent purpose. Robin touched the protrusion with a tentative hand; it felt as cool as marble and as smooth as a billiard ball. As soon as he took his hand away, however, the hemisphere warmed from black to a flickering blue. It was only when "Loading..." appeared in red, pixilated letters that Robin recognized the object as a huge, dome-shaped computer screen.

The computer took a moment to activate, and then the screen was taken up with a satellite image of the Northern Hemisphere. A soft female voice instructed Robin further, "Please speak the name of the party you seek." The voice then began cycling through different languages, presumably repeating the same phrase. Robin stood astonished, but retained enough presence of mind to blurt out the first name that came to mind, "Robin Rodriguez."

Instantaneously, a plethora of red crosses dotted the globe. The neutral female voice said, "Please limit your search by continent." As the voice then proceeded to translate this instruction into various foreign languages, Robin realized that he must be looking at the locations of all the Robin Rodriguezes in the world. He was surprised both by how many Robins there were and by how thoroughly they were dispersed over the entire hemisphere. One cross was inching slowly over the Atlantic, probably indicating a Robin sitting on a transcontinental flight. Robin had, of course, been dreaming about the cosmos since childhood, but he had never before felt quite so small. He was hardly aware of himself saying, "North America."

The globe pivoted and zoomed, and Robin found himself looking at the North American continent alone. Now that he could see with greater detail, he could tell that the majority of the crosses were centered around metropolises such as New York and Mexico City. However, even within East Texas, there were five Robin Rodriguezes. Robin was given the option of narrowing his search further, and he did so, bringing the area around Longview onto the screen. One solitary cross remained.

"Is that me?" Robin thought to himself, already feeling in the pit of his stomach the certainty that it was. "But how could NASA know where I am? Are they tracking everybody in the world?"

The computer's mechanical voice brought Robin out of his confusion. "Your search has revealed one match. Would you like to view this match?"

"Yes," Robin said, without at all feeling that he would like to.

As he had feared, the picture on the screen zoomed in and grew more and more detailed, until he saw a night-vision image of the downed spacecraft in which he currently stood. "Would you like to zoom in further?" the computer asked.

Robin gulped and once again said, "Yes."

The image twisted again and suddenly it was as though Robin were simply looking into a mirror. He was surprised at how pale he appeared. He couldn't precisely say why he felt so uncomfortable at the moment, but it made him profoundly uneasy to see himself reflected in this odd computer. Who else is watching me right now? Robin couldn't help wondering, and he shuddered at his question. He peered into his own eyes, hoping that doing so would somehow resolve his questions. However, his image merely presented to him his own perplexity, and so he cried out, "Get rid of it!"

Robin expected that the image would vanish at his command, but the picture on the screen didn't change. Instead, the computer's voice once again issued from its hidden speaker, "I'm sorry. I didn't understand that. Please repeat your command."

Robin realized that he was dealing with a computer application he didn't know and that, of course, it couldn't deal with commands beyond those it had been programmed to understand. Summoning up his greatest self-possession, Robin made another attempt. "Restart." However, his image remained on the screen, and the voice repeated, "I'm sorry. I didn't understand that. Please repeat your command."

Robin said nothing and, after a moment, the computer continued, "For assistance, please say 'Help.'"

"Help," Robin said.

The soft voice of the computer went on, in a low, neutral tone that Robin found positively off-putting. "To begin a new search, please say 'New search.'"

Robin was about to speak, but the next option seized his attention. "To find more information on this individual, please say, 'Open file.'"

Robin didn't listen to the remaining options. He was completely occupied with a single question – whether or not he ought to open his own file. He generally felt that what he would find would terrify him, but, at the same time, if he didn't look, he knew that he would spend the rest of his life wondering how much of his existence was on record. Preparing himself for the worst, Robin said, "Open file."

The next screen to appear was a long menu with such options as "Biography," "Biography (Executive Summary)," "Fantasies," "Social Network," and "Archives." Robin touched "Archives" and was immediately whisked to a new menu that was simply a long list of consecutive dates. Robin selected a date randomly.

Now the screen was filled with Robin's five year-old self. He was in the backyard of his childhood home in Terrell, pushing a model airplane through the grass. He was wearing an old pair of overalls and a grubby baseball cap, and dirt darkened his fingernails. Suddenly, he saw his mother in the background, standing in the doorway to the house. She was wearing the flannel robe that she used to have, and drinking coffee out of the orange ceramic mug that Robin had all but forgotten about. Robin watched for a few minutes more – his childhood self continued to play contentedly with the airplane, crawling on all fours through the dew-bejeweled grass. Though Robin had no specific recollection of this memory, it seemed accurate down to the last detail: the plastic siding on the house, the chipped birdbath next to the back porch, and the slight curliness that one used to be able to see in his hair.

Robin sat down, breathless, on the floor of the space shuttle. How long had he been recorded? He returned to the menu, only to notice that the string of archived dates corresponded precisely to his lifespan. It seemed that NASA had been watching him since birth. Robin trembled. He couldn't say how this knowledge changed anything, but he felt that everything he used to treasure as uniquely his own was somehow corrupted. His entire life was no longer his, but had been captured by a satellite thousands of miles out of reach. Suddenly feeling fatigued, Robin reluctantly tried another menu. "Fantasies," he said.

The image on the screen permuted into a long, bullet-pointed chunk of text. Robin scanned the list; every item named some hope or aim that he was not even especially conscious of. "Wishes to own profitable investment real estate," he noticed, next to, "Wishes to memorize at least one Shakespeare sonnet by heart." The mundane – "Wishes he could knot his tie more attractively" – was counterpoised against the truly fantastical – "Wishes to be the first man to set foot on the Sun." Again, Robin could not deny that any of what he saw was certainly part of him; and again, he felt robbed of himself, perhaps even more completely than when he had seen his life's externals housed in the archives. My thoughts, and dreams, and fantasies, Robin thought achingly. What am I worth, if everything I am can be represented on a screen?

The thought of rescuing the Las Cruces crew suddenly seemed far distant. Indeed, nothing seemed important anymore. As he gazed at the list of fantasies summarized so succinctly before him, Robin felt as though the fantasies themselves had been wrenched out of him. Seeing them enumerated brought them out of the realm of fantasy and, in a way, made them uninteresting. Robin could think of nothing to do. He did not want to go back into the night; he didn't even want to continue exploring the spaceship or the contents of the computer. He lay on the floor of the space shuttle, its rounded metallic walls arching above him, and wished that he could cease to exist.

At that moment, a familiar tinny ring emanated from his pocket. Robin recalled that, after his meeting with Ross, he had left Vince's cross in his pocket. He now drew out the ringing cross and, without a moment to consider what was happening, was transported bodily to Greater Heaven for the second time in two days.

***

The Greater Heaven that Robin now saw was not the same as the Greater Heaven he had seen the previous afternoon. True, the Gods' house was just as disarrayed as it had been earlier, and nothing had been moved, but everything now gleamed with the filmy, transparent quality of a soap bubble. The aroma of Old Spice and thick cigar smoke that had previously been so overpowering had dwindled into a barely distinguishable trace of its former self. Robin looked in puzzlement at God's desk, the drawers of which were now almost completely transparent. He felt as though he would be able to pass his hand right through them. The biggest change of all, however, had occurred in Ross Tucker's body. Though Ross retained his form and human characteristics, his body was fading in the same way as everything else in Greater Heaven. Robin could see his bones, muscles, organs, and arteries through his skin, all transparent and superimposed on one another. Of everything in the room, only one single object remained bright and vivid – where Robin would have expected Ross's heart to be, a tiny red orb of luminescence gleamed with stellar intensity. As Robin's gaze strayed to the street that he could see through the house's walls, he noticed that similar balls of red light pulsed in the chests of all the men and women of Greater Heaven.

"As you can see, the situation here is dire," Ross began, without giving Robin a chance to fully comprehend his surroundings, "and I will therefore remind you of your crucial role in the salvation of the moral universe." Though Ross spoke with his usual efficiency, he could not avoid betraying his nervousness. His hair – unruly at the best of times – stuck up at all angles, as though it were trying desperately to flee his head. He had also begun picking at his fingernails, which was a bad habit of which he thought he had rid himself during his post-doc years. As he paused, a window shuddered and blinked into nonexistence. "Please be attentive," he said to Robin, with a decided note of urgency in his voice.

"I'm sorry, but what is that?" Robin was still staring at the red light in Ross's chest; the light twinkled like a star, yet with all the lively coloration of stained glass. Robin had never seen anything quite so beautiful or mysterious, even when he had first looked through the enormous telescope at the observatory in Los Alamos.

"Oh, Lord." Ross rolled his eyes. "When the human soul is no longer hemmed in by corporeal constraints, it is able to shine forth in its full brilliance. Now please stop staring at my undiluted essence, and pay attention. You've got a job to accomplish, and if you want to be a hero, you can't be a sentimentalist."

With great difficulty, Robin drew his eyes away from the glistening pulsar that Ross claimed to be his soul, and focused on the face of his deceased higher-up. "I'm listening," Robin said, though he had no desire to be a hero. Even though Greater Heaven threatened to dissolve into nothingness at any moment, Robin could think of nothing he would rather do than remain there. He was tired of his worldly concerns. He was frustrated by the futile search for the Las Cruces crew and by the seeming invincibility of NASA and so he wanted to simply give up the fight. As a former C student who lived in a boxy two-room apartment near the highway, Robin was all too tempted by the idea of something unique and radiant in the immutability of the soul; he felt that, without question, he was meant to remain in Greater Heaven.

"I try to be in error rarely," Ross began, seeing that Robin was not paying full attention to him, but hoping nonetheless that he could convey his urgency in a comprehensible manner, "but it seems I have given you a spot of misinformation." With a muted "pop," one of the walls disintegrated into a shower of translucent dander. Ross increased the tempo of his speech. "It isn't God I need you to help at all, Mr. Rodriguez. It's the fellow that I mistakenly referred to as His son."

At this point, Ross withdrew the photographs he had found earlier from his pocket and fanned them in front of Robin. The pictures were beginning to waver, but Robin could still make out their general features – he could see that each photograph showed three people, all of whom vaguely resembled one another. He didn't know what he was looking at or why he should care, but he hoped that Ross would keep talking. He didn't want to go back to Earth, and the longer Ross took to say what he had to say, the longer Robin would get to remain in Greater Heaven.

"What you're looking at," Ross continued, "is, in some way, a family tree, or a family history. These are permutations of God and His wife."

This sounded highly doubtful to Robin. The men and women in the pictures appeared too normal to be divine. True, some had unusual coloration, or oddly formed faces, but, on the whole, Robin saw nothing but the lopsided smiles, timorous eyes, and gnawed-down fingernails that were, to him, innately human. Even having just been whisked up to a dissolving Greater Heaven from the belly of an omniscient spacecraft, Robin found himself remarkably able to maintain a certain amount of skepticism.

"God and Mrs. God," Ross continued, "are constantly changing in their externals, much as chameleons do. In these pictures, you see Them in some of Their former shapes, along with the visionaries who created Them as such. You see, the currently reigning deities have remained unchanged in essence for over a thousand years, as best as I can gather, but They are constantly being transformed and nuanced by certain singular individuals on Earth who maintain some sort of power over Them. We all possess imaginations as human beings, but certain humans throughout history have been entered by an extraordinarily potent imaginative power, which is, if we are to believe the captions on the back of these photographs, referred to as the Holy Spirit. It is from this Holy Spirit that God and Mrs. God receive Their nourishment and sustain Themselves. If you look at the dates on the photographs, you will see a six hundred year gap, corresponding to God's retirement. This was the great era of religious skepticism, in which the Holy Spirit found it impossible to take root anywhere. In order to prosper, the Holy Spirit requires a fertile vessel with great faith and great imagination. The Gods are consistently being reborn through this imaginative power."

"So now you're saying that They're imaginary after all?"

"Absolutely not," Ross said, grabbing the pictures back from Robin. "And please ask me no more questions. God and Mrs. God are far from imaginary – They are as real as you or I. I said that They are born of the imagination, but so is everything real. The first rocket ship, I'm sure, began as the fancy of some nerdy teenager who lived for stargazing. That doesn't mean that rockets are imaginary. What it does mean, however, is that I got the relationship all mucked up – God is not the father of the kid on your search team. That kid on your search team is, to oversimplify, the father of God."

"Ridiculous."

"It's not ridiculous at all, Mr. Rodriguez, or at least no more ridiculous than your skepticism. Look around you." As if to punctuate Ross's command, the floor of the house sagged downwards as though it had suddenly lost its rigidity. The desk tumbled towards Ross and Robin, but just as it was about to strike the duo, it vanished with an earsplitting bang, sending a flume of documents spewing into the air like water from a violated fire hydrant. "This is the fallout from a devastated faith," Ross continued. Through the walls, the two men could see sections of the roadway peeling from the ground, whipping through the air, and self-annihilating in blinding bursts of light. "You have to get back to Earth, find this kid, and rekindle his imagination. Otherwise the Gods Themselves are going to be too weak to withstand any threats from other potential deities who might be jockeying for power down there."

"So?" Robin asked. He hadn't asked to get involved. He had graduated from Rice, found a cheap apartment, and entered the working world. He had done everything he was supposed to do. He had gone to Career Counseling to get help with his résumé, he had bought a pair of shiny shoes for job interviews, and he had accepted NASA's first offer, even though it hadn't brought him any closer to his dream of becoming an astronaut. All his college buddies were doing precisely the same thing, and yet they hadn't ended up with the onus of salvation upon their shoulders. It seemed cosmically unfair. *I've always hoped for an opportunity for heroism,* Robin thought, *but I suppose it turns out that was never really what I wanted. Fine time to figure it out!*

Meanwhile, Ross was infuriated. Right and left, Greater Heaven was disintegrating into refractive slivers, and the only contact he had with the Earth was through this twerp of a PR-man who couldn't comprehend the enormity of his situation. He silently cursed NASA's policy of hiring lackeys too dense to understand or care what occurred in the upper echelons of the agency. When he had been alive, it had seemed like a sensible enough way of ensuring secrecy, but now he hated himself for ever having believed in its utility. "So?" Ross screamed, finally losing his temper. The red light in his center became still more brilliant, though his ghostlike features were fading. "What do you mean, 'So?'"

Robin looked at the people through the walls of the house; everybody was racing in the same direction, in some cases literally climbing over one another. Sidewalk tiles were popping out of the ground and disappearing in belches of acrid black smoke. Each time something vanished, the swarm of people increased its collective speed. With so many people clumped together, the collective luminosity of their souls made Robin wince. He looked down at his own chest, expecting to find a light throbbing there, but he remained as opaque as ever.

"You're still alive," Ross said, knowing what Robin was wondering. "Your soul's in there, but you won't see it until you've died." He paused. "Mr. Rodriguez, you must find the crew. Otherwise, none of this will remain for you."

"What's going to happen up here?" The disorder of Greater Heaven suddenly became just as unpalatable to Robin as the disorder of Earth. Where was the well-ordered universe that he had learned about in Astronomy 101? Robin felt that he could be safe nowhere from the chaos that surrounded him.

"What's going to happen up here?" Ross repeated. "It depends entirely on you. Find your crew, and soon, and maybe all this mess can be cleaned up. Look, the Heavenly Couple has had a rocky relationship with the people on Earth, but the fact remains that, even if They are flawed, They are, at heart, good. If NASA succeeds in assassinating Them, there's no guarantee that whatever puppet deity it's got up its sleeve will be quite so beneficent." With that, a side of the house that had been flickering in and out suddenly went completely transparent. "Please," Ross said. "Don't be afraid to fight."

As soon as Ross's words had penetrated Robin's ears, Robin found himself flat on his back, staring at the ceiling of the space shuttle. Adrenaline was surging through him like an electrical current. The horror that NASA's computer had caused him had been disrupted, and now his head was swimming with images of the destruction of Greater Heaven. Robin could feel his blood pumping, and visualized a small, red star burning with astonishing brightness in the hollow of his heart. "Robin Rodriguez," he murmured aloud, "Interstellar hero."

Robin rushed to the computer and spoke one of the names he remembered from the Las Cruces crew's roster. "Find Vince Markham."

The Kiss

Amanda woke to find herself draped in warm sunlight. She stretched luxuriantly in bed, savoring the feel of her downy quilt against her legs. She felt spectacular. Her bones moved easily in their joints, she wasn't plagued with the chill she usually experienced upon waking, and she found that she could move without her back shrieking in torment. She awoke without the million pains she had lived with so long that she no longer even recognized them as pains. Indeed, the absence of pain was such a novelty that Amanda felt as though she were an entirely new person – as though she had been reborn in the middle of the night.

As she rose and began to dress, she listened to Arlo fumbling with pots and pans in the kitchen. She found that she could remember him with no difficulty: his name, their history, and where they lived. At her remembrances, joy surged into her heart. So much of her life had been previously obscured by the haze of senility that she now felt as though a curtain had been lifted from her memory, revealing long-forgotten scenes from her long and, largely, happy life. She recalled how Arlo had given her a handful of baby blue cornflowers when he proposed, she remembered the breathless excitement of her first childhood horse ride, and she remembered summer mornings in the garden, the wicker trellises casting shadowy crisscrosses across her suntanned hands. She remembered things that she didn't even remember having forgotten.

With a rapidly beating heart, Amanda looked into the mirror above her bureau. She didn't dare to hope that any of her youthful beauty had returned, but she couldn't prevent a part of her mind from tantalizing her with such a possibility. However, when she saw her reflection, she nearly sobbed. She quickly wiped the tears from her eyes with the lace cuff of her blouse, so that she could better see herself.

She was simply gorgeous. Her hair had recovered its former curliness and, more notably, its soft golden color. Her cheeks were full and healthy, and her lips were no longer cracked and dry. The discolorations of age had been erased; though her skin was not flawless, it was no longer flecked with moles and liver spots.

"Dear me," Amanda said aloud, fighting to keep her voice from trembling. She was surprised to hear that her voice was low and croaky, but she was so prepossessed with the miraculous transformation in her body that she was unconcerned with anything else.

As she walked into the kitchen, enjoying her new ability to straighten her back to its full length, she couldn't help glancing at her protruding abdomen. It wasn't too noticeably large, but it was certainly more rounded than usual. It's almost as though…, Amanda thought, but cut herself off before she could allow herself the joyous speculation that she was pregnant. Amanda knew that she was barren; there was no point in hoping for the impossible.

When she came into the kitchen, she was not prepared for what she saw. Arlo was sitting at the table with a small pot of red poster paint and a pair of eggs. He was painting the ends of the eggs to look like eyes. However, even more surprising than her husband's behavior was his appearance. In the midst of Amanda's happy remembrances of her marriage, she had willfully overlooked one simple fact – Arlo was old. His hands trembled with rheumatism and groves of white hair sprouted from seemingly random points on his chin and neck. When he looked up at Amanda, she could see that the skin under his eyes was raw and sagging. Amanda supposed that, on some level, she had expected her husband to have been visited by an overnight rejuvenation as well. She tried to tell herself that her own sudden transformation should have no bearing on her feelings towards her husband; however, she shamefully felt something bordering on revulsion as she looked at his venous arms and flaking scalp.

Arlo, on the other hand, felt quite the opposite as he gazed at his wife. Rubicund, gentle, and almost plump, she was quite nearly the woman he had married. He allowed his eyes to stray from her sturdy legs to her glossy hair. She had looked quite good the previous night, but her appearance this morning was something else entirely. As he sat with a dripping paintbrush in one hand and Pimp Daddy's makeshift eyes in the other, Arlo experienced the first stirrings of physical love he had felt in a decade. A smile that he felt to be stupid bubbled across his face.

"Morning, sugar," he said, setting down his paintbrush.

"Well, you're hard at work," Amanda replied, hoping that she could mask her reaction to her husband through small talk. Arlo cringed involuntarily when he heard Amanda's voice. Beautiful as the rest of her had become, her voice had wasted into a raspy mess. Her voice had previously been so sweet and well-preserved that Arlo felt that some other horrible entity was speaking through his wife's mouth. However, the physical transformation had been so spectacular that Arlo could, with a bit of difficulty, pass the deteriorating voice off as merely an unfortunate side effect.

"That's right, little lady. I'm putting the last touches on these here eyes." Arlo hoped that Amanda wouldn't follow up on what certainly must have sounded bizarre to her; however, the days of her senility were over, and she quickly responded.

"What in blazes are you spoiling them good eggs for?"

"I ain't got nothing up my sleeve, Amanda. I'm just trying to pretty up our homestead with some sculpturing." Arlo was aware of how lame his explanation sounded, but he really could think of no reasonable way to defend his current action.

"That's a cartful of dog droppings," Amanda said, her voice cracking ferociously. "Now I want you to be straight with me – have you gone off the deep end?" Amanda hated how severe she sounded, and wished that she could soften her tone. However, the sight of her pathetic, old husband filled her with irritation. His eyes started glistening with tears, which galled Amanda further. She had felt so good upon waking that she didn't want to be confronted with age and frailty. Though she knew that the thought was ridiculous, she couldn't help feeling that Arlo was deliberately acting old in order to spoil her mood.

"Honey," Arlo began, not sure what he had done to irritate Amanda, "I don't ever want to be untrue to you, so I'll tell you the whole blamed story from top to tail, but I'm warning you now – there ain't no way in God's grassy earth that you're ever gonna believe me."

Amanda put a hand on Arlo's shoulder as a gesture of peace. "If you tell me it's truth, I'll believe it, sure enough. Now I'm gonna see if we got any bacon left for breakfast, and I want you to unload your mind."

With this invitation, Arlo was about to begin fumbling his way through a narrative of the events of the past three days, but he was preempted by a petulant yowl from the cellar.

"Serving bitch!" shrieked Pimp Daddy from below. "I hear that sturgeon-faced trollop of yours rumbling around up there! Bring her down here – Daddy wants to see her!"

Arlo watched carefully for any reaction from Amanda. He was worried that such an abrupt introduction to the situation would prove too strong a jolt for her weak heart. However, he never could have expected the response that slid across Amanda's face – she smiled broadly, though self-consciously. True, Amanda didn't know what to make of the coarse language, but she nevertheless took guilty pleasure in the sound of Pimp Daddy's voice; she recognized it as the voice of the handsome angel in her dreams.

***

141

Norris and Boris watched the Gods from behind a screen of dripping branches. Even throughout the previous night's storm, they had been able to keep track of the Gods because of Their luminous haloes. Now that day had broken, the sky was clear and, though the forest remained damp, the water-saturated soil was already beginning to dry out and solidify. The Gods were resting on an old tree stump. God was picking at a cluster of purple-headed mushrooms sprouting from the side of the stump. Mrs. God was tracing patterns in the mud with the spike of Her stiletto heel. They had searched all night and had found nothing. Though They avoided speaking to one another about Their apprehension, each knew that the other was disturbed.

"Cheer up, pussycat," God said to His wife, without evincing any particular cheer in Himself. "I picked you a mushroom." God snapped the stem of one of the mushrooms and held it out to His wife. The cap, pregnant with spores, was freckled with minute red dots. Mrs. God took the mushroom absently and sniffed it, as though it were a flower.

"Sure enough," Mrs. God said. "It beith a mushroom." She set the mushroom down tenderly beside Her and heaved a sigh that made the tree branches shudder. Somewhere in the distance, a rustle in the underbrush indicated that the squirrels were up and about. God picked another mushroom and handed it to Her. She set it next to the first. "Hadn'teth We better keep movething?" She asked. "It beith already well into morning."

God inhaled deeply through His nose. He could smell the thick odor of decaying mulch that typically hangs in the air after heavy storms. He spread His arms out like wings and let out a deep-bellied roar, which floated up into the sky and was lost. Mrs. God was overtaken by a sudden surge of passion. Whenever Her husband had a job to do, a virile animalism overpowered Him. However, He never succumbed to savagery. Like a panther, He could unleash great quantities of force, while maintaining His grace and precision. Mrs. God, filled with the vibrations of Her husband's war cry, felt a sudden certainty that all would be well. They would find Vince and, with his renewed faith, be able to battle any challenges that came Their way. Unable to contain Her unexpected optimism, Mrs. God allowed a smile to burst onto Her face as She trilled a clear high note. A bird in a nearby tree responded with a similar call, and this only caused Mrs. God's smile to broaden.

"C'mon, honeybee," God said, as He stroked His wife's cheek. "These NASA heathens have had their run of the world for too long, and now it's time to take out the trash. They've put a frown on the face of My prize dame, and that's a sin this hepcat don't intend to forgive. Catch Me, sweetcheeks?"

Mrs. God put Her hand in Her husband's and felt Her face flush with radiance. "I beith behind Thee every step of Thine blessed way!"

"That's where You're wrong, pussycat," God said with a smile. "So long as I've got any say, You're first in everything." With that, He put His lips against Hers, and the force of Their kiss sent a tremor through the Earth. Boris and Norris, safely hidden behind a stand of pine trees, had to struggle to maintain their footing. They found that they could not look directly at the Gods until Their intimate moment had passed – the gleam that pulsed from Their embrace was blinding.

"Touching," Norris murmured emotionlessly to Boris.

"Maudlin," Boris shot back under his breath.

"Conceded."

When She finally pulled away from Her husband's arms, Mrs. God allowed Herself a moment to glance over God's face. His midnight-black skin gleamed with dew, and His eyes shone like pearls set into an obsidian statue. His toothy smile was soaked with love. This is God at His best, Mrs. God thought. May We never changeth forms again!

"Let's beith off, then!" Mrs. God cried, and started once again to push Her way through the low-hanging branches. However, She hadn't moved ten feet before She emitted a panicked gasp. God, His ears highly attuned to any sound of distress from His wife, hastened to Her. When He saw what had happened, He, too, inhaled sharply.

Mrs. God had scraped Her arm on a thorny vine and against Her snow-white skin was a thin trickle of Her blood. Neither God nor Mrs. God had ever shed blood before and, had anybody asked, God would have laughed the idea off as an impossibility. Mrs. God had never really thought about it, but She supposed She had always thought that something other than blood ran through Her veins. However, the material evidence was now in front of Her face. It didn't resemble human blood – it was thicker and rainbow-tinted, as a puddle of oil is when the sun grazes it at the correct angle – but it was clearly dribbling from the scrape on Mrs. God's arm.

God tried to feign unconcern as He tied His handkerchief around Her wound and said, "Nothing a little whiskey, taken orally, can't fix." However, the vivacious mood of the past few moments had been shattered. Mrs. God's certainty that things would work out for the best suddenly seemed absurd to Her. She stared in horror at the way Her blood soaked into the handkerchief in a small, grey circle. I'm going to die, She couldn't help thinking, before pushing the thought away.

Norris and Boris took advantage of the Gods' moment of hesitation. "Markham is…," Norris whispered to Boris.

"… over that way," Boris continued, pointing to the north. The two agents were equipped with headpieces, over which NASA kept them updated on Vince's current position. They had agreed to wait until the Gods showed significant weakness before leading Them towards Vince. They wanted the assassination to go as easily as possible.

"Mrs. God's bleeding," Norris remarked. "Think that's…"

"…weakness enough? Absolutely." Boris allowed himself a smile. Though he always tried to fight his impulse, he was accustomed to smiling when he felt one of his missions drawing to a close. A tidy resolution pleased him in a way that nothing else could. "Hey, Norris. Think we'll…"

"…get a raise if the Gods bite it? I'm sure of it."

"Aces." Boris allowed his smile to remain for exactly five seconds more before straightening his mouth back into its usual noncommittal line. "In that case, let's get this popsicle stand…"

"…rolling towards its final resting spot. Crackerjacks." Norris deliberately rustled the trees in his area. He cleared his throat and spoke casually to Boris in Vince's voice. "So, you find any trace of the shuttle yet, Chris?"

Boris pitched his voice to sound precisely like Chris's. "This assignment's lame. Let's head up this way." With that, the two agents pushed northwards through the trees, making enough noise to attract the Gods, but not so much noise that they ran the risk of being apprehended.

God, hearing what He thought was Vince's voice, tried to return His wife to Her previously high spirits. "Sounds like Our man has come right into Our open arms, gumshoe," He said with a smile. Mrs. God didn't respond. She felt uneasy about following the voices, but no longer trusted Her instincts enough to speak up. God, too, was not convinced that Their journey had come to such a simple ending, but He really had no other plan of attack. "Taking the bait can't hurt," He thought to Himself, "as long as We're wary. It's not a trap if We know We're stepping into it."

Therefore, although both felt uncomfortable doing so, God and Mrs. God began walking after Norris and Boris, hoping that They would face nothing more powerful than Themselves.

***

Juliet had not spoken since her brush with death. Though Roger had tried many times to get her to say something, each time she looked at him with deadened sorrow in her eyes before turning away. In spite of her reticence, however, her physical energy did not flag; indeed, she seemed to have stepped into mute leadership over the three men, tearing ahead through thickets and brush and making Vince, Chris, and Roger scramble to keep up.

The stretch of forest the crew was now pushing themselves through was less dense than yesterday's, and they found that the vegetation was growing more and more unfamiliar. Bulbous, plum-colored fruits hung from the otherwise barren branches of twisting trees. Bright red roots erupted from the bases of low, thorny shrubs. Delicate sacs of cobwebby material bulged out of tree hollows and sent ropy tendrils down to the forest floor. The ground itself was blanketed with yellow, heart-shaped leaves that crunched noisily underfoot. It seemed to Vince as though they had stumbled into a region of the forest that had actively rebelled against the February frosts, refusing to relinquish its vivacity.

"It's burgeoning with biomass out here," Vince said, not without some unease, to Chris. The two had been sticking together since morning. Vince felt that Juliet was best left to Roger's care, seeing as how he had clearly developed a fondness for her. For his own part, he welcomed Chris's companionship. Vince's wariness about Chris and his sketches had not diminished, but he figured that there was no avoiding the kid now; Vince sensed that the two of them were locked together until the end. Meanwhile, Chris was trying not to allow his own fear to resurface. He found comfort in the sound of Vince breathing beside him as they worked their way through the forest. Since Ana had been swallowed by the earth, Chris felt that Vince had been looking at him with greater consideration. Chris, too, understood that he could not be separated from Vince and that, if misfortune were to come, it would have to visit both of them simultaneously.

"I want to go home," Chris said, as he dodged a low branch.

"Understatement of the year," Vince replied. He strained to see Roger and Juliet up ahead, but they had disappeared into a thicket. He wasn't concerned, though – Juliet and Roger had kept far ahead all day, but would periodically stop to allow Vince and Chris to catch up.

"Hey," Chris's tone was abruptly serious. "Do you really buy all that God stuff?"

"What God stuff?" Vince looked down. Drowned earthworms were coiled among the leaves. Vince recalled Ana's premonition of her own death. He felt trapped, as though he were the subject of a cruel experiment.

"I just haven't seen you praying for a while." Chris didn't want to ask anything inappropriate. He needed Vince's company, and had no desire to offend him. Nevertheless, he couldn't help asking about Vince's faith. The simple earnestness with which Vince exercised his belief had always been a source of inspiration to Chris, though he himself professed no religion. Chris found the recent absence of Vince's piety troubling.

"So, do I believe in God?"

"You do, don't you?"

"Of course," Vince replied thoughtfully. "I've seen Him. And His wife."

"That's nuts, Vince."

Vince took a moment to consider Chris's accusation. Perhaps it was nuts, after all. Perhaps the Gods were all in his own imagination. Perhaps They were the insubstantial outgrowths of feverish delusion. But, then again, were the Gods not real, how could anything be real? How can I have faith in the ground beneath my feet, Vince wondered, if I cannot have faith in Them, who are most real to me?

"You have visions, too, Chris," Vince finally said.

"True, but...," Chris allowed his thought to trail off. For some reason, he desperately wanted Vince to believe – but not in such a concrete way. It might have been okay if Vince had said that he believed in God because he saw His works every day, but to say that he had seen God Himself for some reason cheapened his belief. I suppose it just means his faith is remarkably strong, Chris thought. But still....

"Don't you believe in God?" Vince knew that Chris would say "No," but, at the same time, he found it hard to imagine that anybody existed, who genuinely did not share his belief. To him, atheists were merely those who stubbornly disavowed what they knew to be true.

"Does it matter?" Chris replied.

"Doesn't it?"

"I mean, maybe He exists. I have, after all...Hang on." Chris disentangled himself from a vine. "I have learned that it's best not to disbelieve anything. But say, for the sake of conversation, that He certainly exists, and His existence cannot be doubted. Then what? Does my life change?"

"Well...," Vince would have made the usual argument about belief, or lack thereof, changing the course of a person's afterlife, but would have felt dishonest doing so; he knew God's policy of accepting absolutely everybody into Heaven. Every so often, God would tell His wife that it was time to start making some population cuts, but never actually had the heart to go through with it. "You'd have another friend," Vince finally said. Saying this, however, Vince felt a pinprick of anger. For years, he had indeed had a friend in the Gods, but now, when he most needed Them....

Chris wished that Vince had come up with a better argument. He wanted to see the world with Vince's optimism, but couldn't be convinced by such platitudes. Before he could press Vince further, however, a bright image screamed into his head. Like all of his recent visions, it came from somewhere outside his own consciousness. At first, he couldn't tell what he was looking at – it just appeared to be a pool of blood, with no source. However, the image began to zoom out and refocus, and Chris saw the entire scene with disarming clarity. The moment the image flashed out of his mind, he dropped to his knees and began scrawling in the dirt.

"What?" Vince asked in alarm, though Chris was too focused on his task to hear him. "What?"

As Vince watched, Chris's drawing began to take form. It consisted of two stick figures. The head of one figure had a long crack running through it, and inexplicable curlicues streaming from the crack. The other was lying nearby with X's for eyes. Though the picture was no more macabre than anything else Vince had seen from Chris, he felt cold at the sight of it. When Chris had finished the drawing, he stood up and wiped the dirt from his knees.

"Who are those?" Vince asked.

"Ha." Chris forced a smile and worked to keep the tremble out of his voice. "Those are us."

***

Juliet had been powering ahead for nearly an hour without turning back. Her legs ached from overexertion, and she was acutely aware of the gnawing pain of hunger deep in her belly. Nevertheless, she kept hiking, her breath wheezy and shallow. She felt that she had no right to comfort, after she had been artificially preserved through Ana's self-sacrifice. If she had had a knife, she would have immediately slit her wrists or her throat, but, since she had no other means of self-destruction, she was determined to walk herself to death. She was annoyed at Roger's persistence in following behind her, but she had no will to tell him to fuck off. She needed all her energy for continuing to push forward.

Roger had not failed to discern Juliet's purpose, but he also knew that she was not entirely committed to her suicidal course. After all, she would occasionally pause, ostensibly to allow Vince and Chris time to catch up; however, Roger could see the real reason behind her pauses – to whatever extent a desire for death had overcome her, part of her still sparked with the fierce desire to cling to life at whatever cost. Roger found that monitoring Juliet's mental state provided a useful distraction from his own considerable pain. Though his legs were longer than Juliet's, the breakneck pace she had established was straining his calves and lower back. He had eaten nothing but a pack of peanuts since last night and, in spite of the cold and his relative dehydration, a sticky dribble of sweat was trickling down his back, stinging a scrape he had received two days ago. Nonetheless, he felt that he had to maintain a positive presence for Juliet's sake. This impelled him to motor along behind her, paying no mind to the blisters on his feet or the scratches on his face.

Juliet felt dizzy as blood coursed through her ears. She imagined that her heart was beating so furiously that she could hear it. For the fourth time that morning, she had come up against a crucial decision, whether to continue exerting herself, collapse, and, hopefully, never regain consciousness – or to take a break, restore her energy, and cling to whatever feeble scrap of hope remained in her heart. However, as she stepped into an unexpected clearing, her decision was made for her – what she saw before her was so remarkable that she was unable to avoid pausing to behold it. A moment later, she heard a ragged gasp over her shoulder and knew that Roger had caught up, and was filled with as much astonishment as she.

The clearing was unremarkable in every way except one – it was blanketed with the bodies of dead starfish. Starfish of all colors and sizes were draped from the tree branches, piled on the ground, and caught in bushes.

"There must be millions of them," Juliet whispered, breaking the silence that had weighted her lips since the previous night.

The sunlight streaming from the clear sky bounced off the vibrant reds and oranges of the misplaced starfish. Roger took up one of the starfish in his hand and examined it. It was perfectly ordinary in every way. "Is there water nearby?" he asked.

Juliet shrugged without looking at him. Her attention was entirely arrested by the sheer volume of starfish. She noticed an especially tiny one, no larger than a silver dollar, caught in the forking branches of a nearby tree. She grasped it between her thumb and forefinger. Its skin was textured with tiny bumps. "Millions of them," she repeated, uncomprehending.

"This must mean something," Roger said with a frowning brow. He walked to the other edge of the clearing, looking for anything that might explain this phenomenon. Juliet was too absorbed to watch him leave the clearing; it was only when she heard Roger scream her name that she was startled out of her stupefaction.

"Come here!" Roger screamed from behind a stand of pines.

Juliet dropped the starfish and followed his voice, all thoughts of death swept from her mind. She found Roger crouched low to the ground, examining something carefully.

"They make a trail, Juliet," he said joyfully. He wasn't sure why this discovery was so exciting, but the semblance of order within the chaotic turmoil of the past several days gave him a great deal of reassurance. Though he couldn't begin to guess why a path of starfish should exist in the middle of the Texas wilderness, the path at least suggested something not entirely random. Following a trail of starfish might prove to be just as senseless as scouring the woods aimlessly, but the key difference was that following the starfish felt reasonable. This feeling of rationality was the origin of Roger's jubilation.

Juliet was just as excited by the discovery as Roger was, and she wasted no time in racing ahead. This time, her speed was not motivated by a carelessness for life, but, rather, by an intense curiosity and even hope. Roger tore along behind her, feeling the chilly February air pouring into his lungs. He felt like laughing or sobbing. Instead, he allowed a formless shriek to pour out of his mouth as he ran. He couldn't be certain how long he sprinted behind Juliet, sustaining his scream almost effortlessly. It seemed that the train of starfish stretched on indefinitely, like a royal red carpet leading them to an unknown kingdom. They raced past trees, heedless of the brambles grabbing at their arms and legs, and seeing only their twisting path before them.

Juliet had built up so much momentum that she saw the origin of the trail before she processed it. A large orb of white material loomed before her. It looked like metal. Juliet was traveling too quickly to comprehend the writing on its sides. She saw the figure of a man standing next to the object, though her vision was growing bleary and she could not make out his features. She tried to slow herself before she ran into the object, but found that she could not. As the white orb grew nearer and nearer, she found that her course had suddenly been diverted. It wasn't until a moment later that she realized the man had come forward to catch her in his arms, that her head was against his chest, and that she was weeping from exhaustion and relief.

Robin had observed the approach of Roger and Juliet on the computer when they were still some distance away, and had emerged from the space shuttle to greet them. He had intercepted Juliet when he saw that she was not in control of herself. Roger, on the other hand, had slowed well in advance of the spaceship. Now, utterly winded, he staggered up to Robin and collapsed heavily at his feet.

"Are you okay?" Robin asked Juliet, anxious to unhand her so that he could work on reviving Roger. He received no answer beyond ferocious sobs. "Ma'am?" He tried to separate himself from Juliet, but she only clung to him tighter and buried her face against his shirt. "Ma'am, please calm down. You're safe now." Robin noticed with relief that Roger's eyes were still half open and that he was breathing, albeit unsteadily.

A smile crept across Robin's face. For just this moment, to these two individuals, he was a salvation. And, boy, did it feel good. "Yes," he repeated to Juliet. Now that he could see that Roger was not unconscious, he was happy to let her cry until she could cry no longer. "You're both safe now. Completely safe."

***

Ever since he had sent Robin back to Earth, Ross Tucker had been elbowing his way through the jumbled crowds amassed in the streets of Greater Heaven. The dissolution of Heaven was now well underway – half-formed houses wavered uncertainly at the edges of fading sidewalks. Lusterless lawns were mottled with dead space, and even the very clouds of pollution that had formerly hung so incessantly above the megalopolis were thinning at a remarkable rate. When Ross had first joined himself to the crowd, he had not been certain where he was headed; now, however, as he alternately pushed and was pushed along the streets, he began to develop a guess as to the destination of this mass exodus. It seemed that everybody was heading to the Central Heaven Terminal.

"Are there enough comets for everybody?" Ross asked a woman next to him, straining to be heard over the roar of the crowd.

The woman snorted rudely. One of her arms had already completely dissolved, and her face and skull were entirely transparent. "Of course not." With that, she grabbed a man in front of her by the back of the neck and twisted him out of her way. The man tried to maintain his balance, but his knees had vanished, so he toppled to the ground. At the moment of impact, his body burst as though it were a soap bubble, leaving only his luminous red nucleus. This gleaming soul, now utterly free of its bodily weight, floated lazily up from the ground and disappeared into the sky like a bright red balloon. Ross had only a moment to marvel at the soul's ascendance before he felt himself being grabbed at and shoved by the people next to him.

Ross was not sure why everybody was so intent on reaching the Central Heaven Terminal; if the soul was immortal, he figured, it made no difference whether it fled Heaven on a comet or by virtue of its own buoyancy. Nonetheless, he found it easier to push along with the crowd than to attempt to extricate himself, so he continued allowing himself to ride on the current. As a man whose features had melted away jostled him, Ross issued a silent prayer that Robin would soon track down God's father and bring this mad chaos to an end.

***

"You're a fox," Pimp Daddy pronounced, as he looked at Amanda for the first time since her transformation. He had demanded that Arlo bring the newly constructed eyes down to the cellar and he now used them to stare heavily at Amanda. Unfortunately, Arlo had painted pupils on the pointy ends of the eggs, rather than on the rounded ends, and so they protruded grotesquely from Pimp Daddy's skull. "You gave me tits for eyes, you fart-brained flagellum!" Pimp Daddy had exclaimed when he had first seen Arlo's latest handiwork; however, he now seemed to have forgotten about his own appearance as he admired Amanda's. An enormous grin was spread over his purplish lips. His yellow teeth glistened with saliva.

"If I had genitals," Pimp Daddy continued, "I'd make like a Mongol and invade you."

Arlo felt highly uncomfortable, hearing the head speak to his wife in such a crude manner. He had wanted to keep Amanda from encountering Pimp Daddy again, but once Pimp Daddy demanded it, Arlo knew that it could not be avoided. Arlo had been stunned by how easily Amanda had encountered the head and how little its cruel tones seemed to bother her. He wondered if perhaps, in spite of her youthful appearance, her senility had not been entirely vanquished.

Amanda, however, felt quite far from senile. Indeed, she felt better than she had in the past four decades. She was young again, and she had a suitor. The rational part of her brain told her that Pimp Daddy was disgusting. Bugs crawled out of open sores on his lips and tongue, his thin layer of slime glistened in the low light of the basement, and sections of his scalp were peeling off, exposing layers of grayish substance

151

beneath. However, no matter how much she knew that she ought to be repulsed by his appearance, Amanda couldn't help finding something about him jarringly handsome. She did her best to keep her attraction from being evident, so as not to wound her husband, but she associated Pimp Daddy with the angel in her dreams. They had the same voice and, although Pimp Daddy's was somewhat worse for the wear, the same face.

"Don't get jealous, you old carton of crap," Pimp Daddy said to Arlo, "but I can tell by the way she's looking at me that she's just aching to lick the slime off my lips." He now trained his bulging egg-eyes on Amanda. "Isn't that right, you dirty strumpet?"

Arlo felt a flash of heat that he hadn't felt in years. He was furious. He wanted to pick up the head and bring it down full force on his knee, cracking it like a melon. He wanted to smash the egg-eyes he had built, pick Pimp Daddy up by his empty eye sockets, and bowl him into a brick wall. He wanted to punt the head into a deep lagoon. However, Arlo remembered Pimp Daddy's indestructibility and this further knifed him. Besides, Arlo had neither the energy nor the courage to try anything dramatic and violent. Instead, he seethed silently, troubled both by the disrespect shown to the woman he loved and by his own inability to confront that disrespect. He sighed sadly.

"I won't have you speak so to me, you ragamuffin." Amanda tried to sound severe, but worried that she was only coming across as flirtatious in spite of her hideous voice. She could see the pain her husband was going through.

"You won't have it, you wanton harlot?" Pimp Daddy was clearly enjoying this conversation. He slid his dry, moldy tongue lasciviously over his lips. "But you've already had me! You've been tarting it up for old Pimp Daddy in those steamy dreams of yours."

Amanda blushed. It's true, she thought. That handsome stranger is the angel what's been visiting me these last few nights.

Arlo was too angry and humiliated to notice his wife's reaction. "Amanda, let's get ourselves upstairs," he said. "This is no company for a pretty young thing to keep."

"Leave this cellar, and I'll have you gutted, you outmoded orangutan. I'm enjoying this domestic drama. I've always been a fan of stories about fallen women. Your adulterous wife, you prune-assed fleck of putrescence, is part of a long tradition of slutbuckets and sleazebags. You should be proud."

"I understand what you're tryin' to say," Amanda said. Arlo looked at her in surprise. "But I ain't gonna have you speak such to my beloved."

Pimp Daddy threw open his mouth in an enormous guffaw. His egg-eyes bulged in amusement. "After what we did together, you can still stand there and call that filthsome fuckwad your 'beloved'?"

Arlo noticed Amanda's cowed expression for the first time. Ordinarily, her wrinkles might have disguised any indication of shame, but now her smooth, fair skin readily pronounced her blush. Arlo had known Amanda long enough that he could determine her emotions at a glance. There was no mistaking it now – though Arlo couldn't comprehend how it was possible, Amanda was guilty before him.

"Amanda…?" he asked, heartbroken. He struggled to steady his breath. He felt as though he were at the bottom of a large well that was rapidly filling with water. Amanda said nothing, but instead cast a despondent look at Arlo. His worst suspicions were confirmed. Pimp Daddy was telling the truth.

"It was only in my dream-life…," Amanda began, before deciding that qualifications were useless. Whether sleeping or awake, she had been untrue to her husband; the worst of it was, however, that she couldn't drum up sufficient remorse. Arlo, though sweet, was old and impotent. Amanda was young now, with all the urges that young women feel. She could not renounce her Pimp Daddy.

All Arlo could see was his own despair. He looked around for a means of killing either Pimp Daddy or himself. He saw his old chainsaw, a particularly sharp garden spade, and an old canister of paint thinner. "Do it!" his mind screamed. "Do something! Don't just stand here like a gaping idiot!" However, he could not. After such a long, quiet life, it seemed impossible to end it with a romantic gesture. He could only do what he had done with every other pain and disappointment he had felt in his life – bear it.

"Well, missus," he said, hoping that his eyes were no redder than usual. "If that's your choice, then I reckon I'd be wrong to naysay." He hoped he sounded chivalrous, rather than simply weak. Pimp Daddy, however, would not let this go without comment.

"Is that what you reckon, you spineless dung heap? Won't even fight for your little morning-glory here?" Pimp Daddy cackled once again. Amanda's heart began to pound with youthful excitement. She was an object of contention once again. "It's just as well – you'd lose. But before you shuffle off to die of wounded pride, I'll clue you in to a secret. It's not just your metaphorical testicles that have shriveled like grapes in the Gobi. Think your wife was responsible for your lack of little ones? No, sir. Little Amanda here is fertile as a verdant goddamn meadow."

Amanda found herself short of breath. She felt as though something were swimming in her stomach.

"But that's okay, you impotent ignoramus." Pimp Daddy continued to address Arlo. "You're still welcome at my family reunion. Pimp Granddaddy should be here by tonight. And it looks like Baby Pimp is about to arrive."

Amanda collapsed to the floor and began twisting the hem of her dress in her fists. She felt as though every muscle in her body were taut and ready to burst. The pain in her abdomen grew more intense, and she suddenly felt wet. For a moment, she wasn't sure what was happening, but then she was able to match up her sensations with what she had heard from friends and read about in novels. She was going into labor.

***

The Sun had arched over its zenith and was now at the beginning of its buttery slide down to the western horizon. Norris and Boris had been leading the Gods on all morning, rustling about for a while and then remaining quiet to keep the Gods from finding them. The NASA higher-ups were reporting Vince's whereabouts to them over their headsets. Boris and Norris were bringing the Gods towards Vince, but traveling along a circuitous route, so as to buy more time. The longer they leeched the energy and morale from the Gods, the more likely it was that NASA would ultimately be able to claim victory over Them.

In the early afternoon, Norris paused at the base of a tree. "Cast an eyeball this way," he hissed to Boris. Boris looked down at the ground as well. Norris had noticed a sketch carved into the ground. It pictured two stick figures, one with a split head and the other with X's for eyes.

"Grotesque," Boris said.

"Where there's smoke, there…"

"Must be fire." Boris knelt and sifted through the dirt with his fingers. "Markham's got to be a stone's throw away."

"Cookin'! We'll just keep our course, and we've…"

"Got it made in the shade." With that, the two men continued to skulk along, casting eyes every which way for the remaining members of the Las Cruces crew.

A moment later, the Gods came to the same area.

"I'm feddeth uppeth!" Mrs. God cried. "We're nevereth goething to findeth him."

"Keep Your spirits up, ginger-pie." God paused a moment, thinking that He might have heard something in the distance. "You hear voices again?"

"No," Mrs. God whispered. "Thou beith crazy."

"Sh." The couple crouched low to the ground. Sure enough, two male voices could be heard nearby. The Gods couldn't quite make out the conversation, but it sounded serious. "We might be in luck," God breathed, allowing a smile to enliven His face. Soon after Norris and Boris had begun stringing Them along, the Gods had recognized that the voice They were following was not, in fact, Vince's. Mrs. God, too, felt Her heart leap – the voices She was hearing now sounded genuine. If that's Vince, She thought, We might not be too late to save Ourselves.

Utterly possessed by the desire to find the voices' origin, the Gods eased up from Their crouches and began to tiptoe silently further into the forest. They were so absorbed by Their new hope that neither thought to look down at the ground. Had Mrs. God done so, She would have seen the same crude drawing that had drawn Norris and Boris's attention. She would have seen Her husband tread unknowingly upon it, and She might have avoided stepping on it Herself. However, neither God nor Mrs. God noticed Chris's sketch and, by the time both of Them had walked over it, no sign of it remained, save two divine footprints in the Earth.

***

"Some kind of fuel," Roger said, gazing with wonder at the fish tanks lining the walls of the space shuttle's rear chamber. He let out a low, long whistle. When Robin had made his first pass over the space shuttle, he had entirely failed to notice that one of the wall panels could be depressed to open a concealed door at the back of the ship. Roger had sniffed out the trick wall almost immediately, however, and he was now standing with Robin and Juliet, marveling at the sheer volume of starfish that were being kept aboard the ship.

"Fuel?" Robin said.

Roger pointed out a large metal kiln in the rear of the chamber. "I guess all those dead starfish we saw," he said, "were like exhaust. Or something."

Robin was dumbfounded, though he couldn't deny himself an almost childish outburst of laughter. "Starfish!" he thought. "It makes such perfect sense. Of course NASA would fuel its space shuttle with starfish."

"What about the others?" Juliet said. She had not spoken since coming on board. After she had stopped sobbing and Roger had regained his breath, Robin had been eager to demonstrate the ship to them. Juliet, however, was not impressed by the shiny interior, the omniscient computer, or the profusion of starfish. She was exhausted, emotionally drained, and aching to figure out how she was ever going to be able to lead a normal life again. She asked about the others out of propriety; in reality, she had no concern at that moment for the fates of Chris and Vince. For the time being, her only care was her own survival. If we're going to retrieve Chris and Vince, she thought, let's just do it and get out of this fucking forest.

Juliet's question reminded Robin about the responsibility that Ross had given him so gravely. Robin had been so wrapped up in his feeling of self-satisfaction at having rescued Juliet and Roger that he had almost lost sight of his cosmic duty. Before noticing Juliet and Roger on the computer, Robin had been tracking Vince carefully. He now rushed to the computer and asked it to find Vince Markham.

As the computer processed Robin's request, Roger approached as well. In spite of his fatigue and the pressing need to find the two remaining members of his crew, Roger was excited by the utterly unheard of technology on the ship – between the starfish-burning engine, the seamless interior construction, and the enormous hemispheric computer, he felt lost in a futuristic wonderland. He glanced over the floor around the circumference of the computer. Its sleek metallic surface was entirely unmarred by any indication of its construction. However, Roger's sharp eyes quickly homed in upon a tiny imperfection, no larger than a quarter. He leaned in and recognized the imperfection as a circular inscription; when he read what was written, he let out a sharp, wry chuckle.

"What?" Robin asked.

"This inscription," Roger replied. "I think it's the computer's model number. It's funny."

Robin looked over Roger's shoulder, but the inscription was too small for him to read without bending over. "What's it say?" he asked.

"Ha." Roger chuckled again. "It's really cute. Some jokester at NASA, probably. I guess they're calling the computer GOD2B2012."

**

Ross had never before seen the Central Heaven Terminal in such a state of chaos. The benches that used to house the city's derelicts were gone, and the derelicts themselves – aside from their pulsating souls – had nearly vanished as well. Millions upon millions of half-formed people were crammed into the station's main concourse. When Ross saw how compressed the crowd was, he wished he were capable of avoiding the pandemonium; however, he had already been taken up in the current of the mass exodus, and there was to be no extricating himself.

Ross took a deep breath as he was mashed against the wall of the concourse. He could see through the flickering wall into the infinite blackness of outer space beyond. Greater Heaven's entire fleet of comets had been brought out and, through the wall, Ross could see that five or six comets were departing every minute. Though the comets had been built to hold eight passengers at most, seventy or eighty souls were now being packed onto each. The surfaces of the comets were entirely blanketed with bright red souls, some with traces of their corporeal bodies still flickering around them. Occasionally, Ross would see a straggler who had managed to retain an arm clinging desperately to the tail of a comet. All around him, the citizens of Greater Heaven wailed and screamed as they struggled to compress themselves onto the departing comets.

Suddenly, Ross felt a tingly, though not altogether unpleasant, sensation in his stomach. He looked down and realized that somebody's knee had just penetrated his abdomen. When the knee moved out of the way, Ross saw that nothing was left of his lower half. He tried to move his arms, in order to reassure himself that they remained intact, but was faced with a sudden perplexity – he had no arms to move. Though it was hard to determine in the jumble of disassociated body parts packed into the Central Heaven Terminal, Ross realized that he couldn't actually see any part of his own body. He looked around for his soul, but couldn't see that either. A flash of panic stormed through his mind before his rationality soothed him with an explanation. *Stay calm. I can't see my soul, but I know that I still have one. Perhaps that's all that's left of me. Could that be why I can't see it?*

Ross's surmise was correct. Without his being conscious of it, his body had evaporated in the Central Heaven Terminal. Now, much as a man cannot look himself in the eye, his soul proved incapable of seeing itself. Though an outside observer could easily see the glowing red light that contained Ross Tucker's essence, Ross had become, to himself, entirely bodiless.

Before Ross could fully process the implications of his new form, an earsplitting boom thundered above him. Turning his gaze upwards, he saw that a jagged crack was now running along the concourse's massive concrete ceiling. The wall he had been leaning against suddenly gave way, and Ross was nearly sent hurtling out into the cosmos.

"Get on a comet!" A loud, despairing voice overpowered all the commotion. "Everybody get on a comet! This place is done for!"

Ross couldn't identify the speaker in the mass of souls, but he realized with panic that the voice was right. A flurry of comets all launched at once, spraying light into the inky puddle of space. Ross strained ahead to try to fight his way onto a comet, but before he had come anywhere near the departure gate, he heard a collective scream. In that same moment, he realized that he, too, was screaming, because the floor had suddenly given way, the ceiling had exploded upwards, and he was being propelled backwards into outer space with astounding velocity. As he flew out into the cosmos, Ross managed one final peek at what had been Greater Heaven – it had been entirely subsumed in a supernova of white light. Countless blazing souls shot into space, like sparks from Heaven; they peppered the sky like rubies, each doomed to drift alone in limbo until someone, someday, should come along to rebuild what had just been annihilated.

***

Twilight had crept in silently from the edges of the eastern horizon. Though it was still early, the evening was clear and so Vince and Chris could see the first few stars twinkling in the deep blue sky. The two men lay in the dirt, surrounded by dried pine needles and hidden pockets of sulfurous marshland. They had found a mid-sized clearing and wordlessly decided that they would go no further until the next day; neither expressed the sentiment, but both were fairly certain that the next day would be their last. Branches framed their view of the steadily darkening sky above them. The evening was cool and windless and, though each felt an insistent pang of hunger gnawing at his belly, the men were as physically comfortable as possible.

The night's placidity struck Vince as profoundly eerie. Between the cougars, the storm, and his constant adrenaline, he found it hard to believe that, in the end, the mission had whittled down to something so quiet. Just twenty-four hours ago, he never would have imagined that he could have spent the next night lying with Chris in an open clearing, with none of the other crewmates remaining. He wouldn't have imagined himself able to so calmly picture his own death as an inevitability. Now, knowing that his end could not be too far off, he tried to forget himself in the celestial sphere above him, so that his last evening on Earth might be spent in contemplation of something beautiful.

"Sure was crap of them to leave us," Chris said. When the men had first discovered that they had truly lost track of Juliet and Roger, an initial despair had surged between them. Vince had worried that something had happened to the others, but Chris knew better – he somehow knew that Roger and Juliet had found safety and were no longer concerned with Vince and himself. Even in his fear and anger, however, Chris nevertheless felt a strange sense of joy at having Vince all to himself. It seemed to Chris that they were the last two men on Earth. If this is the end, Chris thought, at least I'll endure it in good company.

"They'll come find us," Vince said, knowing that it was false.

Chris nudged closer to Vince, uncertain about what to say or do. He could feel the heat radiating from Vince's body, and hear his steady intakes of breath. Chris wondered whether or not Vince was as conscious of him as he was of Vince. He doubted it. Of course, I'm all he's got now, Chris thought. As if to emphasize this, Chris said, "You haven't prayed, Vince."

Vince rolled over to look at Chris. Though Chris's green eyes shone with nothing more than sincerity, Vince felt uncomfortable that the subject had been raised. Over the past few days, Vince had come to feel an anger at God that he had never before experienced; however, God had been the center of his life for so long that he felt he could not be mad at God without being mad at himself. He now felt this profound self-loathing with painful acuity and sought distraction in Chris. Looking into Chris's eyes, Vince noticed an essential sadness that had, most likely, been present all along, but that he had not chanced to discover until this moment. The sadness touched Vince deeply.

"I don't think it would help," Vince said.

"Don't you believe in God anymore?"

"Of course I still believe in God." Vince spoke softly. "I just don't think He has as many answers as I used to imagine."

Chris felt self-conscious that he was staring at Vince, and yet he couldn't convince himself to turn his gaze away. Even in his insecurity, Vince was strikingly handsome. "Who has the answers, then?" Chris asked, more to avoid the pressure of silence than because he felt his question had any significance.

"I'm starting to think there are no answers," Vince said, looking up into the purple twilight sky. An especially bright star was suspended overhead, quite luminous in spite of the fact that the sky had not yet finished darkening. A sudden red filigree shot like a tiny thread from the center of the star. After a moment, a couple more red emissions flashed from the star. "Huh," Vince said, uncomprehending. "Look at that."

Chris glanced into the sky in time to see an abrupt shower of bright red sparks spray off the surface of the star. These flares continued to blast from the star, streaking across the purplish twilit sky like comets. The star itself was pulsing and bending, as though something within it were struggling to get out. Chris turned again to Vince, whose eyes remained trained on the heavens. Chris could see the stellar activity reflected in Vince's dark, glittering eyes. Without knowing in advance that he was going to do so, Chris reached over to Vince, grasped him by the back of the neck, and pulled him into a kiss.

As the men's lips touched, the overhanging star finally gave one last shudder, and burst. The entire sky blazed as exploded fragments of the star whizzed across the celestial sphere. For a brief second, comets wailed through the air, orange tongues of flame blasted from the stellar fragments, and a cascade of shimmering starlets rained down from the zenith. As quickly as it had begun, however, the stellar luminescence fizzled out; Greater Heaven had made its last ephemeral imprint on the memory of mankind and had now been swallowed into the blank nullity of a starless night.

The Launch

God and Mrs. God had witnessed both the kiss and the death throes of Their home. A sob rose up in Mrs. God's chest, but She didn't vocalize it. She knew that there was nothing more to hope for. Even if She and Her husband managed to restore Vince's faith, there was no longer any home to which She could return. She felt that Her sense of loss could not be alleviated by anything short of ceasing to exist. Life had just become irreversibly odious.

God had precisely the same feeling in the core of His heart, but, even after watching His home shatter and streak into nothingness across the night sky, He managed an uncertain smile. No matter how close He felt the end was, He knew that despair was unpleasant. He had always sought the most pleasant feelings, and He saw no reason to alter this habit, even in the face of death. Clearing His throat, He grasped His wife's trembling hand. "Things look bad for our intrepid heroes," He said, "but no respectable private ace has ever let himself be stymied by a bout of bad luck. Our right-hand man, Vince, has never left Us high and dry before, and I'm sure he'll pull through in a pinch."

Mrs. God squeezed Her husband's hand. "I beith not so sure," She said plainly, "but I trusteth Thou to the end. But please let Me just sayeth this, God, I loveth Thee. And no matter whatsoever should happeneth, We shall always remaineth together, in death as in life, until the universe cometh to its inevitable end."

God turned His head away, but Mrs. God noticed a single glowing red tear, like a bead of molten lava, rolling down Her husband's cheek. The tear fell to the ground below and burned a sizzling hole into the undergrowth.

"Vince!" God shouted, pushing His way into the clearing in which Vince and Chris were lying. "Our little fighter ace! Long time, no see!" God's gleaming smile shone like a crescent moon in the semidarkness. Mrs. God entered the clearing behind Him, Her pale skin radiating a low bluish aura. "Let's get you out of this forest and on the next plane back to Margaritaville."

Vince leapt to his feet upon seeing the Gods. He felt as though his mind were trying to race in eighty different directions, but remained tethered to confusion. When Chris had kissed him, Vince had been surprised by a feeling of safety. In the middle of the fear of the past several days, Vince had suddenly felt completely secure. A tenderness lay in Chris's kiss that somehow reassured Vince in a way that the Gods had utterly failed to. To Vince, the kiss had not been sexual; he had been too wrapped up in the feeling that he was finally being protected from the world's cruelty to think of it in terms other than emotional. Now, Vince felt a surge of anger as he eyed the Gods. For three days, They had been absent, but now that there was nothing left to hope for, They suddenly had time once again to mingle with the mere mortals. Seized by the sudden release of all the frustration he had pent up in his heart, Vince threw back his head and whipped it forward again, lobbing a wad of spit at God's feet with projectile force.

"Where were You this morning?" Vince asked venomously. He spit again. "Or yesterday? Or the day before?"

"Vince!" Mrs. God cried, Her heart torn at the sight of Vince so barbarously disrespecting Her husband. She felt Her voice quaking, and knew that a flood of tears was welled behind Her eyes, just waiting to be loosed. She simply wanted peace. "Beith not so overtakeneth with thine vengeance."

"Well?" Vince asked. In spite of his anger, he was aching to hear a good excuse. He wanted quite badly to be able to trust God once again and to return to the quiet happiness he had enjoyed just weeks before.

Chris, meanwhile, was not as taken aback as he might have expected. He gathered that the people who had just entered the clearing must be God and Mrs. God from Their physiognomies and speech patterns. However, he felt more confused than awestruck. He had subconsciously believed Vince when he spoke of God and Mrs. God – it seemed to Chris, after all, highly unlikely that anybody should hold such ferocious belief in something insubstantial – and so was not entirely shocked to see Them. What did surprise him was how pathetic They looked. God, though muscular, was drenched with sweat and shorter than Chris would have thought. Mrs. God was beautiful, but She looked haggard and weepy. Chris felt simultaneous tenderness and condescension; though he was pleased by the Gods, he couldn't conceive of Them as worthy recipients of respect.

"Don't worry, hepcat," God said to Vince. "I know you're hot under the collar right now, but the Missus and I are back to take care of you. So cool those jets of yours, bring your new friend if you want," God nodded to Chris, "and let's forgive and forget. Bourbon under the bridge – My treat."

"I beith Mrs. God, by the way." Mrs. God blew a kiss to Chris – Her customary gesture upon meeting a young man. "Thank thee for takething care of Our Vincent." True, the Gods were a little perturbed by what

They had seen of Chris and Vince's kiss – more because They felt that Vince was being untrue to himself than for any other reason – but, as if by silent agreement, They said nothing. The key right now was to win back Vince's faith, and any hint of chastisement could turn him away from Them forever.

"I'm Chris Lester," Chris replied, watching the night's first fireflies blink on and loop circuitously through the cool air.

God replied with His heartiest chuckle. "Wise up, Wilson! We're the Gods – We know you already."

"Charmethed, nonetheless," Mrs. God was quick to reply.

Vince did not lighten at all. "So, which way is out?" he asked God.

"We'll sniff out a grand exit, partner," God replied. "When God's on a mission, He's like a bloodhound on the scent of a prime rib. We'll be out of this shadowy stinkhole before you can say 'Seagram's.'"

"You mean, You don't know how to get out of here?" Vince could feel himself growing hot. He didn't want to be angry with the Gods, but he felt that he couldn't avoid it. He had been walking for three days, he had seen four of his crewmates die, he was sweaty and tired, and he just wanted to escape. For the Gods to fail him now, just as he was beginning to feel the glimmer of new hope burning in his chest, would be inexcusable.

Silence dripped from the tree branches. Somewhere underfoot, a squirrel rustled among the dead leaves. Vince could feel his remaining faith seeping from him.

Mrs. God finally spoke, "We'll findeth a way out, Vince. At least We'll all beith together."

"Two days ago, that might have been good enough," Vince murmured.

A sudden image leapt into Chris's brain. He was back in the dark concrete room he had visited in his dreams – the room with the tools and the dusty wooden shelves. He heard the dream voice – his own voice – speaking to him. "It's time, Chris. Lead him." Unexpectedly, Chris saw with complete clarity where he was and where he was headed. His eyes widened and, with confidence, he said, "Vince. I can get us out of here."

"I'm sorry?" Vince asked.

"I know where we are," Chris said, his excitement accelerating. "Vince, I know where we are! We're no more than five hundred meters from a house. If we walk far enough that way," Chris waved his arm carelessly, "we're saved! Vince!" Chris gripped Vince by the collar of his shirt and pounded him on the back. Chris screamed with giddy, almost maniacal laughter.

Vince remembered the security he had felt in Chris's kiss and the abandonment that he had suffered at the hands of the neglectful Gods. He looked at the dumbfounded faces of the Heavenly Couple and at the absolute confidence in Chris's shining eyes. "Sorry, guys," he said to the Gods, with a little shrug, "I'm going with Chris. You can follow or not. It's all one to me." Vince averted his gaze to avoid looking into Mrs. God's pained eyes. Chris had already grasped Vince's hand and was dragging him towards the safety his vision had assured him of. Vince fought against the urge to look back at the Gods; instead, he followed behind Chris and, after a moment, disappeared behind a stand of trees.

"Vince?" Mrs. God whispered, as Her last hope at salvation turned his back on Her forever. She began to wheeze hysterically. "Oh, woe beith upon Us!" She grabbed Her husband's hand and began shaking it, as though to spur Him into action of some sort. "What shouldeth We doith?"

However, God merely shook His head sadly and ran His hands lovingly down Mrs. God's back. "Well, angel-pie, I don't think there's anything left for these cats in this cruel world. We've had a good run of it, but now Our number's been called. Time to jitterbug onwards to the Great Big Sock Hop in the Sky." He wrapped His trembling wife in an embrace. Safe in God's arms, Mrs. God allowed Herself to give way to the quaking sobs that burst from Her eyes. Her tears rolled down Her cheeks and dripped onto God's face as well. The faces of the Heavenly Couple started to dissolve in these tears and intermix, God's black skin trickling into Mrs. God's white skin, like India ink dribbling into a bowl of milk. The Gods' fingers started to drip like icicles, and the boundaries between Their two bodies began to waver and melt into nothingness.

The soil thirstily gulped up the puddle forming around the melting Gods. The amorphous union of Their bodies shrank and shrank until nothing was left of the Gods but an irregular patch of unusually fertile land and the exhalation of a mournful sigh hanging in the night air. A gentle burst of wind scattered the sigh, causing it to resound to the limits of the forest before fading out.

***

"Quite a spectacle," Norris said to Boris, after watching the dissolution of the Gods.

"Indeed," Boris replied, crossing himself emotionlessly. "The boys at NASA will be…"

"On cloud nine."

"So to speak."

"Godless world," Norris said speculatively. "Doesn't feel too different to me."

"It will," Boris replied. "After..."

"...The launch. That's right." Norris switched on the headset that connected him back to the NASA control center. "All right, base," he said into the headset, "The Gods are swimming with the fishies."

"So to speak," Boris interjected.

"So to speak," Norris repeated. "So now we'll see to it that the other one is similarly dispatched." He switched off his headset, turned to Boris, and laboriously twisted the corners of his mouth into something almost resembling a smile. "And then we can get our raises."

"One pair of false idols down..."

"...And one to go."

***

Amanda was not having an easy birth. For nearly three hours already, she had been wracked by contractions that wrung every muscle in her body. Arlo had been unable to move her upstairs – and Pimp Daddy had threatened him with castration if he were to take Amanda out of eyeshot – so he had tried to make her as comfortable as possible on the cellar's concrete floor. He had pooled together a nest of soft blankets for her to lie on, and found the softest pillow in the house to place under her head. Every so often, he would rush upstairs to fetch her an unsolicited glass of water, which ended up being hurled against the wall as often as it ended up being drunk. Amanda's dress was tented between her legs, as she pushed and screamed, awaiting her first child.

Amanda was conscious of nothing except her pain. She could see the brick walls of the cellar, and Pimp Daddy's bulging eyes, but she could not string together the disparate images she received to produce any thread of sense. She could hear her husband's words, but they simply sounded like incomprehensible noise, as though he were screaming to her through a pool of water. The only thing that was real to her was the periodic constriction of her muscles. She wasn't even aware of screaming. Her mouth was like a safety valve – whenever the pressure of the contractions built up in her body to such a point that there was no room left for more pain, her mouth would automatically fly open and release a yowling wail, which Amanda herself was wholly unconscious of producing.

The screams ricocheting around the echoing basement sent an icy chill to Arlo's skin. His wife's voice had become shredded and raspy ever since her physical transformation, and it was now further distorted by her labor pains. The overall effect grated Arlo's ears with its cracked, gravelly quality. Amanda's voice sounded so aged that Arlo would sometimes go into a panic. She's too old to be birthing! he would think. She ain't gonna survive it! However, he would then glance at his wife's body and his fears would dissipate. Tattered as her voice had become, Amanda had never been in better physical shape for childbirth.

Pimp Daddy was watching the birth with greater apprehension than Arlo had yet seen in him. He had asked Arlo to position him so that he could keep Amanda directly in his line of vision. At one point, when Arlo had returned to the basement after fetching a cold compress to apply to Amanda's perspiring forehead, Pimp Daddy said, "What's wrong with your lady's labia, you prenatal protoplasm? It's been hours, and Pimp Daddy does not like to wait for what he wants."

"I'm sorry, sir," Arlo said, too exhausted to be angry. He wiped off Amanda's forehead. At the sensation of her husband's touch, Amanda instinctively snapped up at his fingers with her teeth. Arlo whipped his hand away just quickly enough to avoid being bitten. "It's her first birth."

Pimp Daddy angled his egg-eyes downwards and stuck out his moldy tongue in contemplation. "It's okay," he said, with uncharacteristic magnanimity. "Baby Pimp can't be born until the last vestiges of the existing Gods have drained from the world." He spoke more to himself than to Arlo, as though comforting himself with the knowledge. "Baby Pimp will come with Pimp Granddaddy." Having reached the end of his train of logic, Pimp Daddy repeated his speculation more confidently for Arlo's sake. "You hear that, you ponderous penile pustule? Baby Pimp and Pimp Granddaddy work in tandem."

"Please, sir." Arlo hesitated. He was trying to hold down Amanda's flailing arms, so that she did not hit herself. Frustrated with her immobility, Amanda began thrashing back and forth. Her animalistic howls swelled in volume. "I think it'd be best not to upset the missus. If I can ask a humble favor of you, please keep your voice down."

Pimp Daddy flushed a deep, bruise-colored purple, and was about to issue Arlo a scathing rebuke, when his attention was diverted by the progress of Amanda's birth; a jet of thick, gelatinous green sludge spewed out of Amanda's skirt, staining the soft blankets beneath her. With a scream that shook the cobwebs free from the ceiling, Amanda tensed her muscles and pushed with unspeakable force. A bloody, writhing tentacle peeked out from beneath the hem of Amanda's dress as she continued to push.

A vast smile of pleasure melted across Pimp Daddy's face. "Here comes baby," he said. Suddenly, a knock sounded on the door upstairs. Pimp Daddy's smile burst into a grin that exposed his rotten, pitted teeth. "Hey!" he called to Arlo, who had effectively been paralyzed by the shock of glimpsing the beginnings of Baby Pimp. "Why stand there gaping, you mound of mutton? Go answer the door. Pimp Granddaddy has arrived."

***

Roger and Juliet, in spite of their fatigue, were busy clawing Robin's truck out of the mud that had entrapped it the previous night. Meanwhile, Robin had volunteered to keep his eyes on the GOD2B2012 monitor, in order to try and figure out where, precisely, Chris and Vince were. The three had agreed that the best course of action would be to avoid trekking back out into the woods, especially since none of them had an intimate knowledge of the area. Robin was simultaneously watching Chris and Vince on broadcast and charting their positions with the onboard GPS. Once the two stranded firefighters had come upon some sort of terrain that Robin could recognize, he planned to pile into the truck, pick up Vince and Chris, treat everybody to dinner at The Chophouse, and wait for the media's accolades to pour in.

Robin was so preoccupied with his fantasy of being honored at a Presidential banquet in some chandelier-laden venue with potted plants and carafes of iced tea that he almost didn't notice the house that appeared on the computer screen. However, something very familiar about the house quickly drew Robin's attention. He could see Vince and Chris standing at the front door next to a bonneted concrete goose. I've seen that goose, haven't I? Robin thought. In an instant, his mind was illuminated, and he leapt with excitement. He raced out of the space shuttle into the evening, screaming to Juliet and Roger before he could see them. "Load in, soldiers! Load in! Your friends are not far, and it's not too late to save them!"

Hearing Robin's exuberant cries, Roger and Juliet looked at one another. Juliet wiped her muddy hands on her pants and said, "Think this is really the end?"

"It's dangerous to hope."

Juliet nodded. "True," she said, as she and Roger climbed into Robin's truck. In spite of her exhaustion and disillusionment, she couldn't prevent a nebulous hope from forming in her heart. "True," she repeated quietly, trying to remind herself not to expect salvation. Nevertheless, her heart began to beat a little faster as Robin hopped into the driver's seat, keyed up the ignition, and started the truck bouncing down the back roads of Texas.

***

Arlo opened the door, but, in spite of all the monstrous images of Pimp Granddaddy he had constructed in his mind, he was not prepared for whom he found on his doorstep that evening. He had prepared a humble speech to offer up to Pimp Granddaddy upon his arrival – "I'm sorry, sir. My house ain't much to look at, but your kin has favored us with a visit, and you're welcome to whatever we got" – but Arlo now found that he could only chew his mouth about ineffectually, saying nothing. He had prepared himself for mutilated corpses, for demoniac wraiths, and for malodorous, gore-drenched barbarians, but he had not prepared himself for what appeared to be a pair of average, twenty-something young men, one of whose faces bore an exact resemblance to Pimp Daddy's.

Chris and Vince were similarly dumbstruck. They had both counted on throwing themselves upon the mercy of the inhabitants of the house, but neither had actually considered what to say when the moment of supplication arrived. Thankfully, the men didn't have to stand long in uncomfortable silence. Pimp Daddy screamed up from the cellar, "The Pimp Daddy's daddy has arrived! Bring him down here, you stinking cesspit of sewage! Pimp Daddy wants to lay eyes on his maker!"

Chris looked quizzically at Arlo. "He'll be wanting to see you, I reckon," Arlo said. "Come on down to the cellar."

As the firefighters followed Arlo downstairs, Vince whispered to Chris, "What's going on? Where are we going?"

Chris whispered back, "I don't know," in all honesty.

Vince was going to recommend that they refuse to go any further, but his thoughts were interrupted by a scream that was only barely recognizable as human. It sounded as though a heavy rock were being rattled about in a washing machine at a high velocity. Vince gripped the banister in discomfort, but Arlo beckoned him onwards. "It's only the labor pains," Arlo said, feeling defeated. "The missus is with child."

Both Vince and Chris were filled with alarm when they saw the cellar. The walls were splattered with blood and greenish slime. A beautiful woman was writhing on the floor, with a venous blob of bloody muscle expanding from beneath her skirt, like an inflating bubble. The sheets upon which she lay were thoroughly saturated with yellowy mucous and warm, rusty splotches. Giggling nearby was a head that looked exactly as Chris's might, had his eyes been replaced with eggs, his skin broken up with scabs and lesions, and patches of his hair torn from his skull. A crude pair of wooden legs stuck out from the base of the head. When Chris noticed the cellar's old tools, stacks of newspapers, and dusty concrete floor, he was hit by a sudden shock. This is the dark place from my dreams, he thought. And that head – his voice is mine, his face is mine.

"Who are you?" Chris managed to stammer, addressing Pimp Daddy, though unable to keep his eyes focused on any one aspect of the macabre scene before him.

"It's such a shame when fathers refuse to recognize their sons, isn't it?" Pimp Daddy replied.

"You're the Pimp Granddaddy, aren't you?" Arlo asked Chris. He couldn't bear to consider his wife struggling to push out whatever demon was clawing its way out of her womb, so he momentarily poured his attention into Chris.

"The Pimp Granddaddy?" Vince asked.

"I don't...," Chris began, before being cut off by another deep-bellied wail from Amanda. Another tentacle – or perhaps it was a tail – had worked its way out of her.

"Don't hand me that crap!" Pimp Daddy exclaimed. "If you're not Pimp Granddaddy, Chris, then Pink Floyd didn't fucking rock hardcore. Don't fill my ears with such patent absurdities, Chris!"

"I don't get it," Chris said.

"Can you deny the family resemblance?" Pimp Daddy said, pursing his lips playfully. Indeed, Chris realized with revulsion, the family resemblance was quite striking. "Now I realize that this is our first formal introduction," Pimp Daddy continued, "so I will try to be more articulate. I, Pimp Daddy, am your imagination, Chris, by the blessing of the good folks at NASA."

Chris could only stare idiotically. Vince did the same. Only Arlo seemed to take Pimp Daddy's proclamation without surprise. He went to Amanda and wiped away a dollop of froth that had dribbled from her mouth.

"Long ago, Chris," Pimp Daddy continued, beginning to savor his role as storyteller, "our resident Quixotes down at the National Aeronautics and Space Administration took it into their heads to depose God."

"Why?" Vince asked. At the mention of his old friend, he felt as though a part of himself were being ripped apart. He could not forget the sad, parting look that Mrs. God had given him as he followed Chris into this new, hellish world.

"Why not?" Pimp Daddy shot back. "Besides, don't interrupt, you brown-nosing Boy Scout. Your Gods are already dead, due entirely to your own fickleness, so, if you have any self-respect, you'll gracefully allow me to tell my tale. My son, after all, is going to be your Heavenly Lord and Master." With this, Pimp Daddy cast a loving glance at the monstrosity being born at the other side of the room. The baby's shape was still uncertain, but a large flap of raw flesh containing an enormous blue eye protruded from one of the tentacles.

"NASA did this?" Chris asked. He felt that continuing the conversation would somehow keep the situation from attaining truly monstrous heights. As long as he was holding a normal, back-and-forth dialogue, some source of familiarity remained in the world.

"No, Chris," Pimp Daddy chuckled. "You did this. As I said, NASA wanted to depose God, but God had been built up by centuries of highly imaginative people, such as our little Georgia O'Keefe here." Pimp Daddy pointed his nose in Vince's direction and then laughed again. "When something's got such a degree of creativity and faith around it, it takes a heavier force than bombs to wipe it out. But luckily for us, Chris, pansy-assed philanthropists are not the only ones who possess the creative urge. So that's why NASA found you, Chris – or, more accurately, us." Pimp Daddy was filled with such filial pride that, had he had arms, he would have thumped himself on the chest, had he had one.

Forgotten memories toyed with the edges of Chris's consciousness. Had there, at one point, been a series of tests? A long series of white rooms, metal implements, and cardiographs? Hadn't he been given injection after injection, told story after story in an effort to scramble his mind? Chris could remember none of this distinctly, but he had seen such scraps and glimmers of these events among his visions. Now that the memory had been brought up by Pimp Daddy's allegation, Chris seemed to vaguely recall some sense of it.

"The question was could the imagination of an exceptionally talented thinker be concentrated and separated from its origin?" Pimp Daddy went on.

Hadn't sketch after sketch been posted on the wall and examined by beard-stroking scientists in white lab coats? Hadn't the tiniest jumps and twitches in Chris's brain been recorded with painstaking precision?

Hadn't Pimp Daddy himself been born of an exceptional frenzy of artistic ecstasy?

"Not to be a spoilsport, but the answer was 'yes,'" Pimp Daddy continued. "And so you birthed me and were sent back out into the wide world, never to know of your illegitimate child. For a while, I was NASA's suck-up. I was supposed to fulfill their lifelong wet dream of eliminating God from the human lexicon. So, I got lobbed up into space with the Daedalus, ready to imagine God into nonexistence."

Amanda screamed and something resembling a foot plopped out from her skirt, along with a cascade of sticky purple substance.

"But God," Pimp Daddy's expression darkened, "swatted down the mission, and suddenly my beef was personal. It was no longer enough for me to lay God on ice and then step aside so NASA could beam up its own new deity. No, sir. Pimp Daddy wanted to take down God for Pimp Daddy's own reasons. And now," Pimp Daddy smiled again, "here comes my little bouncing bundle, a revamped God for the twenty-first century."

With a loud plop, another eye emerged on the form Amanda was birthing. The creature blinked.

Chris felt a vast cosmic energy buzzing about his head. He felt somehow triumphant. As the grandfather of the new God, what wasn't possible? He could recreate the world in whatever form he chose; he could gain immortality. However, he remembered Vince's recent disillusionment. Can I maintain faith in God, even if it is of my creation? he thought. Besides, Chris wasn't certain that he wanted to author a new reality. Try as he might, he couldn't come up with a single material change that he would necessarily inflict on the world. It wasn't that Chris saw no problems with his current existence; rather, he was plagued by such strong insecurity that he couldn't trust himself to impose meaningful changes. Can I really ask everybody to conform to my ideal? Wouldn't I always be worried that I was stepping on people's toes? Chris suddenly wished to get out of the cellar. The stench of mildew and blood hung heavily in the air, and Chris felt almost feverish.

"What's the matter, Pops?" Pimp Daddy asked Chris. "We'll be a duo, you and I. Like Rocko and Jocko. Don't pretend you don't want it. There's nothing going on here that didn't come straight out of your own head."

Unfortunately for Pimp Daddy, he could not have picked a worse thing to say at this moment. Chris, already doubting himself, now looked with greater scrutiny at Pimp Daddy. Within this wisecracking, prophesying, severed head, he saw a cruel parody of himself. His face, his fatalism, and even his subconscious fantasies sat leering before him with necrotic skin and broad, purple lips. He recalled the handsome figures of God and Mrs. God, Their goodhearted whimsy, and Their overabundance of love, which Chris had mistaken for weakness. Next to Vince's creations, Chris's own was horrible and repugnant – and all the more so because he could not deny that it came from his own heart.

Sensing Chris's agitation, Vince put an unsteady hand on his shoulder. However, Vince's gesture was an effort to sop up a tsunami with a paper towel; Chris, with a growl of rage and self-loathing, grabbed the nearest object – a pitted old garden shovel – and swung it in a high, wild arc over his head. One of Pimp Daddy's egg-eyes popped from his head in surprise and burst on the concrete below. Before any further reaction was possible, however, the shovel had struck Pimp Daddy directly on his forehead, cracking open his head. With an inhuman yelp, Pimp Daddy toppled from atop his wooden legs and shattered on the ground, just as his egg-eye had shattered a moment before. Across the room, the baby creature oozing from Amanda's body grew limp and, with a sulfurous exhalation, slowly started to melt into the floor.

Meanwhile, Chris had dropped the shovel. At the precise moment when he had struck Pimp Daddy, Chris's own forehead had split open. He dropped to his knees, grasping doggedly for his last breaths, before collapsing altogether, thick blood flowing from his head like rich, unadulterated Tempera paint.

***

Nobody had answered Robin's knock, so, with all the consciousness of performing a grand gesture, he slammed into the Saunders' front door until the hinges burst under his weight. Having broken through the door, with Roger and Juliet trailing behind him, he called out, "Vince! Chris!" His shouts were met by silence, so he pushed further into the house. Near the kitchen, he observed the open cellar door, so, whispering, "Here goes nothing" to Roger and Juliet, he led them down to the basement.

Robin saw immediately that he had arrived too late. Against one wall, a beautiful young woman on a pile of bloodstained sheets was slumped lifelessly in a puddle of viscous slime. Robin recognized Arlo as the man kneeling over the woman and shuddering with sobs. Not far away, a young blonde man was lying prone on the ground with a fatal gash along his skull; next to him, a replica of his head had been smashed into large, jagged pieces. The head lay in a puddle of black blood and egg yolk. A pair of wooden legs sat splintered and forgotten in the corner of the cellar. In the midst of all the carnage, Robin saw the man he knew to be Vince standing insensibly, with his mouth ajar and his eyes dulled over with dead stupidity.

"Holy shit," Robin exhaled. "What happened here?"

Vince turned to look at Robin with bovine eyes. Vince could hear Robin's voice, but his words meant nothing.

"Vince?" Juliet said. Though she had been preoccupied with her own suffering, the sight before her was so disturbing that it took her over entirely. More disturbing than anything else, however, was the fact that Vince's face had gone entirely dead. His previously expressive eyes were now opaque and revealed nothing. His gaze moved slowly and uncomprehendingly, and he did not respond to Juliet's call. "Vince!" she repeated, but Vince only stared at her.

"Mr. Saunders?" Robin asked, trying now to get Arlo's attention. However, Arlo was just as unresponsive as Vince. His attention was entirely transfixed by his dead wife. "Mr. Saunders?"

Arlo stopped sobbing and, without looking up, said, "Yes, sir?"

"What happened, Mr. Saunders?"

When Arlo finally replied, his sobs threatened to work their way back into his voice; nevertheless, his words remained comprehensible. "You'd best see yourselves out. Ain't nothing to do now but mourn what's lost."

Roger put a hand on Robin's shoulder. "I think the man's right," he said. "Let's get Vince out of here, and then call the police." With that, Roger stepped towards Vince and held out his hand. "Come on, buddy. Let's get you home." Vince made no move to come to Roger, so Roger grasped Vince's hand and led him out of the cellar as though he were a child.

Juliet followed behind the two men. Robin hung back for a moment to speak to Arlo. "Will you be okay, Mr. Saunders?"

Arlo finally looked up at Robin with red, baggy eyes. "Thank you, sir, but I reckon I'll be as fine here as I'll be anywhere. I've just got to..." Arlo, however, couldn't finish his sentence before tears once again overwhelmed him. In lieu of speaking, then, he gestured to Robin that he should go follow Vince, Roger, and Juliet. Feeling a lump enter his own throat, Robin turned away from the old man and began ascending the cellar steps back into the starless Texas night above.

***

Norris and Boris watched the four survivors pile into Robin's truck and drive off into the night.

"Think they've killed off that other one?" Norris asked.

"Chris Lester is the only one who can kill…"

"Chris Lester's own imaginings. True." Norris paused for a moment. "But, do you think…"

"That he did it? Well, I vote we proceed with the launch. If Pimp Daddy rears his ugly head…"

"We'll deal with it. Right on, Daddy-O," Norris said. He switched on his headset. "We have a strong impression that the coast is clear. All Gods have been eliminated. Status of potential deity unknown, but suspected dead."

"What if we're wrong?" Boris hissed in Norris's ear.

"Then we'll just see which is stronger – Chris Lester's imagination or the scientific institution that set it free." Norris replied in a whisper. Into the headset, he said, "Proceed with the launch." Norris switched off his headset and turned to Boris. "All in a day's work."

From deep within the forest, a low rumbling noise could be heard. Norris and Boris turned their gazes upwards just in time to catch the space shuttle containing the GOD2B2012 computer shooting up into the heavens on a cloud of starfish. The spaceship grew smaller and smaller against the dark night sky until it glowed as a solitary star at the zenith of the celestial sphere.

"Ha," Boris said with no mirth in his voice. "Our new God's in heaven…"

"And all's right with the world. Feel any different?"

"Not a whit." Boris shrugged and yawned. "Bedtime?"

"Bedtime," Norris replied. "Think we'll…"

"Get that raise?" Boris said. "Norris, for work like this…"

"For supplanting God…"

"Absolutely." As the two men walked synchronously back to their truck, Boris clapped Norris on the back. "For a job like this, we will most certainly get a raise."

About the Author

Nick Sansone is a current student in the MFA Program for Poets and Writers at the University of Massachusetts-Amherst. He grew up in Champaign, IL, and attended Sarah Lawrence College as a student of economics and Russian language. His short fiction has appeared in several small journals, including *Pear Noir!*, *Pank*, and *Ignavia*. Nick has two years' professional experience as a wildland firefighter and trail services employee through the AmeriCorps National Civilian Community Corps. In 2003, he served on a NASA search and rescue team after the destruction of the Space Shuttle Columbia.

www.ingramcontent.com/pod-product-compliance
Lightning Source LLC
Chambersburg PA
CBHW031112260626
47172CB00001B/326